DECEPTIVE AFFAIRS

A NOVEL

CAROLYN COURTNEY LAUMAN

ISBN: 978-1-7332864-4-2 (Ebook)

ISBN: 978-1-7332864-5-9 (Paperback)

Cover Design by Hampton Lamoureux

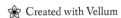 Created with Vellum

AUTHOR'S NOTE

BEST LAID SCHEMES
AUTHOR'S EXPLANATION

Dear Readers, after my second novel, *Deceptive Waters*, was released in February 2020, I immersed myself in the writing of this, my third. My plan was to publish in the summer of 2020. Ha!

As Robert Burns wrote in his poem, *To A Mouse*, "The best laid schemes o' mice an' men. Gang aft a-gley."

I need not speak of the events that rendered my plans, and those of the entire globe, *a-gley*. Nor have I referenced said events in this novel. We have all suffered quite enough.

Thank you for your patience. I hope *Deceptive Affairs* proves worthy of the wait.

Carolyn Courtney Lauman
October 2021

ACKNOWLEDGMENTS

There is such a thing as having too much time to complete a task. Getting *Deceptive Affairs* into your hands is one such example. I wish to thank the following people who helped me reach the finish line of this protracted journey.

Kate Schomaker, my editor, for your expert advice. Please keep pushing me.

Hampton Lamoureux, my cover designer, for your creative mind.

Scott Stein, for sharing your expert knowledge of ice hockey.

Amy Dunmire, my friend and advance reader, for your keen eye and sense of humor.

Pam Sexton, my friend and chief marketer, for taking the leap with my novels.

My readers, old and new.

And Wayne, the strongest warrior on planet Earth, for your unconditional love.

DEDICATION

For Emma and Josh, the epitome
of love, patience, and fortitude.

*All a man's affairs become diseased when he wishes
to cure evils by evils.*
~ *Sophocles*

PROLOGUE

THE SKATERS RACED across the ice with unleashed ferocity, smashing into opposing team members, the boards, whatever and whoever impeded their mission. A ruddy-faced ref went down. His belly thudded onto the frozen surface, and he reflexively covered his head as razor-sharp blades zigzagged alarmingly close to his prone body.

The center, number thirty-nine, tore down the ice, droplets of sweat spraying out from beneath his skull-hugging helmet. Oblivious to the screams of fans and team-mates, he braked abruptly in a fountain of frozen crystals. In hot pursuit, an opponent attempted, but failed, to avoid a collision. Thirty-nine was propelled into the boards, and his head bounced off the glass, smudged late in the game with a blur of sweaty palm prints.

Recovering quickly, he pivoted into position, waving his arms wildly to grab the attention of his left winger. With laser-like precision, the wing launched a perfect saucer pass over the stick of a defender, sending the disc directly onto the tape of his center. In response, thirty-nine executed a flawless one-timer, and the puck blasted toward the goal through the scrum of cold steel and slashing sticks.

Inside the crease, the goaltender dropped to his knees, his legs splaying unnaturally to seal off the tiniest of openings. The lightning-fast puck glanced off his outstretched stick and ricocheted skyward. He thrust his trapper into the air, but the effort failed. Behind him, the puck plunged into the basket.

Thirty-nine's legs collapsed beneath him, and he stretched out his arms in victory. As the camera zoomed in, his body disappeared beneath a sea of orange and black.

***

"SCORE," the man whispered in the hushed room.

He had watched the game hundreds of times, rewinding to the final shot, thousands. His last game as a professional hockey player with the Philadelphia Flyers. The ultimate hat trick. Twenty years and a lifetime later, it remained his finest moment ever.

He reached for the remote and paused the video. Staring at the wall, he allowed the tears to come. A minute passed. Five. When the weeping stopped—had he ever cried so hard or for so long?—he cleared his throat and blew his nose.

The muffled wail of police sirens penetrated the room's soundproof walls.

"Alexa, set lights at twenty percent." His voice was raw.

Subtle up-lights bathed the corners of the room, and he blinked away the last of his tears. An urgent pounding sounded from the foyer, and he pushed unsteadily off the cushions.

Steeling himself, he glanced over his shoulder at the

frozen screen, then up at the ceiling. He pictured her there, two floors above, resting peacefully, her angelic face hinting at long-sought repose. Her hands were folded across her chest, and had he not known her better, he might have thought she was praying.

He had knelt beside her, close enough to wake her, but her unseeing eyes remained sealed by feathery lashes, dark against her porcelain skin. Were it not for the sticky red splatters adorning her naked body, he might have thought to caress her full breasts. Were it not for the jagged slash upon her proffered throat, he might have thought to kiss her lush lips. Were it not for the unspoken sense of relief, he might have thought to cry out in anguish.

1

MARY

A RATTLING from the bedside table roused Mary from her dream—a warm, blissful one, for a change. With eyes still closed, she reached for Jimmy. He was there beside her, snoring softly on his back. The annoying vibration sounded again, and she rolled over to grab her phone.

"Who's that?" Jimmy asked, his voice groggy with sleep.

"Must be Cathy," she said, worriedly squinting to read the screen. "No. It's Diana."

"What the heck, Mary? It's four in the morning."

"I'm well aware of that, Jim. She wants me to call her as soon as I'm up."

"Well, that won't be for another three hours, so go back to sleep." He yanked at the blanket and turned onto his side.

Mary lay staring into the darkness, debating. She had stayed up late, binge-watching *Outlander*, and another few hours of shut-eye would be nice, but she knew herself. Try as she might, she would never doze off again. She slipped from the covers and padded into the bathroom. Gently closing the door behind her, she texted Diana: *Call you in ten.* She changed into the yoga pants and tank draped across her vanity bench, splashed cold water on her face, then tiptoed from the bedroom.

"Thank God," Diana answered.

"What's wrong?" Mary whispered.

"Roger's been arrested."

"Who?"

"Roger Michaud, Mary. Remember? My friend from Bald Head Island."

"The guy you were seeing a while back? What did he do?"

"Nothing. But the police think he murdered his wife."

"Jeez, Diana. He killed his wife?"

"No! He wasn't even there. He was on a fishing trip in Costa Rica."

"Hmm," Mary said. "It's hard to believe someone was murdered on Bald Head Island."

"No, Mary, not on Bald Head. It happened at their house in Pennsylvania."

Mary hesitated, shaking her head. "Diana, this is all very confusing so early in the morning." She heard Diana sniffle. "Are you crying?"

"Yes, I'm crying," Diana replied testily.

"Did you know her, too?"

"No, but still. Roger—oh, never mind. I'll explain everything if you'll please come sit with me for a while. I'm freaking out."

"Okay, okay. I'm leaving now. Put some coffee on."

She scribbled a note to Jimmy and slipped it under the corner of their own coffee maker. She doubted he'd be up before she returned, but she wasn't sure how long Diana would want her to stay. Her friend didn't sound high, but she easily could be by the time Mary got there. Diana always had a ready supply of marijuana, and she jabbered incessantly whenever she smoked. Whenever she drank, for that matter. More often than not, Mary found her nonstop chatter amusing, gossiping and giggling right along with her until they both lost all track of time, but perhaps a murder wasn't the proper occasion to descend into silliness.

Navigating Southport's dark, tree-lined streets was a first in her new car, a sporty white Audi Jimmy surprised her with after *Deceptive Waters* made the *New York Times'* best seller list. She slowed to fidget with the automatic high beams, not sure if the lighted green icon meant they were on or off. Maybe if she had paid closer attention during his in-depth tutorial, the many bells and whistles wouldn't still confuse her. She missed her old, trusty SUV, but they had passed it on to Cathy before she headed back to Penn State in January. Mary was happy her daughter now had a reliable vehicle of her own, especially during the harsh northern winters. Besides, she did look hot behind the wheel of the sleek convertible.

After pulling into a diagonal spot outside Diana's building, she grabbed her keys and phone, then hurried to the door and rang the bell. A buzz sounded, and Mary let herself in.

2

MONKEY

MONKEY DROVE for hours before pulling onto an uncharted overpass near Front Royal. Exiting the truck, he scanned the deserted stretch of road, then limped over to the bridge's railing. Daring to peer down, he watched the murky water of the Shenandoah River moving lazily far below. A wave of vertigo dizzied him, and he clutched the cool metal barrier, shutting his eyes.

When the spinning stopped, he took a deep breath, inhaling the crisp, fresh air. It smelled like home. Sounded like it, too. A pair of whippoorwills called to each other in the distance, and an orchestrated clamor of mating frogs drifted up from the surrounding forest. After a few seconds, he felt steadier and opened his eyes, taking care not to look down. Beyond the not-too-distant hills, a halo of orange and purple painted the western sky. A light breeze stirred his hair, and he rubbed his arms.

The last twenty-four hours had not gone as expected. Not at all. He should have known better. When he set out two days ago, the plan seemed real easy. A quick trip north, get what was his, then head back to home-sweet-home. Nah, it hadn't been easy, but all in all, he was tickled with the outcome. Lady Luck smiled upon him at the last moment, and so long as he wasn't spotted coming or going, he should be in the clear.

Reaching under his untucked flannel, he pulled the gutting knife from the sheath inside his waistband, then wiped the blade on the hem of his shirt. He liked this one, the way it fit his hand real snug. He'd miss it. Winding back his arm, he hurled the knife as far as he could. The shadows creeping up from the hollow made it impossible to follow its trajectory, but holding perfectly still, he picked up the quiet splash, barely audible in the distance.

With a grimace, he stretched out his back, then bent forward, reaching for his toes. The motion tugged at his bad thigh and squeezed his over-full bladder. He righted himself, shook out the sore leg, then unzipped his fly.

Back in his ancient F-150, he checked his phone. No calls, no texts. *Just as well*, he admitted. With a turn of the key, the truck groaned to life. He edged back onto the roadway and headed home.

3

MARY

DIANA WRAPPED her arms around Mary and squeezed hard. Mary hugged her in return. They hadn't seen each other since meeting at Moore Street Market a few weeks earlier. It had become their habit in the past year to get together for lunch at least once a month. That is, whenever Mary wasn't away on a book tour and Diana wasn't tied up at her retail shop, Southport's trendy Seaside Siren.

"Thanks for coming, honey," Diana said, handing Mary a mug of steaming coffee. She wore a flowing silk kimono in tones of lavender and cornflower blue. Her lush, blond curls tumbled messily about her shoulders.

Mary noticed the dark smudges beneath her deep blue eyes. "Of course," she replied. She followed Diana into the living room, where they settled into the plush velvet sofa.

As Mary sipped the coconut-flavored brew, Diana apologized. "I'm sorry, Mary. I realized too late that you don't know I'm back with Roger."

Mary sighed and raised her eyebrows. "I suspected there was someone in your life. Did you two go somewhere romantic last week?"

Diana's face reddened. "No, I told you before. I drove to Atlanta for the gift and accessory show. By myself, I might add."

Mary shrugged. "Why have you been hiding him?"

"I haven't, exactly," Diana said, looking sheepish. "I just wasn't sure how you'd feel about him after, you know, that dust-up with Bobby summer before last."

"Oh, the night they discovered you were two-timing them, and they bolted when you suggested a threesome?" Mary asked. "That dust-up?"

"Two-timing's not exactly how I'd put it, but yeah." Diana crinkled her nose. "Like I told you then, I was bored with the juggling act, so I cooled it. But last August, they, um, took me up on my suggestion."

"Oh, Diana, tell me you didn't."

"Maybe?" she responded with a shrug. She got up to bump the heat up a notch. "You have been keeping secrets from me," Mary said. "Dare I ask how things progressed from cooling it with each of them to hot and steamy with both?"

Diana gulped some of her wine. "I don't know. Summer was in full swing, and I was at Fishy Fishy one night, minding my own business, and Roger shows up. I'd had a few too many of these," she admitted, raising her glass, "and the next thing I know, we're back here in bed."

Mary shook her head. "Bobby, too?"

"Not at that point, honey, but how was I to resist his hot

body forever? You've seen him." Talk of the deckhand's gorgeous physique intensified her Southern drawl.

Mary nodded. "Mm-hm. Cute as they come but a little wet behind the ears."

"Nothing wrong with that. I'm a very patient instructor, and he fills my nights when Roger's not around." Her already rosy cheeks deepened in color, and Mary wondered how many glasses of wine she'd already downed. At least it didn't smell like she'd been smoking pot.

"I wasn't aware your nights need filling."

"Don't get me wrong, Mary. I love living by myself. But a girl's got needs, and they're both so damn good at, well, you know."

"I get it, Diana. I really do, but at the same time?"

"You want details?"

A flash of heat warmed Mary's neck. "Yes?"

Diana stood. "I need another glass of wine for this. Want one?"

"No, thanks. Go ahead, though."

Diana freshened her glass, then grabbed a heart-shaped box of chocolates. "If you're not drinking, at least help me with these."

"Ooh, I will," Mary said, selecting a dark nougat. "Now finish your story."

Diana folded her lean legs beneath her, then draped a throw across her lap. "I can't seem to get warm tonight."

"A little shock, maybe," Mary suggested.

"Yeah, maybe. When my phone rang, I about jumped out of my skin. No one in their right mind calls after midnight with anything but bad news."

"Tell me about it," Mary said with a wry smile. "Jimmy was fit to be tied when your text came through."

"Sorry about that. I guess I'll need to work harder to win him over."

"I'd say so, but I'm not here to talk about my husband. Fill me in on your men."

Diana smiled. "Well, it started innocent enough. Not long after Roger and I hooked back up, I ran into Bobby at American Fish. He asked me to dance, and I said yes. We were both drunk, and it was so damn hot outside. One of us came up with the not-so-brilliant idea to go skinny dipping."

"You didn't! What time was this?"

"I don't remember, exactly. Not too late because the place was still crowded. Anyway, we walked down to the beach, dropped our clothes, and waded on in. We were just laughing and dancing, you know, nothing too scandalous."

"You don't consider skinny dipping in downtown Southport scandalous?" Mary challenged.

"Pshaw," Diana dismissed with a wave of her hand. "But then the music stopped, and I got this weird vibe that we were being watched."

"Not the entire bar?"

"No, it turned out to be Roger. He was standing on the back deck with the strangest look on his face. Not angry, you know. Maybe lustful's the right word? Anyway, I wasn't expecting him until the weekend, but he flew down without telling me. As I mentioned, I was drunk, so I figured, *What the hell?* I waved for him to join us, and the bastard did."

"Please tell me you didn't do *it* right there for the whole bar to see!"

"No. We danced in a circle for a while, kissing a little, but when the band started back up, I came to my senses. We grabbed our clothes and ran up to the Yoga Dock to dress. We came back here, smoked some weed, then Roger took me to bed. Bobby joined in a little while later, and the rest is a fuzzy, but very pleasurable, memory."

"Are you still?" Mary asked, unable to resist.

"Nah, that was the one-and-only night. Turns out the idea of a threesome is more tantalizing than the reality of it. That next morning was weird, even for me."

Mary snorted, then popped another chocolate into her mouth. "Girl, I do love living vicariously through you!"

"I aim to please," Diana said with a giggle.

"That you do. Now, as much as I don't want to be a buzzkill, tell me about Roger's dead wife."

After Mary refilled her coffee, Diana recounted her brief conversation with Roger. How he came home and discovered his wife's lifeless body and was hauled off to jail after the police showed up. Thankfully, his attorney assured him that he would be released as soon as the courts opened in the morning.

"Did he tell you how she died?" Mary asked.

"He couldn't really talk on the jail phone, but as soon as he's allowed to leave the state, he's coming straight here."

Mary picked up her phone and searched *Roger Michaud*. "Nothing's posted to the internet yet, so the press hasn't caught wind of it."

"Good, I guess, but that's bound to change soon enough. Mary, he was just so distraught." She twisted an errant lock of hair, then added, "Which, come to think of it, pisses me off."

"What do you mean?"

"If he's been honest with me that he no longer loves her, why's he so upset?"

"Diana! Whether he loved her or not, she was murdered. And he found her body. It isn't like she died of natural causes."

"I know, I know. But still, I want to be sure."

"Sure of what? That he didn't love her or that he didn't kill her?"

"That he didn't love her," Diana admitted. She pushed her lower lip out in a pout. "He told me their marriage was over a long time ago, even before we started sleeping together, but she wouldn't agree to a divorce. She didn't love him, but she wouldn't let him go. She only wanted his money. Mary, don't tell anyone I said this, but he's better off without her, and if you ask me, she deserved what she got for making him so miserable."

"Girl, this vindictiveness isn't like you."

"Maybe it is like me," Diana said, looking down. "You don't really know me, Mary."

"I think I do, my friend. And I love you, but sadly this is a side I don't particularly like." She stood and pried the wine glass from Diana's hand. "I suggest you go back to bed and get some sleep."

"I'm not sure I can, but you're probably right. As usual." Diana wagged her head. "I went a little crazy just then. I'll up my CBD today and set myself to rights."

Mary rolled her eyes. "You do whatever it takes." Checking her phone, she said, "I've got to get home to prepare for a nine a.m. Zoom interview, but I'll call you this afternoon."

She led Diana into the bedroom, then covered her with a blanket, tucking it tightly around her. "Cozy?" she asked.

"Mm-hm," Diana sighed. "Thanks for coming, Mary. You're the best friend I've ever had."

"My pleasure, and ditto." She kissed Diana's forehead, then whispered, "Sleep tight."

Downstairs, she let herself out and closed the door tightly behind her. After testing to ensure it had locked, she glanced south. The light of the waxing moon, low in the lavender sky, reflected off the dark waters of the Cape Fear River. She breathed in the damp morning air, then headed toward the city pier. Since she was already here, there was absolutely no reason not to take in the sunrise, always spectacular from the Southport waterfront. She had an urge to text Jimmy to join her, but her husband was not a morning person. At least not since his retirement last year. *Maybe I can work on that*, she thought, snickering at the memory of what it had taken to wake him for the one and only sunrise they'd watched together. That little trick, she knew, never failed her.

4

VANESSA

VANESSA MICHAUD BREEZED out the doors of Boutique Sasha as the valet pulled to the curb in her red BMW convertible. The mocha-skinned young man popped the trunk and grinned widely as he accepted her armload of totes. He tucked them into the well around the collapsed roof, then held the door while she lowered her toned body into the driver's seat.

"Have a pleasant afternoon, Mrs. Michaud," he offered with a flirtatious wink.

She slipped a twenty into his shirt pocket, scratching his chest ever so invitingly with her manicured fingers.

He glanced around, then grabbed her wrist. "I get off at five."

She battered her long eyelashes and pulled her hand free. "Not tonight, Javier." With a wave, the Z4 darted into traffic, resulting in a cacophony of angry honks from drivers forced to slow their navigation of Rittenhouse Square.

Stopped at the intersection of Eighteenth and Market Streets, she checked the dashboard clock. Roger was due home in two hours, and she was running out of time to do everything she wanted, not least of which was getting her purchases inside and hidden upstairs. When the light changed, she expertly shifted gears, accelerating the sports car in a display of speed and impatience.

Her husband knew full well of her shopping addiction. Sometimes she tried to contain it. God knows she didn't need one additional thread of clothing. Hell, she didn't need ninety-nine percent of what she already owned. But Sasha's seasonal sales were far too tempting to pass up. So long as Roger didn't venture up to the third floor of their Main Line home, she was in the clear. Without his knowledge or approval, she had secretly contracted for the entire space to be transformed into her enormous personal suite, complete with an elaborate closet system, an alcove for a custom-made canopy bed, and an elegant bathroom with hot tub and rainfall shower.

She hired the contractor four years ago before Roger left on an extended fishing expedition with a group of men from Bald Head Island. He had asked her to fly as far south as North Carolina with him, then wait on that godforsaken island for three miserable weeks while he gallivanted around the Caribbean. She refused, pouting that she would be bored out of her mind stranded by herself, when all along she was counting down the minutes until he left.

She found the entire barrier island far from the romantic retreat Roger had promised when he built the home several years earlier. He, on the other hand, absolutely loved it, flying down often for weeks at a stretch. She hadn't joined him since Hurricane Jasmine—in answer to her silent prayers—wreaked havoc on the island in the summer of 2018. Since then, he had found himself a local floozy to keep him entertained, and she doubted she would ever go back.

She loved the majestic house in Radnor, as well as the charming cottage in Bethany Beach, Delaware, which was a far closer escape than Bald Head Island, so desolate that it was reachable only by private boat or ferry. She didn't begrudge Roger's spending time there without her. Just the opposite. She relished her solitude and freedom when he was gone, shopping during the day and dressing up in her beautiful gowns at night. Even without someone to admire and gush over her.

Smiling at the thought of her stunning new evening gown, a Badgley Mischka from last fall's collection, she gunned the engine and merged into the mass of streaming metal otherwise known as the Schuylkill Expressway.

ROGER

THE BARRED cell door clanged loudly behind him, and Roger surreptitiously crossed himself in gratitude. The uniformed deputy snorted, then prodded him down the garishly lit walkway, stopping short at a solid steel door. With a click, the door slid open into an interlocking vestibule. Once inside, a plastic zip bag containing his shoes, belt, and other belongings was shoved through a gated opening in the glass. After signing for the items, he asked, "What now?"

"Leave," the surly officer replied.

Roger glanced around the tight space, a look of uncertainty on his face. "Which way to the exit?"

The officer scowled and pressed a keypad set into the wall. A second door swung outward, and Roger hurried through to his freedom.

In the reception area, he spotted his attorney and

made a beeline for the man. Wallace Leonard looked tired but dapper in a tailored navy Brooks Brothers suit, his striped lavender-and-yellow tie a nod to spring. He accepted Roger's extended hand, then motioned for him to sit down. "Put on your shoes, and we'll head to my office."

"I'd rather go straight home," Roger countered, pulling his tan docksiders from the bag and dropping them to the floor. The right shoe landed sole-up, and a wave of nausea hit him at the sight of the deep red splotch etched into the tread. He swallowed back the bile that burned his throat, then quickly righted the shoe and shoved in his foot.

"Your home's a crime scene for the foreseeable future. My assistant is arranging an apartment for you, but it won't be ready until this afternoon, so you're coming with me."

Roger followed Leonard outside. A gaggle of reporters, many with mics and cameras, came alive when the two men exited the building. "Keep your head down and don't say a word," Leonard ordered.

"Roger, why'd you kill your wife?" called a female voice. Roger flinched.

"Was she cheating on you?" A microphone was thrust under his nose.

"Were you cheating on her?" another voice yelled.

Roger hesitated. He had to set the record straight. The attorney squeezed his arm. Hard.

Leonard's limo was waiting at the curb, and the burly chauffeur hustled the men inside. Behind the tinted windows, Roger watched the frenzied media give chase, hurling accusatory questions at the departing vehicle. His shoulders drooped in exhaustion.

"Just how screwed am I?" he asked.

Leonard looked up from the papers he had pulled from

his briefcase. "Unless the cops have another suspect, you're it."

"But what about my alibi? I was in Costa Rica, or on my way back, when Van—" His voice caught. "When Vanessa was killed."

"The police know that," Leonard said, "but they'll say you hired someone to take care of her while you were away."

"You mean a hit man? I didn't. I couldn't. Sure, we had issues, but—"

Leonard cut him off, then pressed the button to close the privacy window between the front and back seats. "No one wants to hear about your issues. From this point forward you speak only when I say 'speak,' and you never, ever volunteer information that could convict you. Understand?"

Roger nodded.

"Good. It's neither your job nor mine to prove the prosecution's case."

Roger dropped his head against the seat back and stared up through the sunroof. He was screwed big-time.

MARY

MARY WAS SHOWERED and dressed by the time Jimmy bounded down the stairs. Kissing his wife on the top of her head, he asked, "So, what the heck's up with Hippie Chick?"

Her husband had never warmed up to Diana, whose laissez-faire lifestyle bristled against his conservative, law-enforcement sensibilities. She understood and had stopped trying to force the two together.

"Do you really want to know?" she asked.

"No, but I would like to know what was so darn important that you were compelled to sneak out of the house before dawn."

"I hardly snuck," she insisted. "I left you a note." She waved it at him.

Jimmy snatched it from her and wadded it into a ball. "You can tell me in person now."

"If you insist." She handed him a mug of coffee. "Do you remember that guy from Bald Head Diana was seeing a couple summers ago?"

"No. Should I?"

"You asked," she replied.

"All right. Tell me."

"Well, the guy, Roger Michaud, was arrested last night for murdering his wife."

"Diana's seeing a married man?"

"That's what your take-away is from what I just told you?" She opened the fridge and grabbed a lemon from the crisper.

"Yes, but it hardly surprises me. You should tell her that husbands murder their wives all the time." He poured his coffee into an insulated travel mug with the UNCW logo, then tamped down the lid.

"And wives murder their husbands all the time," she countered, waving a citrus reamer in his direction.

"How'd he do it?"

"Diana says he didn't. She's pretty upset." Mary elbowed him away from the sink.

"If you ask me, she should be grateful he was arrested. If the dude's a killer, she could've been his next victim."

"I'm afraid that's not how she sees it. She says he's coming back to town as soon as his lawyer gets him released."

"That's just great, Mary." He pulled his phone from his pocket and hovered an index finger over the screen. "Should I call Joe Vickers right now?"

Mary narrowed her eyes. "Why?"

"To warn him what you're up to. You'll recall he asked for a heads-up the next time."

"Ha! I'm in no way involved in this, Jim."

"Yet," he said, pocketing his phone. "I gotta run. I have that meeting with Sheriff Franklin this morning. If you want, I'll fill him in, too."

Mary jabbed the reamer in his direction again, and he sidestepped her as he headed for the garage. Pausing, he turned back, a curious look on his face. "Did you say this guy's name is Roger Michaud, as in the Philadelphia Flyers all-time star Roger Michaud?"

"I vaguely remember Diana saying he played hockey," Mary replied with a shrug.

"Hmm, wouldn't that be something?"

Mary's cell phone buzzed, and she waggled her fingers in Jimmy's direction as she answered the call. "Good morning, this is Mary Branson."

MONKEY

THE UNTIDY PATCH of crabgrass needed mowing, and the weeds along the rutted concrete walkway were propagating like rabbits. Monkey was trying his best to fix up the place, but it was a never-ending job. He got the chimney repointed last week, and the bats were finally chased from the attic, but his to-do list seemed to multiply itself every night while he slept. The missus sure wouldn't be happy when she got home if the place didn't look tended to.

He stood at the sink and stared out the window, swallowing the last sip of cold coffee. A thick dusting of pollen, like the fine fur of yellow cockscomb his ma used to grow, clung to the porch railing and aluminum siding. The window screens, too. With a heavy sigh, he rinsed out the chipped cup and placed it on the drain board.

Later, exhausted and frustrated by his unproductive day —each repair uncovered something else that needed fixing—

Monkey pushed himself up from the sofa and shut off the ancient TV. Not a damn thing worth watching until he saved up the money for cable service. At least his parole officer had helped him hook up the internet and buy a new-to-him cell phone. It was amazing how much you could get done these days on a little mobile phone.

When he was first sent up to Mountain City Penitentiary, he never imagined how things would change while he was serving his time. But he watched it all from the inside. He even trained on computers as part of his mandated work rehabilitation. At the time, he dreaded those classes, hated missing out on a single hour in the yard to take them, but he was glad now. Those lessons were how he managed to track down Ina Rose.

He pushed his spectacles up the bridge of his nose, then swiped a finger across the phone screen. As the image loaded, he squirmed in anticipation. There she was, still so darn pretty. He could almost feel her soft body lying beside him, in a big bed now, not the tiny twin from when they first got hitched. They would have this house and the master bedroom all to themselves now. He would buy a new mattress first, of course. He had thrown out his parents' old one after discovering an entire brood of mice had set up housekeeping inside.

He sighed heavily. He was doing that an awful lot lately. He glanced around the frigid room, eying all the things that needed sprucing up. The blue plaid couch was far rattier than he remembered, and the rag rug beneath his feet was faded and threadbare. Ina Rose would want everything fresh and new, of that he was sure. She liked pretty things, and he wanted her to have them. Hell, they both deserved nice things. He would figure a way to make some money. At least enough to buy a piece or two of new furniture, another rug, maybe even paint the walls. And he'd need gas to get where he needed going. To finish what needed doing before she came home. Willingly, he hoped, but if not...well, he had plenty of time to worry about that. Being locked up taught him that fretting about things never changed them. It taught him...what was that word the prison preacher used? *Long-suffering.* He had long-suffering in spades. If nothing else, Monkey Parker was a very patient man.

VANESSA

VANESSA CLICKED THE GARAGE REMOTE, but the door didn't budge. She pressed the button again, to no avail. She'd have to open it from the inside. Precious time lost, and she was hoping to get in a sweat-invoking Pilates session before her shower.

Once inside the front door, she hurried through the foyer, her three-inch-high Manolo Blahniks echoing off the polished travertine. In the rear breezeway, she kicked off the stilettos, then barefooted it into the garage. When the door opened, she hurried to her car and steered it into the bay. Stupidly, she tried to close the door behind her using the same defunct remote. Embarrassed, she lobbed it across the garage, where it hit the wall and disappeared behind a fire-engine red cabinet.

"Just great," she muttered. She shouldn't have done that. The cabinet was massively heavy, laden with every conceivable tool known to mankind. Not that Roger had ever used a single one. Her husband was decidedly not a handyman. He only bought the cabinet and tools to impress her early in their marriage when she expressed dismay that he didn't own a single wrench. The only other person those tools had impressed was the contractor she hired to do the work on the third floor. He'd also been quite impressed, she recalled with a tingling sensation, with her own handy skill set.

After jumping from the car, she gathered the shopping bags, and with arms loaded, she hurried up the back staircase to her secret suite. She was practically salivating at the thought of trying on the gown again, but it might have to wait for another day. Inside the closet, she unzipped the plastic bag containing the billows of silver chiffon, snipped off the tags, then tore them into tiny pieces. As she gently parted two gowns of a similar shade on the long rack of evening attire, she paused. Maybe, if she cut her workout down to twenty minutes and grabbed an even quicker shower, she would have time. She laid the gown across the chaise, then dashed down to her gym.

FORTY MINUTES LATER, Vanessa lifted the gown from its padded hanger and slipped it over her head. The silky lining caressed her naked skin, causing her to shiver with ecstasy. She stepped into a pair of dainty heels with straps lined in Swarovski crystals, then she all but floated onto the pedestal in front of the wall of floor-to-ceiling mirrors. Closing her eyes, she twirled, humming the refrain to Reba McEntire's "Fancy."

When she stopped, she opened her eyes and grinned at the fairy princess staring back at her. The gown was so much lovelier under the glittering prisms cast by the over-head chandelier. The delicate beads sewn onto the fitted bodice sparkled as she swayed back and forth, the full skirt swishing elegantly to the music in her head. *If only Mama could see me now.*

With a start, she froze, gooseflesh rippling up her arms. Someone was downstairs. Was Roger home earlier than expected? She hadn't even called out for their dinner yet.

She reached back to unclasp the gown, allowing it to drop in a heap at her feet. As she stepped over the folds of fabric, a heel caught the edge of the pedestal. She squealed as she fell, her arms outstretched to catch herself. She landed in a tangle on hands and knees, then rolled over quickly to inspect the damage. The plush carpeting had saved her from any lasting injury, but a coppery taste filled her mouth and both knees were blooming with droplets of blood. She rubbed her throbbing right shoulder for a second, then pushed carefully to her feet.

Dangit, she thought, examining the errant shoe. The heel was snapped clean off. They'd been perfect with the dress, and now they were worthless. She bent to gather the gown, inspecting it for damage. It appeared to have survived the calamity. She held it in front of her body for one last, longing glance in the mirror. The reflection of the chande-lier's crystals twinkled like ethereal fairies above her head, and she sighed dreamily.

ROGER

SEEKING to avoid both the press and Wallace Leonard, Roger ordered an Uber to take him to the airport. His attorney would be sending his limo to collect him for their scheduled appointment, but Roger had no intention of sticking around for that. As far as he understood it, the terms of his release did not require that he stay in the state, only that he not leave the country. And last he checked, Bald Head Island was in the US of A. He was good to go.

At the counter, the airline attendant checked his ID, typed into her computer, then shook her head.

"Is there a problem?" he asked nervously.

"No, it's just that our system is annoyingly slow this morning."

He smiled, holding his breath until the woman returned his driver's license along with a business class boarding pass.

"Have a nice flight, Mr. Michaud," she said with a pleasant smile.

He passed through security and headed toward the gate. He'd timed it so there wouldn't be much of a wait before takeoff. Just enough time to grab a double Bloody Mary. He might agree to stay in the country, but he had no intention of adhering to the court's order that he not consume alcoholic beverages. Now was not the time to sober up.

The news streaming on the bar's TV concerned last night's storm, an early spring nor'easter that had knocked down trees and power lines as it raced north to New England. Amazingly, he hadn't heard the rain or wind, but it appeared to have been a doozie. He had been so exhausted when Leonard's driver dropped him off at the extended-stay accommodation, he had gone straight to bed, passing out within moments of closing his eyes. His sleep had been deep and, fortunately, dream-free.

As the vodka hit his bloodstream, he felt his shoulders relax, the tension draining from his neck and back. He could almost smell the salt air and feel the sun warming his skin. He loved the house on Bald Head Island. The peace and quiet, the absence of prying neighbors, the general lack of nosy attention. He was counting on the home's remote location, away from the small village and marina, to ensure the privacy he so desperately needed now. His only desire was to hunker down until he figured his way out of this mess.

Diana popped into his head, and he smiled. He was finally in a position to invite her to the island, have her stay overnight with him. She had never come across on the ferry before. Why, he wasn't exactly sure. It was highly unlikely Vanessa would have ever caught them. And even if she had, so what?

Downing the last of the cocktail, he flinched when his photo flashed on the TV screen. The closed captioning read: *Legendary Flyer Roger Michaud released after murder of second wife. The woman's body was found—*

The empty glass slipped from Roger's hand and struck the lacquered bar top. The bartender glanced up from his phone and sauntered over. "Need another, buddy?"

"No," Roger replied, laying a twenty on the bar. "Gotta catch my flight." He dropped his head and all but ran from the bar.

10

MARY

MARY PEDALED her bike into town and dropped the kickstand outside Diana's shop. The display window was dark and a *Closed* sign hung in the window, so she rang the bell.

"Hello?" came Diana's voice through a small speaker.

"It's Mary."

The door buzzed, and Mary let herself in. Upstairs, inside the apartment, she called out, "Where are you?"

"Bedroom," came the reply.

As she wandered through the small, eclectic space, redolent with the scent of patchouli, she smiled. Pausing in the doorway to the bedroom, she watched as Diana rolled a brightly patterned skirt—one of the full-length bohemian numbers she was so fond of—before stuffing it into a canvas carryall.

"Going somewhere?" Mary asked.

Diana looked up with a wide grin. "Yes, ma'am. Bald Head Island." She giggled like a teenager. "I'm meeting Roger at the four o'clock ferry."

"He's here already?" Mary asked.

"He will be this afternoon." She glanced at the clock and shimmied.

"I'm surprised he's been allowed to travel," Mary said.

"I'm not," Diana sniped, a flash of annoyance crossing her face. "He isn't guilty, Mary."

"Okay," Mary said as she cleared a spot on a chair overflowing with colorful clothing. "He didn't kill his wife. What's her name, by the way?"

"Vanessa." She practically spat the word.

"Vanessa," Mary repeated. "I'm willing to give him the benefit of the doubt if you are. But, come on, Diana, how will it look if you're seen together so soon after her death?"

"When have you ever known me to care one hoot about how things *look*?"

"Never, but then again, this isn't a typical situation."

"No, it's not, but he needs me, Mary, and I'm going to be there for him." She zipped up the bag before picking up a glass of wine from her bedside table. She raised it toward Mary with a lift of her eyebrows.

Mary shook her head and tried again. "Beyond how it'll look, then, there is such a thing as being too caring. Don't let your soft heart prevent you from using your head. You'll want to keep an eye out for anything that might seem off about him."

"I'm not exactly sure what you mean by *off*, but there's truly no need to worry about me. Or Roger, for that matter. Trust me, he'll be seeing a lot more of me than my soft heart." She sat on the mattress, then downed the remains of her wine.

Mary smiled. "I have no doubt about that, girlfriend. Again, if you're not concerned, neither am I."

Diana set down her empty glass, then sighed. "There is one thing I am fretting about."

"What's that?"

"Bobby. He's out shrimping today, so I can't tell him I'm leaving town again. Not that I'd tell him where, mind you. Or who I'm going with. Knowing him, he'd only come looking for me."

"He might figure it out on his own once the story about Roger comes out. You know how fast rumors spread around her."

"God," Diana said, shaking her head. "I hate that about this town."

"Maybe you should stay under the radar while you're on the island."

"We will."

"Because when reporters learn where Roger's hiding," Mary continued, "they'll surely sniff him out. I wouldn't give the locals more than a day or two to give him up. Stay in touch, please?"

"I will, but don't expect to hear anything until we come up for air." She held up a bottle of massage oil before dropping it into an outside pocket of her bag.

Mary laughed. "God, don't hurt him."

"Only if he begs me," she teased with a wink. "That reminds me. I need to beg a favor of you. Would you receive a delivery for me if it comes in while I'm gone?"

"Sure, just let me know when."

"Thank you, honey."

Mary got up to leave and glanced around the tiny bedroom. "You won't know what do with yourself in Roger's big house."

Diana looked away and mumbled something.

"What?" Mary asked. "I didn't hear you."

"I said I once lived in a grand house." Her voice was wistful. "Before I came to Southport. It was outside Las Vegas and had more rooms than I could count."

"Nice," Mary observed with a nod. "You never told me that."

"There are many things I haven't told you, honey. Most of which I've tried very hard to forget."

"We all have a past, Diana. You're no different than the rest of us, no matter how hard you might try."

Diana grabbed a tissue off the nightstand and dabbed her eyes. "That's the cruelest thing you've ever said to me, Mary Branson."

Mary patted the top of her friend's head. "Glad to be of help."

11

JIMMY

AS THE GARAGE door lowered behind his parked truck, Jimmy stepped down from the cab. Heading for the mudroom, he noticed that Mary's bike wasn't leaning against the wall in front of his bumper. She was out and about again. He wished she had waited until he got home, and he would have gone with her. Since his retirement last spring from the University of North Carolina at Wilmington, where he'd served as the university's chief of police, he tried hard to embrace a more-relaxed lifestyle. His new part-time gig as a personal firearms and defense instructor took up a portion of his time, and Mary's book tours still more, but like his wife, he now enjoyed walking and biking through their little slice of coastal heaven.

The side door to the garage opened, and Mary pushed her bike through, startling when she saw Jimmy standing there.

"Oh, you're home!"

"Just got here. I was on my way in to fix a late lunch. Want something?"

"Yes, I'm starved," she replied.

Jimmy helped her with the bike, then hugged her tight to his chest. She smelled of perspiration and patchouli. "You okay?"

"I'm fine. Why?"

"Just wondering." He spanked her rear end with affection.

"You?" She asked as she kicked off her sneakers.

"Never better."

Inside, Jimmy opened the fridge, taking out all the fixings for turkey sandwiches. As he laid everything on the counter, he considered asking Mary what was going on with Diana and, far more intriguing, Roger Michaud. He didn't especially like the woman, and he had little to no interest in her life. Except when it impacted Mary. From what he could tell, she was well-liked in town, and Mary considered her a dear friend, but something about her rubbed him the wrong way. Maybe it was her pot-smoking disregard for the law, but even setting that aside, he could tolerate only so much of her.

Mary intercepted his thoughts. "Diana's going to Bald Head with Roger this afternoon."

Jimmy puffed out an impatient breath. "She's a grown woman, Mar."

"That doesn't stop me from worrying about her. She swears he's innocent, but like you jokingly said, he could easily be a wife killer."

"Not so jokingly. There are plenty of studies that confirm uxoricide accounts for nearly half of all female homicides."

"What?"

"Women murdered by their romantic partners," he explained.

"Not much comfort, honey."

"What do you want me to say? I'm not going to lie to you."

"I know. Just hear me out."

"That I can do." He carried the plates to the dining table.

Mary grabbed a bag of chips from the pantry, then asked, "Beer or tea?"

"Sweet tea. I can't stomach that black stuff you drink."

"To each his own," she said, selecting two bottles from the fridge.

They munched in silence for a moment, then Jimmy prompted, "So talk."

Mary wiped a napkin across her mouth. "Despite what Diana says, I don't think she knows Roger all that well."

"His wife probably didn't either."

Mary nodded. "Exactly. Which leads me to my next thought. Do you think George might be willing to take a drive up to Philadelphia to nose around? Find out who Roger Michaud really is?"

Jimmy shrugged. "Jumping right into the fire, aren't you, Mary?"

"Well, I've got to do something! The police in Pennsylvania don't care anything about Diana. They'll be focusing on the evidence as it pertains to the victim and suspect, or suspects, in their jurisdiction. But the prime suspect will be down here, romancing my friend, who, sadly, is looking at him through rose-colored glasses."

"Fair argument. If George is willing to do his thing, dig

around a little, what do you see him accomplishing that the police can't?"

Mary sighed with frustration. "I don't know. Maybe talk with his employees. His neighbors. Figure out what kind of man he really is. Just so I'm more comfortable with Diana being with him."

Jimmy rolled his eyes. "I thought you promised not to become personally involved in your next story."

"Who said this will be my next story?"

"I recognize that glint in your eyes, Mary Branson."

Mary purposefully closed her eyes and took a big bite of her sandwich. Jimmy waited while she chewed. He knew all about the itch to pursue a case. He had felt the rush time and again during his career, but he was now more than content to let others do the pursuing. His wife, on the other hand, had only recently tasted the rush of criminal intrigue. Sadly, that first thrill had nearly cost her her life. He'd joked about it earlier, but it was hardly a laughing matter. While her wounded body and psyche were mostly healed, he continued to worry whenever they were apart. He'd never tell her how much, but he lived every single day with the dread of losing her.

Mary swallowed and opened her eyes. "I can't help it, Jimmy. This murder has all but fallen in my lap. And with Diana's indirect involvement, I can't not look a little deeper. Or at least let George to do it for me."

Jimmy knew when he was beat. "Call him. See what's on his plate, but don't guilt him into it. If he's busy on another case, drop it."

"I would never," she protested. "Not on my first call, anyway."

. . .

LUNCH OVER, Mary joined Jimmy in his study, and together they called George Purnell. They were introduced to the private investigator when Mary was looking into the deaths detailed in her best-selling novel, *Deceptive Waters*. Jimmy knew him to be a good and honest man, and with their law enforcement backgrounds in common, they'd become fast friends. He trusted George, who had come to care for Mary and would assuredly do everything in his power to keep her safe.

"Hey, pretty lady. What can I do for you?"

"What's going on, George?" Mary asked.

"Just waiting on you. Are you ready to leave Jim and live on the wild side with me?"

"Not just yet, but give me time. His retirement has him underfoot way too much for my liking. He's here with me now, by the way."

"Hey, buddy, how ya doing?" George asked.

"Good, George. I hope we're not interrupting anything, but Mary's got a bee in her bonnet and won't let it go."

"You need to write another book, Mary. That'll keep you busy."

"Funny you should mention that. There's something—or rather, someone—I'd like you to look into."

"I'm all ears."

"Guy's name is Roger Michaud, and he's been accused—"

"Of stabbing his wife to death," George finished. "I know. I'm a Caps fan, but I'm well aware of who Michaud is. The murder's all the talk on sports radio."

"Then you're ahead of the curve."

"Just why and how are you involved, Mary?"

"My question exactly," Jimmy interjected.

Mary gave him her best evil eye. "I'm not involved, but

my friend, Diana, is. She's been having an affair with Michaud for a couple years now."

"I heard rumors he's a dog, but that particular detail escaped me," George said. "Tell me more."

FIFTEEN MINUTES LATER, they disconnected the call.

"Happy?" Jimmy asked her.

"We'll see what he comes up with," she said. "Regardless, it was nice catching up. We should invite him down for another visit."

"It was, and we should," he agreed.

"I'm heading up for a shower," Mary announced, holding out her hand. "Care to join me?"

"Tempting," he said, rubbing his belly, "but if I'm going to lose this winter girth, I need to get on that bike. If you wait for me, I'll be back in an hour or so."

She walked around the desk and wrapped her arms around his neck, kissing his ear. "Oh, I'll wait," she whispered.

12

DIANA

THE FERRY WAS right on schedule, but Roger was not. Diana's disappointment was as heavy as the bag she dropped beside a wooden bench in the open-air waiting area. Sweat trickled down her back, and she blew a few straggling hairs not yet plastered to her forehead. After watching the departing vessel back away from the dock, she sat down in exasperation. She had rushed to get here with ample time to spare, waiting excitedly in the warm afternoon sun while other passengers passed her in line. When it became apparent they would miss the four o'clock ferry, she texted him, then called. Nothing.

She dropped her head against the back of the bench and closed her eyes. She had slept very little in the past week, and her deep disappointment mixed heavily with the exhaustion pulling her down. Should she have listened to

Mary and turned down Roger's invitation? Maybe it wasn't her smartest decision to be with him just now.

"Glad you waited." The deep voice roused her from her drowsiness.

She opened her eyes and squinted in the afternoon sun. "Roger!" She jumped to her feet and hugged him. He held her tightly, then kissed her long and hard. When they separated, she pouted, "We missed the ferry."

"Not to worry. I hired a private boat to take us over. It'll drop us off at the marina, and we'll avoid the crowds altogether." He reached down to pick up her bag and grimaced. "What the heck did you pack in here, woman?"

Diana blushed. "Enough for a few days. I didn't know how long I'd be staying."

"As long as you want," he replied, taking her hand.

He led her to the deep-water marina, stopping beside the fuel dock where a center-console, its two outboard motors idling, was tied off.

Roger stepped onto the fishing boat, handing Diana's bag to the skipper. He held out his hand for her, but she hesitated. "Come on, baby," he urged. "I won't let you fall in."

She sucked in a breath, then hiked up her skirt. After tentatively setting a foot on the gunwale, she leaned forward. Roger grabbed her by the waist and hoisted her aboard.

"I've never been on a boat this little before," she admitted as he set her down.

"Well, ma'am, I'm sorry about my tiny Grady-White here, but I promise you she's seaworthy," the captain said as he threw off the dock line.

"No, no," Diana apologized. "Your boat's great, and to

be honest, it's the only one I've ever been on. Where I come from, we're pretty far from the ocean."

As they tooled through the marina and out to the channel, Roger and Diana settled into the bow for the short trip to the island. As they picked up speed, the spray from the river canceled out the heat of the late afternoon sun. Diana wrapped her arms around herself, and Roger pulled her in close, nuzzling her ear.

"Just you and me against the world, baby," he whispered. "Just you and me."

THE BEACH HOUSE WAS MAGNIFICENT. Not as big or architecturally impressive as the mansion she had lived in near Vegas, but the endless views of the ocean were breathtaking. As Diana pirouetted on the back deck, she had an overwhelming desire to drop into the lotus position for an impromptu meditation.

Roger called her name, and her heart dropped a little. Couldn't he feel the fierce pull of the setting sun? She reluctantly bowed toward the western sky, then followed his voice through the open French doors.

She found him at a long bar that dominated the tastefully decorated great room. The teak surface was polished to a high gloss that reflected the pendant lights dangling from the crisscrossed beams high above the room. She flinched when the cork popped on a bottle of Moët & Chandon. Watching as he poured out two flutes, she conceded that a fine champagne might serve to relax her just as much as a sunset meditation.

She accepted the flute, and he toasted, "To time alone with the most beautiful woman on earth."

"Sir, you do flatter a girl."

She turned her longing gaze to the wall of windows. "Why don't we take these outside to watch the sunset?"

"Screw that," he said, his eyebrows arching mischievously. "I'm taking you to bed."

She stepped into his arms. "Miss me, did you?"

"Yes," he answered before proving it with another deep kiss.

The aromatic taste of champagne filled her senses, making her head spin. She hadn't eaten a thing all day, not since yesterday afternoon, actually, but mistaking her swaying for desire, his arms tightened around her waist. She struggled to catch her breath and pushed herself away.

When his face took on a puzzled expression, she reassured, "You took my breath away."

His grin returned, and he grabbed her free hand. "Baby, I haven't even started."

She followed him up the winding staircase to the third-floor master bedroom. A massive bed encompassed one entire wall, its four sleek posters rising eight feet from the floor. Roger pulled back the plush down comforter, then picked up a small remote from the nightstand. Aiming it toward the opposite wall of draperies, Diana watched as the panels parted to reveal yet another expansive view of the Atlantic.

"Roger, this is stunning," she observed.

"I know, and I'm so happy you're finally here to see it."

Walking over to take in the full view, she was suddenly shy, unsure of herself in all this opulence. Long-suppressed feelings of unworthiness threatened to bubble up, and she shook her head to scatter them away.

Roger came up behind her and ran his hands down her bare arms.

"I'm serious, Diana. You're gorgeous, and I'm so glad you're here with me."

She felt the warm flush rise from her chest and spread into her face. He seemed so serious. Suddenly her doubts were gone. Roger wanted her, and she needed him. She lost herself in his embrace.

TWO HOURS LATER, Diana awoke to the sound of muffled shouting. Opening her eyes in the dim light, she didn't immediately know where she was, but the waning pink in the distant sky brought it back.

She glanced at the mattress beside her. It was empty. The voice carried up from below, outside on the lower deck. She slipped from the bed and padded to the wall of windows. A sliver of moon hung just above the water, now the shade of deep, ripe plums. She unlatched the sliding door and stepped onto the balcony. The evening air was cool on her naked skin, and she shivered.

She could hear him more clearly now, on the deck below. His voice carried over the soft whoosh of waves, and it was obvious he was angry.

"Screw that, Leonard. I don't care how it looks. I'm not coming back."

Diana couldn't hear the other voice, but she assumed it was Roger's attorney.

"Then you and that detective can get yourselves on a plane if you need to see me. I swear, Leonard, make this go away, or I'll find an attorney who will." The door slammed below her.

She tiptoed back into the bedroom, closing the slider behind her. She found a bathrobe on a hook inside the closet and slipped it over her body. Pausing at the bedroom door, she smiled at her reflection in the mirror above the dresser. *Look where we are*, she thought.

"Roger?" she called, stepping onto the spiral staircase. She paused on the second-floor landing to count the closed doors. Five bedrooms on this level, he'd told her. Had they ever been slept in?

As she descended into the great room, she saw him standing in front of the fireplace, staring intently into the blue flames. He was wearing a T-shirt and cargo pants, but his feet were bare.

"Hey, there," she said, walking up behind him. "It's gotten chilly."

He turned and smiled. "Come here. I'll keep you warm."

He draped an arm around her shoulders, then offered her his glass of deep amber liquid. She took a sip. It was warm and aromatic, and it burned her throat as she swallowed.

"Mm. What is it?"

"Cognac. Want one?"

"I do."

He walked to the bar, and she wandered into the kitchen. The space was bathed in cool light from the circular pendants above the island. In contrast to the great room's polished wood bar and beams, the kitchen cabinets were stark and modern with a matte black finish and glass-fronted doors. She ran a finger over the white marble-topped island, then turned to open the fridge, an enormous Sub-Zero twice the size of her own.

"Hungry?" she called over to him. "I'm not much of a cook, but I think I can manage scrambled eggs and"—she pulled out a drawer—"bacon?"

"Or we could just order a pizza and save the eggs for breakfast," he suggested.

"Perfect," she agreed. "Do they deliver?"

He handed her his phone. "Not a chance. Besides, it'll be quicker if we pick up, although you should be the one to go. Here, I have them on speed dial. Delphina's. The Margherita is great, if you don't mind garlic breath."

"As long as we're both eating it, we're good."

Upstairs, he watched her dress, then he led her down to the garage to show her how to operate the golf cart. "Follow the beach road back to the ferry terminal. Delphina's is right before the marina entrance."

"Got it," she said, accepting the fifty he handed her.

He kissed her gently, then slapped the cart's roof. "Take it easy on those curves. The official speed limit here is eighteen, but thanks to a buddy of mine, this baby will go a lot faster."

"Will do," she replied, shifting into drive.

As she meandered along the coast, protected from the ocean breeze by grass-covered dunes, she marveled at Old Baldy, the island's imposing lighthouse. She reflected on the generations of ships navigating their way home by its steady light. Hadn't she done much the same thing since fleeing Tennessee? Like those seafarers, she had docked temporarily in other ports, but she eventually found a safe harbor, a safe home, on the Carolina coast.

A cart heading in the opposite direction honked as it passed, the family of passengers waving a friendly hello. She returned their greeting. *I'm one of them now*, she told herself, honking again for good measure.

13

MONKEY

MONKEY WAS PISSED AND POOR, and no one would hire him. Even if there were jobs to spare in this has-been town, he would be the last man hired. His parole officer had warned him against returning to his tiny home-town, suggesting Knoxville, or maybe farther away in Nash-ville or Memphis, where the jobs were more plentiful. But he had to come back here. Ina Rose would want to live in their home again.

THEY HAD no choice but to move in with his mama, into his old bedroom. Hell, they were only eighteen, barely out of high school. They graduated one day, got hitched at the courthouse the next. Their dream was to move to California, get good-paying jobs, have a bunch of kids. Ina Rose would become an actress, or a singer. She was sure pretty enough, and her voice was sweet as an angel's. Better than Dolly or Reba, even. In preparation, she would practice her award-winning acceptance speech:

"And finally, I'd like to thank my handsome husband, Michael, who's been my number one fan since we was in kindergarten."

Monkey would stand and wave to the imaginary audience. Yes, indeed, Ina Rose was going places.

He didn't have no talent himself, but he could take a car engine apart and slap it back together faster than anyone. He had learned by watching his pa, then by doing it himself while the old man shined a light under the hood, offering tips and encouragement. Pa had been a quiet man, beaten down by life and Mama, but loving in his own way. Until the morning a '68 GTO slipped off its jack and crushed him. He yelled for help, but no one heard his desperate pleas. He up and died right there in a puddle of gunked-up motor oil and piss.

After Pa died, Mama took to her bed. She hadn't been real happy with Ina Rose before, but she turned downright mean after. Ina Rose couldn't do nothing right in Mama's eyes, and the more she tried, the more Mama harped. She demanded Ina Rose scrub the toilets and the kitchen floor, scour the scum from the bathtub, and wipe down the baseboards crusty with grime and cat hair.

Ina Rose complained to him at night, whispering because the walls were paper thin. They were wasting their lives in Unicoi County; they ought to leave and leave soon. But he couldn't bring himself to deepen the fracture in Mama's already-broken heart. Every time he mentioned heading west with Ina Rose, Mama cried and moaned so desperate-like that she couldn't catch her breath.

Mama's emphysema eventually got so bad, she would practically pass out from the coughing. She couldn't even get herself to the toilet, and she'd cry out for Ina Rose to empty her bed pan and clean her up with a sponge bath. Then Ina Rose would blubber to him at night. He couldn't win for losing.

AS HE TRUDGED along Main Street, his head down to avoid tripping over cracks in the debris-strewn sidewalk, he heard his name being called. He stopped and glanced around at the boarded-up doors and windows. This part of town was pretty darn deserted, and it didn't look to him like no place was open for business.

"Hey, Monkey. Hear you're lookin' for work."

He whirled toward the voice, his hand slipping below the hem of his shirt. He'd be sent back up if he was ever caught with a weapon, but he didn't care. If push came to shove, he'd be the one walking away.

A tweaker stood just inside the gaping doorway to the abandoned Bubbles and Suds laundromat. He was emaciated and toothless, more skeleton than man. Greasy hair flopped over his brow, and a hand-rolled fag dangled from his collapsed mouth.

"Did you say something?" Monkey asked, backing into the street.

"Yeah. Dontcha recognize me, a-hole?"

Monkey squinted. "No. Who are you?"

"Been a long time, but I guess I don't much look like I used to."

"What's your name?"

"Banjo. You and me graduated high school together."

"Banjo Boxer? Well, I'll be darned. What the heck happened to you?"

The man picked at a scab on his cheek, then coughed out a phlegmy plume of smoke. "Crank and shine, s'pose. I didn't go away for more'n dozen years with a cot and three hots, like you."

"Yeah, well, you look like a zombie just out of the grave."

"Tell me something I don't know. You want a job or not? I ain't got all day."

"What kind of job you talkin' 'bout? I ain't sellin' no drugs, if that's what you got."

"Never mind then." Banjo turned and disappeared into the darkened building.

Monkey wavered. He needed money bad, but he'd cleaned himself up a long time ago. Cold turkey in the joint had sucked big-time, and he wasn't stupid or desperate enough to jump willingly down that critter hole again. There had to be some other way of making decent money.

He stomped on a rusted-out can of Schaefer beer, kicking it into the gutter. Life outside sucked almost as bad as inside. He angrily pulled out his phone.

"Hey, chicken little, I'm calling in my chit."

"Who is this?" came the nervous reply.

"Here's a hint. It was me who saved your sorry ass from Big Darrell Deekins. Double D. You remember him, dontcha?"

"Parker? You out?"

"About four months now," Monkey answered.

"Good for you, man. How ya doing?"

"Not good, Raskins. There ain't no jobs for me here, and I'm outta bread."

"Sorry 'bout that, Monkey, but how can I help?"

"Remember how you begged me to take out that crazed monster?"

"I don't recall much from the joint," Raskins claimed, "other than the daily grind to stay alive."

"Well, let me refresh your memory. Double D had a hankering for you, but you was too scared to tell him your scrawny backside wasn't up for grabs. So, I did it for you, and it cost me a week in solitary. Now you're gonna show me a little appreciation."

"Monkey, come on. No way did I want to be his plaything. I...I just couldn't."

Monkey ignored the pathetic whining. "Your dad's a big bank president or something, right? Lives in a fancy house outside of Philly?"

"Yeah, and he wants nothing to do with me since I got locked up. I haven't even seen him since my release."

"Well, it's about time you paid him a visit. I think ten grand will take care of me real nice. I been thinking about heading out on a little road trip, so I'd be happy to make a detour to come along with you. Offer moral support, you know. Or muscle, like before."

"Oh, hell no. That's all it'd take for him to disown me for good. Let me call my mother. See if she's willing to grease him up for me, but hell, Parker, ten thou's a lot of dough."

"Pfft. You talk to your mammy and get back to me by the day after tomorrow. If I don't hear from you, consider me on my way."

"You don't know where I live," Raskins said, laughing nervously.

"Upper Darby, apartment 3B."

"Shit, Parker, you stalking me?"

"Nah. Not yet, anyway."

"I'll call you back, I promise. Just please, Monkey, don't come up here."

Monkey hung up.

14

ROGER

"WHAT THE HELL, Roger? You're hardly ever home anymore. Why not move out altogether?" Vanessa wore multicolored yoga pants and a pink, too-tight tank top that plunged low across her chest. She'd gotten so thin in the last few years, but her fake boobs stood at full attention, threatening to tip her over if released from their skintight harness.

"Don't tempt me, Vanessa. I'd move south in a heartbeat, but you seem to forget this house doesn't pay for itself. My hard-earned income covers the expenses here, on Bald Head Island, and in Bethany Beach. And thanks to your outlandish spending, I'm forced to work myself ragged running Slap Shots."

"Poor, poor you," she jabbed. "Yet you still manage to jet off to North Carolina whenever the hell your dick twitches."

"Don't be crude," he chastised, grabbing a beer from the

fridge. "You've made it perfectly clear you want nothing to do with my dick, twitchy or otherwise, so I'll take it wherever the hell I please." He took a deep pull from the bottle. "But just so you know, my dick and I will only be in North Carolina through the weekend, then I'm flying down to Costa Rica for that fishing tournament."

"So basically you'll be screwing around on me in two countries."

"If that's how you want to look at it." He shook his head and trudged up the back steps, ignoring the audible protests of his right knee.

"You think you're fooling me, Roger Michaud, but you're the fool." She chased after him, bursting into their bedroom with a screech. "I'm your wife, dammit. You will not ignore me."

He did just that, pulling folded shorts from a dresser drawer, then placing them into an open suitcase atop the bed.

She threw herself onto the mattress and exhaled dramatically. "Fine. Do whatever you want."

"I will, thank you very much," he replied, grinning back at her. He watched her wince as she rolled onto her right shoulder. "What's wrong with you?"

"Nothing," she replied, sliding off the bed and following him into the bathroom. She sat on the edge of the tub. He felt her watching him, and when she caught his eye in the mirror, she pushed out her lower lip. "It's just that I get so scared when you're not here."

He snorted. "So come with me."

"God, no," she replied. "But extra spending money might help me feel safe while you're gone."

"Safe from what?"

"I don't know. It just will."

"You get more than enough now." He pushed past her. "You simply spend too much."

As he packed his toiletries, then zipped his bag, she grabbed him from behind, her nails digging into his biceps. "Listen, Roger. You might as well give me what I ask for, because if I divorce you, it'll cost you way, way more."

Roger laughed. "Prenup, Vanessa—remember? You know as well as I do that if we divorce, you get a measly one percent for every god-awful year we're married."

"Then you're stuck with me forever, just like you vowed on our wedding day."

The very thought of growing old with her made Roger's blood curdle. He yanked himself from her grip and shoved her out of his way. It wasn't a strong push, but she fell dramatically to the floor, squealing in rage. Kicking out a leg, she struck him on the side of his bad knee, and the breath caught in his throat. Quickly sidestepping a second strike, he moved toward the door.

Scrabbling after him, Vanessa grabbed onto his pant leg. He dragged her tiny body behind him, and she wailed, "I'm sorry, Roger. Don't leave me."

He stopped. She was pathetic, but he couldn't summon an ounce of pity for her. They'd danced this dance before. She didn't want him around anymore than she missed him when they were apart. She only wanted things her way. And money. She always wanted money.

"Let me go, Vanessa. I don't want to hurt you, but I've got a flight to catch."

"Too late. You've already hurt me."

She pretended to cry, but she wasn't fooling him in the least. He glanced at his phone, calculating how much time he had to get to the airport. He released the handle of the suitcase and reached down, grabbing her high ponytail. "Get up."

"Ouch!" she screamed, digging her bare heels into the floor and her acrylic nails deeper into his legs.

He knuckle-punched her upper arm to loosen the grip on his leg. She yelped, but he had to get her off him. He had to leave. "Okay, okay, you win. Let me go, and I'll increase your allowance."

Her sobbing stopped immediately, and she retracted her talons. Sniffling, she wiped her forearm across her nose. "How much?"

He shook his head. Her greed never ceased to amaze him. But he only had himself to blame. His early generosity had turned her into the insatiable wretch sitting at his feet now. "Will an additional five thousand suffice, your highness?"

"If that's all you can come up with, I guess it'll have to." She rolled to her knees and grunted, her mouth grimacing in a show of pain.

"You can stop with the drama, Vanessa. I'll call the bank in the morning." He thrust a hundred-dollar bill in her face. "This should tide you over til then."

She snatched the bill and shoved it down her cleavage. "Gee, thanks."

His head was close to exploding, and he clenched his fists to stop himself from punching her again. He picked up his suitcase and strode from the room.

15

MARY

"HEY, GEORGE."

"Hi, Mary. I've got an update on Michaud," the PI replied. "Got a sec?"

"Sure. We're heading out for lunch in a few minutes, but shoot."

"Is Jim there with you?"

"He can be. Hang on." Mary carried the phone into the study, switching to speaker mode as she set it on the desk.

"How ya doing, George," Jimmy asked.

"I'm good, man. You?"

"Still a little worried about Mary's new undertaking, but otherwise I'm fantastic."

"You won't be for long if you continue with those snide comments," Mary threatened. "Go ahead, George."

Papers rustled over the line, then George said, "I'll start with what I've learned about Michaud himself. I've just gotten started, mind you, but he seems well-respected by his employees at Slap Shot Sports, of which there are about two hundred spread between the six stores. Most are part-timers in their late teens and twenties."

"Given his hero status on the Philadelphia sports scene, it's no surprise that he's liked," Jimmy observed. "How are the stores doing financially?"

"I visited three yesterday and will get to the other three today and tomorrow. From the looks of them, they're in good shape. Lots of inventory, plenty of cars in the lots and shoppers in the check-out lines."

"So he's not in money trouble," Jimmy speculated.

"Wouldn't say that just yet. I did go by his house, and it's real big. I talked up a neighbor who was out walking her dogs, and she claims to not really know him. He keeps to himself, as did wife number one when she lived there, as did Vanessa, a.k.a. wife number two, when she was alive."

"Where does this neighbor live in relation to Michaud?" Mary asked.

"Two houses down, on the same side of the street. But like I said, the houses are big, and the lots are sprawling. Michaud's property is two and a half acres by itself."

"What's it look like, George?" Mary asked.

"I'll send photos, along with the most recent MLS listing for the property."

"It's for sale?" Mary asked.

"Not now, but it was about ten years ago, which I assume was around the time of Michaud's divorce from numero uno. Anyway, I took some photos of the rear of the property, too. It backs up to public parklands, and I was able to reach it from a trail that runs from the welcome center, about a mile east."

"Didn't know you were a hiker, George," Mary said.

"I'm a man of mystery, Mary. Anyway, this neighbor lady told me she tried to make nice with both wives, but her efforts were not reciprocated."

"What about the men? Are they on good terms with Roger?" Jimmy asked. "As a sports star, you'd think they'd want him as a poker or drinking buddy."

"Not that kind of community, from what I gather. Many of the residents are every bit as *impotent* as Roger Michaud, if not more so. A bank president, two big-time portfolio managers, a lady news anchor with the local Fox affiliate. Even a seventies pop star whose name escapes me now."

"Hmm. Anything else?" Mary asked. "You said you heard he was a dog, so could he have been messing around with one of the neighbor ladies, and her *impotent* husband took out his revenge on Vanessa?"

"Not that I picked up on."

"Let me spin Mary's idea," Jimmy proposed. "Could Vanessa have been messing with one of the husbands, and his jealous wife killed her?"

"Again, I didn't catch wind of any neighborly impropriety relating to either Mr. or Mrs. Michaud. I did speak to a FedEx driver, though, who was in the hood making deliveries. It's his regular route, and he told me that the missus received lots and lots of packages. Like, every single day. He drops them outside the garage door, rings the bell, then takes off. He rarely saw her in person, but once a week, usually on Fridays, he would find a hundred dollars inside an envelope taped to the door."

"How'd he know the money was for him?" Jimmy asked.

"I asked the same thing. He said the envelopes were addressed to *Delivery Driver*."

"So, she was a shopper," Jimmy said, pointing a finger at Mary. "I got one of my own."

George laughed.

"Guilty as charged," Mary said, scrunching her nose at Jimmy. He seemed to be enjoying himself, getting involved despite his initial reticence. "But, getting back to Roger, did his employees have anything to say about Vanessa? Or wife number one? What's her name, by the way?"

"Veronica."

"And a pattern emerges," Jimmy said.

"What pattern is that, oh, wise man?" Mary asked with a laugh.

"Both names begin with *V* and end in *A*?" George offered.

"That's a coincidence, not a pattern," Mary replied, tossing a wadded ball of paper across the desk and hitting Jimmy on the forehead.

"Ouch!" He grinned as he knuckle-balled it back at Mary. "George, the wife's getting feisty here, so I'd better feed her. If you need a lackey, maybe I can fly up to give you a hand."

"I'm good for now, Jim. I'm sure Mary has you tackling a lengthy honey-do list, anyway."

"Why do you think I'm offering my help?"

George's rich laugh echoed through the line as Mary picked up the phone. "I'm ending this conversation. Talk soon, George." She set the phone down and walked around the desk, pushing back Jimmy's chair.

"Hey, what are you doing?" he protested.

Dropping to her knees, she replied, "Reminding you why it's best to stay right where you are."

16

GEORGE

GEORGE PULLED his Ford Explorer into the lot of Slap Shot Sports in Middletown, Delaware. A smattering of vehicles were evident, most parked at the far end of the lot. He checked the time: 9:59 a.m. The store should be opening in less than a minute, but no customers were milling about at the front door.

He drove up to the entrance and observed a hand-lettered sign taped to the glass. Something about a late opening, but he couldn't make out all the words. He put the truck in park, then strode to the door. The sign read:

Opening Late Due to
Death in Family

Hours: 1:00 p.m. – 8:00 p.m

Whose death? Vanessa Michaud? Were all the stores closed today for some sort of memorial? If so, it would take place without a body or Roger Michaud, who, according to Mary, was in North Carolina. George pulled on the door, but it was locked. He peered into the darkened store and watched as two men headed his way.

The door opened, and the older man, tall with steel-rimmed glasses and a receding hairline, pushed through. Noticing George, he smiled and said, "Good morning, sir. Sorry, but we won't be opening the store until one."

"I read the sign," George acknowledged. "Who died?"

The younger man, still a kid, really, volunteered, "Vanessa. It was on the news and everything."

"Ah," George said. "Was she an employee?"

"Not anymore," the kid answered, frowning. "She was Roger's wife. He found her body, and they arrested him."

The older gentleman cleared his throat. "That's quite enough, Ben. Remember what I told you about disclosing too much information."

Beet-red splotches emerged on the kid's face. His full, wet lips twisted in a grimace of embarrassment, and he dropped his head. George couldn't help but notice his over-size feet sporting a pair of Air Jordan Blue the Great sneakers. The garish colors, in his opinion, only served to enhance the young man's childlike appearance.

"Sorry, Dad," the kid mumbled.

"My condolences for your loss," George offered. "I'll come back some other time."

The man thanked him, then pulled his son by the arm. "Let's go, Ben. We can't be late."

George watched them walk away. He waited a few moments before returning to his SUV, then as the man's truck pulled from the lot, he shifted the Explorer into drive and followed.

THE FRONT ENTRANCE to the King of Prussia store was locked, so George waited by his truck until a carload of teens pulled into an adjacent parking spot. When they exited the beat- up sedan, he quietly tagged along, slipping inside the building through the employee side door.

Inside the vast warehouse-style structure, a hundred or more people, most wearing the signature Slap Shots jersey, gathered around a small-scale ice rink. George had noticed similar rinks in the other stores he'd visited.

A male voice echoed over the cavernous store's address system. "Friends, quiet down." When the voices subsided, he continued. "As you all know, we've gathered here in memory of Vanessa—Vanessa Michaud—who sadly passed away last weekend."

Murmurs echoed through the assembled crowd, and a few women dabbed their eyes.

"Not all of you knew Vanessa, but those of us who did loved her dearly."

George focused on the man speaking. He stood in the center of the rink facing away, but he was undoubtedly the man he'd talked to earlier, Ben's dad.

"I first met Vanessa when she came to work in our ladies' clothing department. Some of you worked with her then, others met her only after she married Roger."

Employees nodded their heads.

"When she was one of us, a mere worker bee, there wasn't a kinder, more caring young woman. Always in a joyful mood, her contagious smile lit up whatever room she entered. She was as beautiful as she was talented, and to this day, I can still hear her singing those country songs she loved so much."

"*Fancy*," a woman called out.

"She could've been a star," another said.

"You're right," the man agreed, smiling sadly. He cleared his throat, then took a moment to blow his nose. "Who knows? Maybe Vanessa and her voice would be alive today if she'd remained a mere mortal like the rest of us.

"If you'll indulge me, I'd like to share a few memories of the Vanessa Ben and I knew. Then, if any of you would like to say a word or two, the mic's yours."

George scanned the crowd, spotting young Ben grinning ear-to-ear. He listened while the kid's dad regaled the crowd with charming stories of Vanessa as a younger woman, before she'd become Mrs. Michaud number two.

When he wrapped it up, he handed the microphone to a woman who skidded beside him on the ice. As she began speaking, George wandered off. At the rear of the store, he slipped into the men's room to relieve himself. When he stepped from the stall, Ben was standing at a sink, making goofy faces in the mirror.

"Hi," George greeted with a friendly smile. "You're Ben, right?"

"Yeah. You were at my store this morning. Are you here for Vanessa's memory party?"

"I am," George said.

"Cool." The kid turned and scooted onto the counter, his long legs and color-blocked feet dangling to the tile floor.

"So, your dad said you knew Vanessa real well. You're too young to have worked with her, though, aren't you?"

"Yeah, but she babysat me when I was little."

"Hmm, that must have been before she married Roger."

"Yeah," he snickered.

"Why are you laughing?" George asked.

"I can't tell you," the kid said, shrugging his sloped shoulders. To George, he seemed to be bursting at the seams to spill something.

"Why not? Something funny happen with her?"

Ben looked around, then whispered, "One of the stock guys—Sammy—told me that Roger and Vanessa used to—" His ears turned bright red. "You know, in the dressing room."

"The dressing room? Really?"

"Yeah. That's where I work now when we're not busy. Not on Saturdays, though, 'cause I can't keep up with putting away all the tried-ons."

"I'm sure Saturdays are crazy busy," George said. "Did your dad know about Roger and Vanessa? In the dressing room, I mean."

Ben snorted. "I told him, but he said I shouldn't be gossiping and should just zip my mouth." Ben mimicked zipping his mouth. "He was really sad for a while after, though."

"Why? Were you telling fibs?"

"No." Ben looked slightly panicked. "It's just that Dad really liked Vanessa. She made him smile after Mommy died."

"Huh." George checked his phone. "Shouldn't you be getting back to the service?"

"Nah, as soon as Dad was done talking, I didn't care what anybody else said."

Drying his hands, George asked, "So, Ben, aside from what he and Vanessa did in the dressing room, what do you think of Roger?"

"He's cool, I guess. But he can be mean, too. He yells at my dad a lot."

"About what?"

"Numbers, or something like that."

George smiled at the kid. "Your dad manages the Delaware store, right?"

"Yeah, but he's a partner, too," Ben said, beaming.

"Good for him. I didn't know Roger had a partner."

"That's 'cause Dad's a silent partner. He was a Flyer. Did you know that?"

"Roger? I did."

"No, my dad."

"That, I didn't know. What's his name?"

"Bart Nixon. And I'm Ben Nixon. BN and BN."

"Huh! I think I remember him. A winger, yeah?

"Yep. The best winger ever."

"I'm a Caps fan myself" George said.

"How lame," Ben teased.

"I know, I know," George said, chuckling. "Let me ask you something else. If you've got the time."

"Sure."

"Do you think Roger took other girls to the, um, fitting room?"

The kid glanced toward the door, then held his hand over his mouth. "I'm not supposed to gossip about that either."

"You can tell me," George prompted, punching Ben's arm playfully.

The door banged open, and Bart Nixon walked in. Recognizing George, he demanded, "What the hell are you doing here?"

"I thought I'd pay my respects," George improvised.

The man gave him a doubtful look. "Come on, Ben. You've been in here long enough."

Ben jumped down from the counter and followed his dad. At the door, he looked back at George, grinning as he fashioned an L with his fingers against his forehead.

17

BART

DRIVING BACK to Delaware after the service, Bart struggled to keep his attention on the road. Thankfully Ben was quietly playing Minecraft on his phone, so he didn't have to listen to the boy's mind-numbing chatter. When he nearly missed the exit for Route 202 South, he turned on a talk radio station to keep himself alert, but Ben promptly changed it.

"That station's annoying, Dad."

"You're right, it is," Bart agreed. As the countryside rolled by, his thoughts drifted back to Vanessa.

HE TIMED IT PERFECTLY. They put Ben to bed early, and he and Vanessa enjoyed a quiet dinner by themselves. A rare treat. After the dishes were done, Vanessa retreated to the living room to watch her favorite program, *American Idol*. She'd confessed that it was her dream to be discovered like the show's winner, and Bart told her he was sure it would happen one day.

When the program ended, he turned off the television and pointed the remote toward a small stacked stereo system. As the strains from "The Music of the Night" filled the room, he knelt in front of the sofa and pulled a ring from his pocket.

Vanessa looked at him with a confused expression, but he persisted. "Vanessa, darling, will you marry me and be Ben's mother?"

Tears spilled from her eyes as she shook her head. "I-I don't know," she stammered.

"It's all right if you're not sure," he reassured her, though his heart was already breaking into millions of tiny, jagged pieces. "Take your time. We're not going anywhere." He brushed a tear from her cheek and smiled. "I love you, Vanessa, and I want you for my wife."

She gulped down a sob, jumped from the sofa, then raced downstairs to her small apartment in the finished basement.

IT WAS ONLY a few days later that Roger stole her out from under him, and once they married, he rarely ever saw her. Then last summer, they ran into each other quite by accident at the King of Prussia Slap Shots. She did her best to ignore him at first, acting as though she didn't recognize him. He cornered her in the parking lot before she was able to get her car door open.

"Hello, Vanessa."

She squinted in the sun, then lowered her gaze to her

purse where she'd been fumbling for her keys. Her arms were loaded with Slap Shot bags, full of God-knows-what unneeded items.

"Hi, Bart."

"Can I assist?" he asked, reaching for her packages.

"Thanks." She grudgingly handed him the bags. When she located her key fob, she popped the trunk and motioned for him to drop the bags inside.

"I haven't seen you in a long time," he said, for lack of anything better. "Ben would love it if you came for dinner one night."

"Oh, he doesn't even remember me." She waved her hand, still not looking him in the eye.

"He does. I do."

She grimaced, looking decidedly uncomfortable. And sad.

"Everything okay with you?" he asked.

"Sure," she said. "Everything's great."

Roger was out of town, which was why Bart had been called to King of Prussia. There was a crack in the ice rink cooling grid, and hundreds of gallons of brine had flooded the showroom floor. The on-duty manager discovered it when he arrived that morning, but the maintenance company refused to conduct the necessary cleanup and repairs until one of the owners authorized the expenditure.

"You obviously heard about the flood."

"Yes, they called the house looking for Roger. I figured I might as well rescue a few things before they became a total loss."

"Let me guess," he said. "Workout wear and sneakers."

She nodded and smiled. Her smile was as captivating as ever, and his heart missed a beat.

On a whim, he asked, "I'm about to grab some lunch before I head back to Delaware. Care to join me?"

She took in a sharp breath. "I really don't think I have the time."

"No? By the looks of you, you could stand to eat something."

Anger flashed in her eyes, and she turned away. He put his hand on her shoulder.

"I'm not being critical, Vanessa, I promise. You're as lovely as ever. It's really that I could use the company."

She hesitated, then looked at her watch—a Rolex, if he wasn't mistaken. "If we make it quick. I have a hair appointment at two.

He followed her to the mall, parking beside her outside Bonefish Grill. They found two seats at the bar, and after ordering their meals—a cheeseburger for him and a side salad for her—he slowly got her to open up. By the time he paid the bill, the iciness of the past decade was ever so slightly thawed.

After that, they spoke periodically by phone, usually when Roger was out of town. Their conversations typically centered around her, what she was doing, when she was going down to the beach, how she spent her day. He even managed to convince her to join Ben and him for lunch one afternoon, but that turned into a most regrettable meal.

Vanessa was undeniably uneasy around teenage Ben, who was far bigger and ganglier than when she'd last seen him at the age of seven. Ben, on the other hand, instantly fell back in love with her, to the point of embarrassing himself by snuggling against her in the booth. Vanessa picked at her salad until making an excuse to leave before the meal had ended. As much as Bart wanted to deny that nothing had changed in the years since she'd lived in their home, he was only fooling himself.

Then late last year, she phoned him in tears. Roger had decided at the last minute to spend New Year's in North Carolina, most likely with his local girlfriend. Nothing new there. She didn't even mind spending the holiday without him. It was just another night alone. What upset her so was the news that he was carrying on with yet another female employee, an assistant manager at the Willow Grove store. Bart had already heard of Roger's latest conquest, the Slap Shots grapevine being faster than Twitter.

"What do you want me to do about it?" he asked her bluntly.

"I'm just so over this," she cried.

"He'll never change, Vanessa," Bart said. "You've known that since day one. What you need to do is leave him."

"I can't."

"Why not? Ben and I would be thrilled to have you stay with us until you find your own place. And your old apartment just happens to be available."

She huffed out a breath. "I'd go to the cottage in Bethany if it came down to it. But I'm not leaving him."

Bart sensed his hopes slipping away. "Then, I repeat, what do you want from me? If you won't leave, there's not a thing I can offer you."

"Just someone to talk to. That's all."

"Sure. Talk."

"Don't be angry with me," she pleaded.

"I'm not angry, Vanessa. Just frustrated."

"I know, and I'm sorry. About so many things." Her voice choked, and then she whispered, "Will you come over tonight?"

His breath caught in his chest. He wanted so very much to say yes, but he couldn't get the word out.

"I shouldn't have asked," she said quickly. "Never mind. I'll be fine."

Ben was staying the night with a school friend whose parents were having a ball-drop party. Nothing was stopping him. Except for the minor detail that Vanessa remained married to his business partner.

"Yes," he blurted before he could change his mind. "So long as you're absolutely sure you want me to."

"I'm sure, Bart. It's the night for auld lang syne, isn't it?"

"Give me an hour," he told her, heading for the stairs. "Can I bring anything?"

"No, I've got plenty of wine, unless you prefer something stronger?"

"Wine's good. I'll see you soon."

"COME ON, DAD!" Ben said, shaking Bart from his thoughts.

Somehow, they'd arrived back in Delaware and were parked outside the store. "Go ahead in, Ben. I'm right behind you." He took a deep breath, then pulled his aching body from the truck, following his son into their nothing future.

18

MONKEY

MONKEY LAY on the soiled sofa in the poorly lit room, staring at the muted TV. He was bone-tired and his stomach roiled with hunger, but he had neither the strength to fix himself dinner or the gumption to put himself to bed. The doldrums—his mama's word for his crippling depression— had him by the balls. His prescriptions had run out five days ago. He'd meant to refill them when he was in town yesterday, but his visit to the unemployment office was so disheartening, and then he ran into Banjo Boxer, he plum forgot. Plus, his money was so low, he barely had enough for food, let alone pills.

The shrink in the joint had diagnosed his clinical depression a few months after he was sent up. Finally forced to stop self-medicating, he descended into a detox hellhole. Sadly, it was when the Oxy and meth completely cleared his system that the real demons took over. A bottomless, black despair settled upon him, and terrifying night-mares came on even when he was wide awake. When he went berserk one afternoon in the day room, swearing that Vanna White was his missing wife, he was carted off to the psych ward. He spent five weeks bouncing off padded walls before a cocktail of meds steadied him enough that he could return to a cell. By then, he'd lost so much weight, his prison jumpsuit hung from his body like folds of a shroud, and his teeth jiggled in his gums. He'd later gotten his teeth, decayed and putrid from meth and neglect, capped by a dentist who offered pro bono services to long-timers.

Monkey ran his tongue along his upper teeth now. They sure felt and smelled a heck of a lot better than his old chop-pers. He was looking forward to showing them off to Ina Rose. He would smile so big when he saw her, she'd be blown away. Not that his smile had been so bad when she up and left, but there'd never been money for braces when he was a teenager. 'Course, Ina Rose's teeth had been shiny and perfect.

His cell phone startled him from his stupor, and he reached for it on the floor in front of the sofa. His arm felt as though it weighed a hundred pounds.

"Hello?" he whispered weakly.

"Parker?"

"Yeah."

"You don't sound so good, man. You sick?"

"Yeah."

"Well, this'll make you feel better. I convinced Mother to cough up two thou. It's all yours. I just need your address, and I'll mail it on down."

Monkey dropped the phone as he stood, his legs trem-bling beneath him. He reached for it, and the room spun around him.

"You there, man?"

"I'm here, but I'm pissed," Monkey huffed. "I told you I need ten, and you're telling me two."

"I'll get you the rest, I swear. It's just that I gotta talk to my old man first. My mom won't cough up more until I do."

"That ain't good enough," Monkey said, steadying himself against the fireplace mantel. "I need it all. Now." Another wave of dizziness assailed him, and he lowered himself shakily to the cold hearth, his head dipping between his knees.

"I know that," Raskins shouted. "I said I'll get it to you, but I need more time. You can either take the two, or I'll find a good use for it."

"It's mine, Raskins. Don't you mess with me."

"Okay, it's yours. Now what's your damn address?"

Monkey shook his head. He needed his meds bad, or there'd be no telling what would happen to him. How bad he'd get. He gave Raskins the address.

"Okay, man, I'll get this to the post office. Just sit tight, and I'll let you know when I can send more."

"Call soon, Raskins, or like I told ya before, I'll get in my truck and come find you."

Raskins hung up, and Monkey stared at the phone. "Pathetic," he muttered. He should head to Pennsylvania now, but he needed to get himself to the drugstore first thing in the morning. Get the pills back in his system.

He shoved to his feet and staggered into the kitchen. He pulled half a cold sub left over from yesterday from the fridge. It was probably soggy, but he couldn't complain. He cracked open a can of Coke and chugged a little. The bubbles stung the back of his throat.

Leaning against the counter, he gulped some air, then took a huge bite of the sandwich. As he chomped, the calories registered first in his gullet, then slipped through his veins into his brain. The fog was lifting, and he felt steadier. He'd give himself another day or two to pull himself together, get the cash from Raskins, then he'd start crossing more tasks off his to-do list.

He moved to the table and pulled out one of the rickety chairs, mentally adding tightening the table and chair legs to the list. His lips shifted into a weak but determined smile. He recollected the last meal he and Ina Rose had shared together, right here at this table. The details were a little sketchy now, but he sure hoped she'd learned to cook in all the years they'd been apart. His ma had tried to teach her, but that didn't go over well either, as evidenced by the black scorch mark on the wall above the stove top. One more thing to add to his list.

19

VANESSA

VANESSA PICKED herself up off the floor, muttering, "Bastard," at Roger's retreating back. Her little tantrum had worked, though. She was pretty good at getting whatever she wanted, but the issue of his North Carolina hussy, all his hussies for that matter, niggled at her. She'd known all along that he wouldn't be faithful. That he hadn't been faithful to his first wife long before she allowed him to lure her into the dressing room. It wasn't in his DNA. But she'd been so turned on by him, she hadn't the power to resist his seduction. Their first time was exhilarating, her back pressed against the full-length mirror, her legs wrapped around his hips as he ground himself into her.

They managed a few quickies in hotel rooms that ensuing year, but it wasn't until Veronica finally moved out that he invited her to spend an entire night here. She was so desperately in love by that point, she married him a week after his divorce was finalized.

Now, she could barely stomach the thought of touching him. Or of him touching her. Yet she would never agree to a divorce, and she would never sign away this house, like Veronica had. Come hell or high water—one of Mama's favorite expressions—she'd hold onto her status as Mrs. Roger Michaud. With the help of a private investigator, she was cementing a fail-safe plan to ensure it, and she was neither too shy nor too proud to implement every last step of that plan.

In the meantime, with Roger away with his buddies, she craved a companion of her own. A real man to hold her, to touch her, to take her to the heights of ecstasy. She picked up her phone and dashed off a brief text. The reply came within seconds, and with a grin, she headed upstairs. She knew the perfect party dress to wear, and if she came home at all tonight, she wouldn't be alone.

20

MARY

DIANA WASN'T ANSWERING her phone or replying to Mary's texts. She'd only been on the island with Roger for a few days, but still. Mary was concerned and needed to know her friend was okay.

George had called a short while ago with an update on what he learned at the company-wide memorial for Vanessa Michaud. As Mary had feared, he picked up some bad vibes about Roger.

"He's not as well-liked as you originally thought?" she asked.

"Yes and no. The male employees, for the most part, idolize him. I heard a lot of, 'He's the GOAT.'"

"The what?"

"Greatest of all time."

"Oh. Is he?"

"Some say so, others say it's Wayne Gretzky or Gordie Howe."

"Whatever. Get back to your but. I know it's coming."

"Yeah, it is. But, I met Bart Nixon, the manager of the Delaware Slap Shots, and according to his son, Ben, Bart and Roger argue all the time."

"That's not the kind of thing you want to do and hold onto your job," Mary said.

"Not unless you're a silent partner in the business and a former teammate of Roger's."

"Hmm. So what do they argue about?"

"Ben said it's usually over money. Nixon gave the eulogy, and from what I read into it, he was a huge fan of Vanessa's before she became Mrs. Michaud. Maybe not so much after, but he seems truly devastated by her death."

"I wonder if she was the source of tension between the two men."

"Could be. I'll follow up."

"Good. In the meantime, if he's the *GOAT* to the men, what is he to the women?"

"Before I go there, a little background on Vanessa. According to the kid, she and Roger first hooked up in the women's fitting room."

"Seriously?" Mary said. "Was the store open for business at the time?"

"From what I gathered, yes."

"Eww!" She envisioned black-lit body fluids splattered on a dressing room mirror.

"Yep. And worse yet, it appears good ol' Roger continued his shenanigans even after he married Vanessa."

"Dang," Mary said. "If she wasn't his last, chances are she wasn't his first."

"Very probable. It shouldn't be too hard to find out who

his other conquests were. I think I might have met one already."

"Who?"

"She didn't give me her name, but she did tell me to pound sand, using the tried and true one-finger salute."

"Rude. Maybe she pegged you as a reporter."

"Could be, but being the suspicious type, I'd say she's one of his recent, if not still-active, conquests."

"Ok, or maybe she doesn't want to be disloyal to her boss."

"Or," George went on, "she fancies herself as wife number three."

"Yeah, I could get there," Mary agreed. "He's suddenly a widower, and her fantasy of being married to him magically jumps from farfetched to promising."

"Magically, except for the whole murder thing. I've added her to my list of suspects."

"Where to next?"

"Home to DC. I put a call in to a Detective Molino with the Radnor Police Department, but he's off til the weekend. He's the friend of a friend, so I think he'll talk to me. What about you?"

"I'm waiting to hear from Diana on how things are going with Lothario."

"Think you should warn her about his reputation?"

"She's been with him off and on for two years, while all along they've been seeing others, so I doubt she cares."

"She should care about her security, though, don't you think?"

"I've warned her to be careful. There's not much else I can do."

21

DIANA

DIANA WANDERED LANGUOROUSLY along the water's edge. With each step, the fine, wet sand pulled at her feet. Hiking up her skirt, she waded in up to her knees, feeling the tug of the receding tide. Closing her eyes, she swayed in the soft waves and imagined herself being sucked under, like the quicksand in *Blazing Saddles*.

The whir of an outboard motor broke the spell, and when she opened her eyes, she glimpsed a dark tailfin disappear beneath the surface twenty yards out. Splashing out of the surf, she clambered up a dune, ignoring the threatening sign but careful not to disturb the razor-sharp grasses. Focusing on where she'd spotted the disappearing tail, she steadied her cell phone in time to capture a pod of dolphins dancing in the wake of the passing speedboat.

As she stood in awe of the view and her surroundings, a light breeze caught her skirt, billowing it up around her hips. An irresistible urge to dance bubbled up inside her, and with arms overhead, she twirled. Oh, how she wished Roger was with her.

Waking to discover him missing, she'd found his hurriedly scrawled note taped to the bathroom mirror: *Appointment in Wilmington. Be back after noon.*

His absence wasn't ideal, but at least he wouldn't be gone long. In the meantime, she could relax and enjoy the island's beauty in solitude. And if the last few nights were any indication, he would certainly more than make up for his disappearance.

She swiped open her screen and composed a message to Mary, attaching the dolphin photo: *Good morning! Check out these happy locals. All's great here. Loving island life and will stay through weekend. Favor: can you meet delivery at SS Monday? Will call with details. Xoxo, D.*

A dog barked excitedly on the beach, and she spotted the golden lab bounding into the surf after a just-hurled slab of driftwood. The dog grabbed his prize, muscled it ashore, then proudly deposited it at his master's feet. As the pup shook himself vigorously, spraying seawater in all directions, the man's deep laugh carried across the breeze. He bent to retrieve the wood, then yelled, *"Tráelo!"* as he tossed it back into the waves.

His command stirred up a long-forgotten memory, and Diana momentarily froze. She dropped to her knees behind a swaying patch of sea oats, squinting through the tall grass to get a better look at the dog's owner. His back was to her, but as the lab again dropped the stick at his feet, she realized it wasn't Alejandro. The guy might sound like him, but he was far too tall and beefy. Besides, Alejandro was dead. With a nervous giggle, she stood and brushed the sand from her skirt.

22

ROGER

ROGER STRODE through the revolving glass doors, taking a moment to read the tenant directory before pressing the *up* elevator button. Joshua Mason, in suite 618, had agreed to a meeting before the start of the official work-day. He and Roger had known each other for several years, having met at the Bald Head Island Marina. They, along with four other island dwellers, travelled frequently to the Caribbean and Central America to fish, drink, and party with pretty women. The six men were all successful in their chosen fields, and it was understood that if any of them was in need of a service offered by another, it was only a call away. Roger had phoned Josh Mason yesterday afternoon.

"Roger, how are you?" The stocky, red-faced man hugged his friend, then locked the door behind them. "I didn't think I'd see you again so soon, but come on in."

"Thanks, Josh. I'm about as well as can be expected, given that I'm the prime suspect in my wife's murder."

"Yeah, I heard. Frankly, I'm surprised you're down here. When you called, I figured I'd be visiting you in a Pennsylvania jail."

"You know darn well I've got a solid alibi," Roger said "I was in Costa Rica with you and the other guys when she was killed. They had no choice but to release me on my own recog."

"True that." Josh said, moving to the wet bar. He poured from a decanter of brandy, then handed a snifter to Roger.

"Thanks, man." They each took a sip, then Roger added, "I didn't kill her when I got home, either."

"I wouldn't care if you did," Josh replied, motioning for Roger to sit. "But seeing as I'm not a criminal attorney, what do you need from me?"

"Help with hiding my money. I want it to stay in my hands, and mine alone."

"You've come to the right man, then," Josh said, raising his glass. "You know you could have asked for my help earlier."

"Didn't realize just how important it was until all this happened. I've been managing fine on my own til now, but I can't afford a single mistake from here on out."

Josh opened his laptop and typed for a few seconds. "Okay, how much are we talking, where is it, and who else has access to it? Give me the deets."

Roger pulled a folded sheet of paper from his breast pocket and slid it across the desk. "Everything's there, and last I checked, it's all where it should be. My question for you is, do I move it? If so, I need you to make it happen. Bury it so that it no longer exists for anyone but me."

Josh smoothed out the paper and read it over, glancing up once or twice with raised eyebrows. "Nice portfolio, my friend. Hockey must have been very, very good to you."

"Hockey, hell. Most of that came after I retired. I've been working my ass off for twenty-plus years to amass every dime you see there."

"Who'd you say's been advising you? Maybe I should talk with him about my own investments."

"I told you, you're talking to him. I might be a jock, but I'm sure as hell not a dumb one. At least where money's concerned. Women, I'm not so sure."

Josh leaned forward and reached his right hand across the desk. "I'm impressed." He settled back into his chair and punched a few keys. "Cayman account is intact." He typed again. "So are the two Zurich funds. Who specifically do we need to hide these from? The IRS? Your family?"

"Anyone and everyone who might want to take advantage of me. I don't have kids, and far as I know, Vanessa had no family. At least no one she stayed in touch with."

"What about your ex? Your own family members? Anyone who might think they're entitled to a piece of you."

Roger shook his head. "Not a one."

"Perfect," Josh said. "Try as they might to find these, give me an hour or two, and I'll make that all but impossible." He pecked at his keyboard for a few moments, then paused and pointed at Roger. "Got an idea. With a number this big, we might want to move some to an on-shore account. Maybe a hundred K in a simple money market where it'll be easy for the IRS to find. It might satisfy their bloodthirst and stop them from digging deeper."

Roger grimaced. "If it's certain to be found, I'd be a heck of a lot happier if it were only fifty grand."

"Sure, whatever you want," Josh agreed. "How 'bout

this? We put some in an IRA then invest a little more in a small-scale business. A local one here in Carolina would be a convincing touch. You do the owner a solid, and the cash isn't immediately recoverable by the IRS."

"I reinvest in my own stores every year," Roger said. "I can move on that earlier than usual. Will that be good enough?"

"Nah, not under the circumstances. Pick a legit business in real need of the money. One that will spend it immediately, maybe to cover capital expenses or inventory. Something like that."

Roger nodded. "Yeah, you're right. That's the advice I'm looking for. I'll give it some thought and let you know in a few days. Thanks."

"That's why I'm here, buddy. That's why I'm here."

MARY

MARY'S PHONE dinged with an incoming message, and she pulled it from her hip bag. She was walking into town this morning for a change of scenery from the trails surrounding her neighborhood. The sun's glare made it impossible to read the screen, so she turned her body into the shadow of an oak tree and lifted her sunglasses atop her ball cap.

Thank goodness, she thought. The message was from Diana. With a smile, she darted off a quick, *Of course, but still want to talk to you.* She'd helped out at the Seaside Siren in the past, most recently during the tedious year-end inventory. Diana's part-time employee, a retired woman from Oak Island, would be returning in time for Easter weekend, which, Mary realized, was right around the corner.

There was so much she wanted to tell Diana, but how

much should she? Roger's reputation as a ladies' man? As she told George, her friend no doubt knew that much already.

Her phone vibrated again. Jimmy, this time. *Heading to Potter's for shrimp. Pick you up?*

She smiled and responded: *Meet you in an hour.* She needed a longer walk to sort through her jumbled thoughts. Anyway, she suspected Jimmy's trip to the seafood shack was his way of keeping tabs on her. But she was perfectly fine, and the shrimp would wait.

Not only was her husband still adjusting to retirement, he had yet to accept that Mary needed time to herself, to walk and to bike and to think, without his tagging along. While she'd welcomed his comforting presence in the aftermath of her brutal assault, she was now determined to recover her independence.

Who could have imagined a contract killer in Southport? And while it was never proven that the man had been hired to kill Mary, it was indisputable that he'd been stalking her. Worse yet, she came very close to dying at his hands, regardless of whether he'd been paid. Fortunately, Jimmy shot the man dead before that had happened.

A shiver ran down Mary's spine, and she glanced behind her. No one was there. She no longer had valid reasons for being nervous or paranoid. The mysterious cowboy—who, to this day, remained nameless—was dead and presumably buried at sea. The experience, however, had demonstrated she could never again let her guard down. She patted the small revolver nestled in a holster under her arm.

She and Jimmy went target shooting at the local range a couple times a month. It was during one such practice that he came up with the idea of teaching his own classes in self-defense. Mary hoped he would eventually become so busy that he wouldn't worry about her quite so much.

She removed her cap and whisked away a sheen of perspiration from her forehead. The early spring air still held a chill, especially near the waterfront, but the sun was bright and warm. She checked the step count on her Fitbit, then turned in the direction of the ferry terminals.

"MARY!" a voice called out.

Mary squinted toward the commercial harbor where Bobby Moore was posed atop the wheelhouse of a shrimp trawler docked at a finger pier. He held a thick white hose as he washed down the boat's nets and outriggers. A half dozen squawking pelicans flapped in the air around him. He directed the stream of water at a particularly pesky bird, and it screeched before diving bill-first after a morsel of discarded catch.

She'd spoken with the young deckhand several times in the past, once next door at Fishy Fishy when he was dining with Diana, and another time at the Seaside Siren when she was there helping out. He is, she now observed with a guilty smile, candy for tired eyes. Tanned and muscled with a mop of sun-kissed curls, he could easily pass for an earthbound cherub. Not to mention his sleepy, come-hither eyes, freckled cheeks, and full, kiss-me mouth. *No small wonder*, Mary thought, *Diana finds him irresistible.*

She waved and headed over. "Hey, Bobby. Just get in?"

"Yep, about an hour ago. Long overnighter, but it's my last outing for a few days."

"Good for you. I'm picking up tonight's dinner, so thanks for the fresh haul."

"No problem." He smiled his incorrigible grin. "Seen

Diana today? I texted her about going out later, but I haven't heard back."

Uh-oh, Mary thought. "No, not today."

"She's probably tied up at the store," he replied with a shrug. "I'll head over there when I'm done here."

"Probably," Mary agreed. "Good to see you, Bobby."

"You, too," he replied.

She turned as an uncomfortable feeling settled in her belly. Inside the small yellow shack, she reviewed the chalkboard specials. Fresh shrimp, scallops, triggerfish, and grouper. What did she want to prepare for dinner?

"Hey, beautiful!" Jimmy said, draping an arm over her shoulders.

"Hey, yourself. What sounds good?" She nodded at the board.

"I have a hankering for shrimp and scallops. Is there pasta at home?"

Mary thought a moment. "Yes, but I can't remember how much."

"That's okay. Whatever's left in the box should be enough for one night. John Franklin called and invited us over for dinner tomorrow. He and Maria have been taking cooking classes, and they want us to be their guinea pigs."

"That sounds fun."

"I thought so, too," he said, squeezing her shoulder. "He's given me the okay on the conceal carry classes, by the way."

"I knew he would," Mary said as she hugged him.

While they waited at the counter for their order, Mary stared out through the shack's back door. Beyond the docks and across the channel, the graying, weathered roof of a gazebo was visible above the marsh grasses. A vision of the mystery cowboy flashed in her mind, and she closed her eyes. She hadn't gotten up the nerve to return to the marsh walk since the day the hit man startled her there. What at one time had been a favorite spot of hers, peaceful and inspiring, haunted her still. She wanted—no, she needed—to get over her trepidation. *Baby steps*, she told herself.

"Ready?" Jimmy asked, shaking her from her reverie.

"Yep."

As they crossed the street, she glanced over at Bobby. "That's...," she started.

"That's who?" he asked, following her gaze.

"Oh, never mind," she replied, deciding her husband needn't know about Diana's other lover. "It's not who I thought it was."

24

WILL

WILL RASKINS, sick to his stomach and clammy-cold, paced in his dingy apartment. God willing, he was coming down with a deadly virus that would take him out in a matter of hours. He'd just hung up from talking with his mother, and she'd been adamant that he show up for tonight's dinner. His father would be there, and in addition to wearing a jacket and tie, she insisted that he arrive bearing a bottle of senior Raskins's favorite, and very expensive, Scotch whisky.

"It's long past time, William," his mother said. "He's not the unfeeling fiend you make him out to be. He's hurting, too."

Will could dispute her claims, but he held his tongue. Mother wouldn't bide whining of any sort, let alone any concerning her husband. Will had paid dearly for that at an early age.

"Mind you, William," Mavis Raskins continued, reproof in her carefully modulated voice, "I expect you to swallow that pride of yours, establish that you have rehabilitated yourself." She then listed her conditions. First, he would sincerely apologize for being such a miserable, inconsiderate loser (his slant on *promise to make amends for your past defiance*). He would then swear on a stack of Bibles to never screw up again (i.e., *vow to never again besmirch the family name*). Then, bending over, he was to lift the tail of his jacket, drop his drawers, and take it up the keister. Figuratively, of course. While seven years in the joint had given him a thorough understanding of the literal act, listening to Howard William Raskins, *the third*, rant about what an ungrateful son-of-a-bitch he was, how he'd tarnished his silver spoon beyond all repair, would no doubt be just as unpleasant.

A needle jabbed behind his right eye, and he winced. Maybe he would succumb before seven thirty. And then there was Monkey. Would he really come after him if he didn't cough up the rest of the money? Will didn't think so, but could he be sure?

Crap! His entire skull now throbbed, and he stumbled into the tiny bathroom to puke up the dregs of his morning coffee. Droplets of cool water splashed back into his eyes, but the pounding eased mercifully. At the sink he rinsed his face, then stared at his reflection in the mirror. Bloodshot eyes stared back. He badly needed a haircut and a shave. And what about a jacket and tie? Or a crisp, collared shirt, for that matter? His job on a landscape crew required only jeans and T-shirts, and he would need to make a trip to the mall, spend a little of his stash, before Mother rang the dinner bell.

The phone in his pocket vibrated. Monkey. Will

reached for a bottle in the medicine cabinet and tossed back two ibuprofen tablets, slurping them down with water from the faucet. The phone vibrated again, but he ignored it. There were more important things to do just now, and Monkey Parker would have to get in line.

25

BART

BART CIRCLED the parking lot twice before settling on a spot beneath a towering pine that offered a miniscule triangle of shade. Even with the sunshield covering the dash, the interior of his shiny black Ram 1500 could get deadly hot, even in the middle of winter. He hadn't thought of that when he ordered the truck's deluxe package in the hopes of impressing Vanessa. Money wasted.

He checked his appearance in the rearview mirror, smoothing the retreating wisps of graying hair into submission. He hated that the older he got, the homelier he got. Not that he'd ever been much to look at. Unlike Roger, who seemed to be transitioning effortlessly from rugged and youthful to mature and distinguished. It wasn't fair.

He should have joined a gym or hired a personal trainer years ago when there'd still been a fighting chance, when his thighs and arms were strong and muscular from years of skating. But he couldn't justify it then when he had a vast array of fitness equipment at his disposal. While he tried to work out a few nights a week after closing the store, his formerly athletic physique was irretrievable at this point. What he should've done all along was work harder. Work smarter. If he had, everything in his life would be better now.

He practiced his smile. Thanks to implants and the molded braces he'd suffered through the past two years, he was no longer snaggle-toothed, the result of an errant stick to the face late in his career. Not that he felt much like smiling these days. Not since New Year's, after which Vanessa, for all intents and purposes, had gone into hiding.

He slammed his fist into the steering wheel. "Get a grip, Bart," he scolded himself. He grabbed the red-and-white paper sack from the passenger seat and jumped down from the cab. Maybe, if he stopped shoving fast food into his face, he'd get rid of his embarrassing paunch. But nothing tasted good to him these days, so he ate whatever Ben wanted. Today, his son had asked for Chick-Fil-A, so Chick-Fil-A it was.

Inside the lunch room, he laid out the sandwiches and fries in the precise arrangement Ben demanded. Heaven forbid the waffle fries sat to the left of the sandwich. Or the napkin was grease-stained before Ben wiped it across his own face. Bart loved the boy with his whole heart and soul, but the kid's idiosyncrasies were trying at best.

Ben burst into the room. "I'm starving!"

"Well, you're in luck."

"You took forever," his son complained, plopping down in front of the food.

"You know how busy their drive-thru is, son," Bart

explained calmly. "But I did manage to score you an extra sauce." He held out the small plastic container.

"You're the man," Ben said, snatching the cup and kissing it.

As they ate, Bart did his best to listen to Ben's aimless banter, but his melancholy thoughts continued to drag him down. When Ben belched loudly, Bart looked up at his son and shook his head.

"Excuse me," Ben apologized dramatically.

Before his passionate night with Vanessa, Ben's birth had been the highlight of Bart's life. Sadly, the carefree joy of being a father ended when Ben's mother Becky died.

WHEN HE FIRST MET BECKY, she was so young and pretty, in a fresh-off-the-farm way. From Lancaster County, Pennsylvania, she was a die-hard Flyers fan, waiting outside the locker room after almost every home game. Toward the end of his final season of play, he worked up the nerve to ask her for a date. Whether she was simply starstruck, he couldn't say, but when she agreed to marry him later that summer, and got pregnant shortly thereafter, he stopped questioning her motives. Life post-hockey was full of promise, and having a doting wife and an adorable, healthy son was more than he had ever hoped for.

By Ben's third birthday, there was no denying something wasn't quite right with the toddler. He'd not only missed many developmental milestones, but he began to experience seizures that were both alarming and foreboding. The diagnosis of significant cognitive impairment devastated them both, but Becky took it especially hard, blaming herself and the heavy drinking she'd done in college. She became despondent, and by Ben's fourth birthday, she stopped caring altogether—for Ben, for Bart, for herself.

Busy with the growing chain of sporting goods stores, Bart sought out a nanny to take over young Ben's daytime care. Initially, he believed that Becky would come around rather than permit a strange woman in the house. But by that point, it was too late. She couldn't find her way past her deep disappointment and shame.

It was a cold, dreary afternoon when Bart received the call that changed his life forever. Ben's nanny at the time, a grandmotherly woman who'd been referred by a well-respected care agency, had discovered Becky, cold and unresponsive, on the floor of their bedroom. An empty bottle of Elavil, the anti-depressant her physician recently prescribed, was found on the nightstand beside an equally empty bottle of cheap vodka.

BEN'S VOICE invaded Bart's thoughts. "So, can we?"

"Sorry, Ben, can we what?"

"Dad, you're not listening. Can we go to the shore this weekend for the air show? I want to see the Blue Angels."

"I have to work, Ben. You know that."

"Then can I go with the guys?" Ben asked, chomping loudly on a waffle fry. "I don't have to work."

"And just who are the guys?"

"I told you!"

"Calm down, son, and tell me again."

"Mike R. and Sammy." Ben dropped his chin to his chest in frustration.

"Tell you what," Bart placated. "Let me see if I can get someone to cover for me, and if I can, I'll take you myself."

"Pfft," Ben uttered. "Like that'll ever happen. Just so you know, I'm going no matter what. I don't need you or your permission."

"And what genius told you that? Mike R. or Sammy?"

Ben looked away, but the blush in his cheeks deepened.

"Finish your lunch," Bart said, pushing his chair back from the table. "There's still a boatload of stocking to do."

AN HOUR LATER, Bart sat at his desk going over an income statement when a flurry on the surveillance monitor caught his attention. Lo and behold, Vanessa was strutting through the front door. His heart stirred at the sight of her gazelle-like legs, a vision in a hot pink, flirty skirt. He zoomed the camera in, and his smile and growing erection wavered. Her carefully made-up face was pinched, oozing with a mix of pissiness and arrogance. She held no resemblance whatsoever to the angel he'd kissed goodbye their last morning together.

When she stopped at a brightly colored display of Patagonia leggings, Bart watched, mortified, as Ben ran up behind her. He could almost see the excitement radiating off the boy as he wrapped his gangly arms around her waist and lifted her off the ground. Vanessa screamed and slapped at him, but when Ben set her down, he was laughing. She shoved him away, dusting herself off.

Fortunately, Ben didn't pick up on the brush-off, or the posture of distaste Vanessa assumed when she realized who had man-handled her. Wanting to save his son the humiliation, Bart quickly paged him to the warehouse before heading down to see what the prissy Mrs. Michaud wanted.

"Hi," he greeted her, hoping his matter-of-factness masked both his excitement and his irritation. He'd found her in the shoe department lacing up a pair of soft pink Skechers. "It's lovely to see you again."

She didn't look up. "I only have a few minutes. I forgot my running shoes, and I need some for the beach. Is this all you have?" She waved her hand at the shelves overflowing with rectangular boxes.

"I'm afraid so," he said, biting his upper lip.

"They'll have to do, then." She pried off the shoes and shoved them into the box. "Gotta run." She stood, smoothed down her wrinkled skirt, and turned toward the exit. Bart stopped her. "Those need to be scanned out of the system before I can let you take them."

She huffed impatiently. "Whatever, but hurry up." She thrust the box into his outstretched hands, then dropped her eyes to examine her bright pink manicure.

"What's with you, Vanessa?" he asked.

"Nothing." She scowled. "I'm in hurry, so please just scan the box."

"Yes, ma'am," he replied with a salute. "I'd be happy to kiss your ass, too, if you'd bend over and lift that pretty little skirt."

Vanessa's neck and face reddened, and she sputtered, "That's rude and uncalled for." She clenched her fists and stomped her foot.

"No, Vanessa, you're rude and uncalled for." He turned his back to her and walked to the nearest register. He scanned the box, then placed it on the counter, crossing his arms.

After a full minute, she approached the register. Her head was down, but Bart noticed the tears threatening to spill over her lower lids. Clearing her throat, she muttered,

"Thank you, Bart." When she reached for the box, he grabbed her wrist.

"Vanessa. Talk to me."

"I don't have time for this today."

"You won't take my calls, so when is a good time?"

"Never."

"I can't accept that."

"You have to. I promise not to bother you again, so please don't bother me."

"So that's what happened over New Year's? We *bothered* each other?"

"Yes. And it was a huge mistake."

Bart swallowed hard to stanch a regurgitation of his lunch. "You're wrong, but if that's how you want to remember it." He took a deep breath. "Keep in mind, though, your simple proclamation doesn't change how I feel or how I remember that night. When you finally come to your senses, I'll be here."

"And if I do, what then? What can you possibly offer me?" She yanked her arm away. "I sure as hell don't need an *I told you so.*"

"I would never say that, I promise. Just give me the chance. It's literally killing me that you're so unhappy with him. He'll never love you as much as I do. You've got to know that by now."

Vanessa looked into his eyes. Her lower lip was quivering, and he desperately wanted to stop it with a kiss. "Bart, you're sweet. You really are. And I know you want what's best for me." She took a breath. "But that isn't you. I'm sorry."

Bart felt the all-too-familiar stab of rejection. "That's where you're mistaken, Vanessa."

Vanessa swiped angrily at a tear slipping down her

cheek. "No, I'm afraid you're the one who's mistaken." Annoyance was back in her voice. She grabbed the shoebox and spun around, her swirling skirt teasing him as she stormed away. The clicking of her heels echoed in his ears long after she left the building.

26

MONKEY

THE CASH from Will Raskins arrived in a cardboard box wrapped with multiple layers of brown kraft paper. Monkey counted out the bills on the kitchen table: two thousand in tens and twenties. It would do for now, but he'd need the rest to carry out his long-term plan. He'd give the a-hole another week max to come up with eight more, or he'd be paying him a visit.

After stuffing the money under a floorboard in the hall closet, the same hidey-hole where Pa had hidden his small, army-issued revolver, he stumbled into the bedroom to lie down. Though back on his meds, the fogginess persisted, and he found he couldn't function without a nap most afternoons. He'd never felt this lethargic in the slammer, at least not once his body and mind adjusted to the pills, but then again, he hadn't done much to tire himself on the inside.

Just yesterday, he took down the shutters and covered

them with a fresh coat of black paint. They had needed a good sanding first, and that alone tuckered him out. This afternoon, after his nap, he would paint the front door— bright red, of course—then tackle the porch railing and steps.

He was hoping to drive over to Big Lots on Route 26 this weekend, use some of the cash for a new sofa, a mattress set, and a living room rug. Depending on how much that set him back, he would see what Ollies had in the way of lamps and pretty things, tchotchkes, and such.

As he lay there, unable to still his mind, he made a mental list of other items he might pick up: nice bath towels and fresh sheets, a flowery bedspread, or at least a warm blanket, a couple of pillows, shiny pots and pans, dishes, glasses, and cooking utensils. *Monogrammed coffee mugs would be a nice touch*, he thought, knowing that Ina Rose wouldn't be too pleased with the stained and chipped ones he was drinking out of.

Yawning, he turned onto his stomach, but despite his fatigue, he couldn't relax. After twenty minutes, he pushed to his knees. *No sense wasting time*, he thought, *when I can be finishing my chores*. Staring down at the threadbare blanket, he pictured Ina Rose beneath him, moaning softly like she always had when they made love. It had been far too long, but when his penis stirred, he bounced off the mattress. He'd waited so long to have her again, he could certainly wait a few more weeks. Afterall, it wasn't like he was still in the slammer. Those desperate and interminable nights were far behind him.

Rubbers, he thought with sudden panic. Should he pick up a box? Could Ina Rose even get pregnant? The vision of a little baby sleeping in a cradle beside their bed made him smile. To heck with the rubbers. He would buy one of those pregnancy sticks he remembered from high school, before Ina Rose started on birth control pills. He didn't imagine she was still taking them after all this time, but if she was, he would make her stop. Suddenly re-energized, Monkey banged out the front door, hopped down the three steps to the walkway, and retrieved the can of red paint from the back of his truck.

27

VANESSA

VANESSA GUNNED the engine of the BMW and merged onto Route 1 South. Her heart was pounding crazily, but not from the car's speed. She should have known better than to stop at the Middletown store. She shouldn't have risked running into Bart and allowing him to dim her spirit. She punched on the stereo and turned up the volume. She needed to calm down, to surrender her stress to the siren call of the ocean.

She had an entire week to herself while Roger was out of the country. She'd seen his itinerary, along with his passport, laid out beside his suitcase, and if she remembered correctly, his final flight would land in Liberia, Costa Rica, within the hour.

At least he was no longer with that Southport woman. From what Javier told her when they met up at the night-club the night Roger left, wives and girlfriends of American gringos were not especially welcome in Guanacaste, the land of mocha-drenched señoritas with dark, wavy tresses and enticingly exotic dialects. These women were renowned for offering unaccompanied men a legal state of *pura vida* for the duration of their stay. All for less than the cost of round-trip airfare for the missus.

But, again, Vanessa reminded herself, she didn't care. She was done servicing Roger, especially knowing what she did about the caliber of women he bedded behind her back. The only one who truly bothered her was the woman in Southport. She knew that wench's identity, but she refused to say her name.

But here she was, thinking about her. She unwrapped her fists from the steering wheel and forced herself to smile. To grin so wide that it hurt her cheeks. Bumping up the bass, she willed her heart to beat in cadence with "Every Breath You Take." Sting's soulful voice always helped to soothe her.

Passing a state trooper idling in the median, she dropped into lower gear, then reduced the volume. Fortunately, the music had already done its job, and when the trooper pulled up beside her to motion for her to slow down, she waved apologetically, mouthing, "Sorry." When the cruiser sped on, she hit the lever to retract the roof, cranked up the volume, and sang out at the top of her lungs

ARRIVING IN BETHANY BEACH, she let herself in the cottage and immediately scrunched her nose. A stale, damp odor permeated the air from weeks of being closed up in the humid coastal climate. With warmer spring temps, she'd make certain to leave the air conditioning on when she left later in the week. She dropped her bag, then proceeded to open all the windows, letting in the soft breeze off the ocean. Within minutes, the stagnant smell dissipated, replaced with the life-affirming essence of sand and sea.

She loved this little place. *A little place with an astronomical price tag*, she granted, grinning with pride. From the outside, it looked like an original beach cottage from the 1950s or 60s, which is exactly what had drawn her to it in the first place. The unassuming screened-in porch facing the street reminded her of the lakeside cabins her family had vacationed in back in Tennessee. Not that they'd gone every summer, and never after Daddy was gone, but still, she half expected to find Mama shucking corn behind that screen.

But it wasn't the porch that had sold her on the cottage. Instead, it was the completely revamped and modernized interior with its unobstructed view of the Atlantic Ocean. Water as far as the eye could see. As she took in that view now, she had no idea why Roger had ever built that monstrosity on Bald Head Island.

She located a bottle of Perrier in the fridge and poured herself a tall glass over ice. After the first bubbly sip, she opened the sliding screen to the deck, breathing deeply and willing the tension out of her shoulders. If she could just figure out how to fit her closet into this small space, she would live here forever.

She brushed sand off the bistro table and settled into an Adirondack chair to watch a flock of seagulls on the beach. Some people hated the birds, calling them flying sand rats, but she thought they were magical. Their laughing calls meant the sea was near, and she was home.

An entire week to herself. Alleluia! As her taut neck relaxed, she reviewed her agenda for the week. This evening, she would head out for a crab cake appetizer at Off the Hook, maybe drive to a dance club in Dewey after. Sadly, today's run-in with Bart had zapped the appeal of picking up a man for a little fun. No big deal. The memory and aftereffects of her night with Javier would hold her for a while longer. The young valet, his muscles rippling beneath his sweat-glistened skin, had been insatiable, with each round kinkier than the one before. He had left no part of her body untouched or unscathed. Vanessa wiggled in the chair as she recalled his never-ending blitz.

With a giggle, she returned to her list. Tomorrow morning, she would visit Hocker's Market to stock up on a few prepared meals, beverages, and fresh flowers. Her afternoon would entail lounging on the beach and reading the paperback she had picked up for the trip. Depending on the temperature and cloud cover, she would stay out til most other sunbathers called it a day, then lace up her new sneakers for a sweat-drenching run down the beach. Like always, she would stop at the World War II tower, then kick off the shoes for a cooling dip in the surf. Dinner would depend on her energy level and mood, as would any post-dinner entertainment. She ought to feel up for some by then.

As she reveled in the sights and sounds around her, her encounter with Bart shoved its way back to the surface. *No, I don't want to think about him or Roger!* She was sick and tired of men insisting they knew what was best for her, something they'd been doing her entire life.

When she was little, her father demanded she be a good Southern girl, seen but rarely heard. Try as she might, it wasn't in her DNA to be good or quiet for long stretches of time. She still felt the sting of his belt striking her backside.

Later, after she married her high school sweetheart, he did his very best to turn her into an obedient, stay-at-home wife, like his mama. By the time she called it quits—less than a year after the wedding—he had taken to locking her inside their crappy little house, forcing her to cook and clean during the day and feign adoration of his sexual prowess at night. Foolish boy.

Fast-forward to her move north, when she had gone to work for Bart, both at the sporting goods store and in his home, caring for young Ben. *Poor Ben*, she thought, feeling guilty for her reaction when he surprised her earlier. If there was one thing she regretted in the last decade, it was that she had broken the boy's heart. To hell with his dad's heart.

Angry at herself for permitting the intrusion, she picked up her glass and went inside. Time to select a pretty dress for dinner and dancing.

28

MARY

"DIANA, YOU'RE ALIVE!" Mary greeted her friend.

"I assumed my earlier text was evidence of that," Diana responded. "I told you not to worry yourself."

"Well, I did," Mary said. "For a hot minute, anyway."

"Well, this is me safe and sound," Diana replied with a laugh, "and I'm staring across the water at Southport right now."

"It's a gorgeous day, isn't it," Mary noted. "What are you up to?"

"Out and about shopping for tonight's dinner. Roger's off-island til later, and I thought I'd have steaks marinating when he gets home."

"Sounds delicious. Roger left the island?"

"Yes, he had an appointment in Wilmington."

"And you're okay with that? I mean, there's nothing weird going on with him?"

"Honey, you don't have a thing to fret about," she assured. "He's the same as he's ever been, and we're having a marvelous time together."

"All right. I trust you, but don't let your guard down."

"Hush now. I'm fine. But I do need you to accept that delivery Monday. Maybe unbox and price it all, too? I left the invoice on my desk."

"Sure, but what am I unpacking? Something you picked up last week in Atlanta?"

"Uh-huh. Just some lightweight scarves and wraps. It won't take you but an hour or two."

"I'm sure I can handle it, but I am surprised they shipped out so quickly, but with tourist season gearing up, that's a good thing. By the way, when will Rosalie be coming back to work? It's getting awfully close to Easter."

"Dang. I've been meaning to call her, but it keeps slipping my mind. Do you want me to ask her to go in instead?"

"No, I said I'll do it, and I will. I have the key you gave me earlier."

"Mary, I sure appreciate your helping me out, so I don't have to hurry back."

"When are you coming home?"

"I don't yet know, honey. Roger says I can stay as long as I want, even after he goes back to Pennsylvania."

Mary bit her lip. "You're not afraid of staying there by yourself once he's gone?"

"Of course not," Diana said. "This house is a fortress. But as you've reminded me, I do need to get the Siren decked out for Easter. I'll give it some thought and let you know. Anything else?"

"There is something I need to tell you."

"What's that?"

"Bobby's looking for you. I ran into him outside Potter's this morning."

"I know," Diana admitted. "He's texted me half a dozen times already."

"And?"

"And I can't decide what to text back."

"How about: 'I'm away for a few days. Be in touch when I get home.' Short and sweet works every time."

"I guess, but that's what I told him last week. I hope he doesn't get the idea that I'm cutting him loose. How'd he look?"

"Scrumptious as ever. Bib overalls covering nothing but his magnificent, naked body. Or at least that's what I imagined."

"Girl, you're probably right there. He is a proud peacock, isn't he?"

"Mm-hm," Mary muttered.

"Maybe I will come back after Roger leaves."

"You're irrepressible," Mary laughed.

"I am, aren't I? Ah, well. I'm not hurting anyone."

"No, you're not. Let's just make sure someone doesn't end up hurting you. Okay?"

"No arguments there. All's well with you and yours?"

"Yes, we're good. Sorry if I've been a worry wart."

"No reason to apologize. I appreciate your concern, but rest assured, I'm in no danger."

"Thank God for that. Be safe, and we'll talk again soon."

"You too, sugar."

After hanging up, Mary's thoughts switched to the upcoming dinner at the Franklins. She didn't know them all that well, having met Maria only a time or two at her small studio just outside of town. She was a talented designer and seemed like a lovely woman who, sadly, had also been the victim of a horrific crime the year before Mary and Jimmy moved to Southport. *It'll be nice getting to know them better*, she thought, *especially for Jimmy's sake*. She knew her husband missed the camaraderie of his fellow police officers, and a night of shop talk with the Brunswick County sheriff would do him a world of good.

Her phone rang, and she swiped it open.

"Hey, Mary," greeted George, his deep voice muffled by a cacophony of car horns.

"George, what's all the racket?"

"A vehicle fire on the beltway has everyone merging into a single lane. No one's very happy about it."

"What else is new?" Mary asked.

"Not a darn thing. Listen. I learned the DA is looking to revoke Roger Michaud's bail."

"Why?"

"From what I'm told, Michaud was ordered to stay in PA."

"Then he lied to Diana." Mary said sadly.

"I doubt it was the first time," George said, before yelling, *"A-hole!* Sorry, Mary, not you. I'll have to call you back once I get home. I have more dirt from his employees that you'll want to hear."

"Oh, great," she said, as George uttered another curse. Mary cringed and set down the now-dead phone.

29

BART

BART TURNED his truck onto Wellington and drove slowly along the tree-lined street. It was dark here, with few other cars out at this hour. The slip of paper with Vanessa's address was damp in his clenched fist, and after pausing at the intersection, he put his truck in neutral to collect himself. He checked his surroundings, then opened the center console where he'd stowed a stainless steel flask. He twisted off the cap, then swigged the entire contents. The vodka hit his stomach hard, but he willed the liquid courage to slip quickly into his veins. With a final glance at the dashboard map, he flicked on his turn signal.

Vanessa's signals—rude and dismissive one minute, teary-eyed and apologetic the next—had left him baffled. *Well*, he thought, *she might not know her true feelings, but I know mine.* By showing up at the store, she reopened the door, and he was determined to reclaim what had rightfully been his from the start.

Surprising even himself, he agreed to drive an ecstatic Ben to Ocean City for the air show, allowing his son to spend the night with Mike R. and Sammy at a beachfront condo. He booked himself a motel room around the corner, but he had no intention of sleeping there.

After arriving, he spent an hour with the boys watching a little of the pre-show rehearsal from the condo balcony. When the last fighter plane disappeared to the south, he reminded the boys that there was to be no drinking, carousing, or troublemaking. An embarrassed Ben sheepishly agreed, but the other two boys, looking decidedly guilty, remained mum. Bart considered checking out the contents of the refrigerator, but when Ben grumbled, "We'll be fine, Dad," he shook his head and left.

The motel room was shabby but clean. He showered and shaved, then watched HBO in his underwear until he was fairly certain the boys wouldn't require bail money.

Now, as he sat in his truck staring out over the darkened dunes, his heart thumped crazily in his chest. He was such a fool, a glutton for punishment, and he knew it. But there was no turning back now. He shifted into drive and turned up Atlantic Avenue.

He spotted her sports car easily enough parked in front of a rather small and unassuming cottage that stood atop five-foot pylons. Not the grandiose beachfront home he had expected, but the view of the ocean from the other side had to be awesome. The dashboard clock read eleven fifteen. She might be asleep by now, but that might actually work in his favor. *Okay, Bart,* he told himself, *it's now or never.*

He pulled the truck around the corner, then jumped down from the cab. With dread, he realized he had to pee.

Shit! How awkward would it be to surprise her, only to ask to use the toilet. Not quite the romantic scene he was aiming for. Slipping into a portable toilet at an under-construction house, he relieved himself, then took a moment to pull himself together before heading toward Vanessa's cottage.

From street level, the cottage appeared dark and quiet. With every step up to the screened-in porch, Bart's heart beat faster and faster. As he pulled the screen door toward him, the metal hinges squeaked noisily, and he groaned inwardly. Holding his breath, he listened for sounds coming from inside, but he heard nothing but the distant whoosh of waves on the beach. Pausing at the door, painted a bright coral pink with glass insets, he knocked gently three times. Nothing. Summoning his nerve, he knocked harder.

A light flickered on inside, and he picked up a woman's voice. Vanessa. He smiled when he saw her glide into view. She was a vision of loveliness, her long, blond hair tousled wildly around her angelic face. He was so right to have come. She approached the door tentatively, tying her robe as she squinted through the glass. The moment she recognized him, her beautiful face twisted with fury.

The door flew inward, and she rushed out. "Bart, what the hell are you doing here?" she whispered angrily.

Bart was dumbstruck, and his legs threatened to buckle beneath him. He took two steps backward, nearly tripping over a wicker footstool.

"Well?" she demanded. "Oh, never mind. It doesn't matter. Just leave!" With both hands, she shoved him toward the screen door.

When her robe slipped open, exposing one perfect, voluptuous breast, Bart found his voice. "Don't be angry with me, Vanessa. I brought Ben down for the OC air show, and I knew that being so near would give us the perfect opportunity to talk things through. Calmly and uninterrupted. Like on New Year's Eve."

"No, no, and no!" she hissed. "You've got to get out of here."

Undeterred, Bart stood his ground, smiling down at her despite his growing fear. "Come on, Vanessa. I'm here now, so you might as well let me in."

"Who's he, Vanessa?" a young man asked from the doorway. He was tanned and muscular, with dark hair streaked with blond. And he was naked.

"No one, Patrick. Go back inside." The naked man did as he was told.

"Oh," Bart said, nodding toward the pink door. "I see how it is." He clenched his fists and rocked back on his heels.

"Now you know," Vanessa said, shaking her head. "I'm sorry if you're hurt, but I've been trying to tell you for months that I don't want you in my life."

A bolt of lightning-hot pain flashed deep in his left eye. He blinked hard, then cleared his throat. There had to be something he could say to change her mind. "I'm willing to overlook—"

Vanessa held up her hand. "Just don't. Don't even go there."

Turning, he slammed through the screen door and cleared the five steps with a single leap. He ran to his truck and climbed into the cab. After fumbling with the key, he revved the engine. Gravel sprayed from the rear tires as he tore onto the roadway. Somewhere between Bethany and Fenwick Island, he pulled onto the shoulder and jumped out. Bending at the waist, his tears mixed with vomit as his liquid courage spilled into the roadside brush.

30

WILL

WILL'S hands trembled as he pressed the number for Monkey Parker. He dreaded making the call, had nothing to tell him. Dinner with his parents had been painful and unproductive, his father as remote and priggish as ever. Despite pleading his case, explaining that the money was needed to fund a sure-fire venture, he might as well have been talking to the wall. Howard Raskins acted as if his only son wasn't even in the room. The man finished his dinner, then retreated to his study without so much as a *good to see you, son* or *I'll mull over your proposal.*

In the kitchen afterward, his mother hastily wrote out a check. "William," she whispered, "your father's still deeply hurt and humiliated. I was hopeful, but it's obviously going to take more time and effort to break through to him." She handed Will the check. "I can't give you more without his finding out, but come by next Sunday, and we'll try again."

She walked him into the foyer, kissed his cheek, then closed and locked the door behind him.

"You better be callin' with good news," Monkey answered.

"I've got two more for you," Will replied.

"That's not enough, Raskins," he snarled before the phone went dead.

"Shit," Will swore. Was Parker serious about driving up here? He sure hoped not, but he never could read the crazy SOB. He needed to score the remaining six thousand or run. Waiting around and doing nothing was a risk he wasn't prepared to take.

He dropped onto his bed and pulled the pillow over his face. Frustrated, he screamed, not stopping until he ran out of oxygen. If only he could asphyxiate himself, hold his breath long enough to fall into a deep, bottomless sleep. At this point, there was nothing to live for. If dead, he would be off the hook. Maybe his dad would even feel a touch of remorse.

Senior's smug, pompous demeanor as he carved last night's roast flashed behind Will's eyelids. He envisioned himself grabbing the knife and stabbing it through his dad's heart. But as much as he wanted the man to suffer, it would never happen. Will was too much of a coward. But...

"Perfect!" he shouted, tossing the pillow across the room. *With me gone, the lunatic will head straight to dear old Dad for the money.*

Would Howard Raskins, the third, be smug or scared shitless when confronted by the scrappy ex-con? Will hoped for the latter. What he'd give to be a fly on the wall when Father soiled his perfectly tailored Brioni slacks.

Will's smile transformed itself into a wide grin. Nope, he wasn't going to off himself, but he would disappear. *How much time do I have*, he wondered. *Two days tops*, he figured. Sucking a deep breath, he opened the door to his crammed closet and pulled out his old high school gym bag. Within fifteen minutes, he shoved in a few days' worth of underwear, socks, and T-shirts. Enough to buy himself a week or more, but not so much that anyone would notice things missing.

What else, he wondered. He had Mother's check, which he would cash in the morning, and a few hundred left over from her first gift. What about a toothbrush and toothpaste? Nah, too obvious. He yanked open the nightstand and routed around for his phone charger. There was no one he needed to call, but you never knew when the GPS might come in handy.

Until he settled on a destination, he would head west on the turnpike. No, not the turnpike—too many cameras. He'd take 611 North, then pick up 80 West. Beautiful drive along the river, and the Pocono Mountains would be good for his soul.

Buoyed by his plan, he took a final piss, then grabbed a few bottles of water from the fridge, leaving behind the six-pack of Dogfish Head IPA, his all-time favorite craft beer. He'd pick up another once he stopped for the night, wherever that might be.

31

MONKEY

MONKEY DROVE THROUGH THE NIGHT, pulling up outside the seedy apartment building just before noon. He had stopped only twice to pee, and as he stepped down from his truck, his bum leg buckled. He glanced around, but the only other person in sight was a mail carrier busy at a bank of boxes at the rear of the parking lot.

Inside the foyer—the door was propped open by a broken cinder block—he allowed his eyes to adjust to the gloom, then took the steps slowly, one at a time as his leg loosened up. The pace gave him a few moments to review his plan: gain access to the apartment, subdue Raskins, call Dad and demand a ransom, pick up his money, head on home. Easy as can be.

He found apartment 3B, ripped off a small length of silver duct tape, placed it over the peephole, then knocked loudly twice. When no one answered, he knocked again, more urgently this time. Still no sign of Raskins, he slid his driver's license behind the latch and was inside seconds later. The place was a shit hole. A very tiny shit hole. *Just like Raskins*, he thought.

He found the head first, pissing for what seemed like forever. He had been holding it since DC, and he grunted as his jaw muscles spasmed. With his bladder empty, he went in search of the refrigerator. Finding the cold six-pack, he grabbed a bottle, then rummaged through the nearest drawer for an opener. After a deep pull of the cold beer, his shoulders dropped down from his ears. He grabbed a half-eaten bag of nacho chips from the cupboard and plopped down onto the cracked pleather sofa to wait.

With his belly quiet and his head buzzed by two beers, Monkey yawned. Was he ever tired. He figured Raskins would get off work around four, five at the latest. A quick check of his phone told him he had a couple good hours to rest up before his old friend would arrive home. He laid down on the sofa and closed his eyes. As his exhausted body relaxed, something jabbed at his belly, and he pulled the knife from its sheath on his belt. Without opening his eyes, he placed the blade on his belly, covering it with his right hand. He was asleep in minutes.

HOURS LATER, a honking car stirred him from a dream of Ina Rose. She was so darn pretty dancing around their kitchen in her bare feet, a radiant smile lighting up her face. "Dance with me, Monkey," she called to him, and he twirled her around the room.

Awake now, a sense of loss settled over him. He wanted the dream back. He wanted Ina Rose back.

He rolled over and willed himself back to sleep, but the

dream had vaporized. In a burst of rage, he stabbed the sofa cushion, stopping only when he heard voices in the hallway.

He jumped up and moved quietly to the door. When the footsteps retreated, he relaxed and re-sheathed his knife. He checked the time. Four thirty. Raskins would be home soon.

At seven, Monkey's stomach wouldn't shut up, and after hunting through the kitchen cabinets again, he uncovered a pack of cheese crackers. He used his knife to cut through the plastic, then downed the squares one at a time, following each with a swig of beer.

At eight, he was ticked. Where the hell was Raskins? By ten, he was long past ticked and done waiting. He slipped out of the apartment and down the stairs. In the glove box of his truck, he pulled out a notepad. "Radnor," he read aloud. Scrolling through his phone, he pulled up the address to the home of Mr. and Mrs. Howard W. Raskins, III. From the suggested route, it looked like he would be paying them a visit in time for the eleven o'clock news.

32

BART

WALKING through the Slap Shots showroom, Bart stopped to organize a messy display of thermal gloves and face masks. Looking around, he spotted a bored sales associate who was failing miserably to appear busy. He beckoned him over.

"Relocate this display to the front of the store, then mark everything down fifty percent."

The kid stared at Bart like he had four eyes, then turned and huffed away. "Get someone to help you," Bart shouted after him.

He was in a foul mood, had been for days. Despite trying desperately to move on after Vanessa's memorial, to forget all about her, he couldn't shake his devastating heartache. Or the anger that gripped him without warning.

Then there was that man nosing around the stores. The guy who first showed up the morning of Vanessa's service.

Bart figured he was a reporter trying to dig up dirt, but regardless, he was pestering the employees and stirring up unnecessary gossip. Ben had even brought him up at dinner last night.

"Dad, you remember that big Black dude?" his son asked.

"What Black dude, Ben?" Bart replied, distracted by ESPN's recap of the previous night's match between the Caps and Islanders.

"You know. That bald guy with the beard. At the store the day of Vanessa's memory party."

Bart looked away from the TV. "It was a memorial service, Ben, not a party. And yes, I remember. What about him?"

"He's a Caps fan. That's all."

"He told you that?"

"Yeah. He probably watched the game last night." Ben pointed at the TV, then shoveled a spoonful of macaroni and cheese into his mouth.

"What else did he tell you?"

With his mouth full, Ben garbled, "Nothing. Just some questions about Vanessa." He swallowed noisily. "And Roger, too."

"What did you tell him?" Bart asked, muting the TV.

"Hey, I'm watching that!" Ben protested.

"I'll turn it up in a minute. What did the guy want to know, Ben?"

"It doesn't matter." Ben grabbed the remote and maxed out the volume. Bart stood and yanked the plug on the TV. The screen went dark.

"Dad!" Ben yelled, knocking over his chair as he jumped up. He shoved Bart out of his way, then stomped into the den.

Bart allowed him to calm down for a few minutes, then he reheated the mac and cheese in the microwave and carried the bowl and a fresh glass of milk into the den.

"Sorry 'bout that, Ben," he relented. "It's just that I get nervous when you talk to strangers. You remember what happened at the park."

"I was twelve, Dad! I'm not a kid anymore, so stop treating me like one."

"I will. I promise. Didn't I let you stay at the beach condo without me? I just want you to tell me when someone bothers you."

"He wasn't bothering me," Ben said, defiantly digging into his dinner.

"If you say so, son." He ruffled Ben's hair, then returned to the kitchen.

Bart dropped it after that, but he still worried about what the man might be up to.

The company grapevine was also abuzz with rumors that Roger was back in town. Not that his business partner had notified Bart directly. That would be asking far too much of the man who used people then tossed them away like trash. And yet, here he was, free to come and go wherever, whenever, and with whomever he pleased, while poor Vanessa lay dead and buried.

But wait. Was she even buried yet? Had the medical examiner released her body, and if so, to whom? Who arranged for her funeral and burial? Or had she been cremated? The thought of her tiny body disintegrating in a thousand-degree fire made him suddenly nauseous, and he raced for the toilet.

33

MARY

JIMMY AND MARY drove up the Franklins' private drive, shielded from the road by a canopy of massive oak trees, and came to a stop in front of a charming clapboard cottage beribboned with a wraparound front porch.

"Jimmy, look at that," Mary said breathlessly, pointing beyond the house to the Intracoastal Waterway. The water was aglow with the rays of the setting sun which were radiating from a fissure in the cloud cover.

"Beautiful," Jimmy agreed.

"Can we live here?" she asked.

"I'm not sure there's room for us, but feel free to ask," he replied with a laugh.

John and Maria met them on the front porch with a tray of iced tea and canapes. "Welcome," John said, beaming as he shook Jimmy's hand and kissed Mary's cheek.

"Yes, welcome to our humble abode," Maria said. "I

thought we'd sit out here for a while before dinner. Unless the rain starts up again, that is."

"Thank you," Mary said, accepting a glass of tea. She set a small, wrapped box on the tray in its place, then added, "And this is for you."

"Oh, you didn't have to do that, Mary," Maria graciously said.

"You're cooking for us, so of course she did," Jimmy joked, winking at his wife.

"It's nothing," Mary said, though she'd struggled with what to bring for a woman who specialized in home decorating. She'd finally settled on a set of three hand-painted oyster shells that she found at Southport's weekly craft fair.

When they were all seated, Mary said, "Your property is so lovely. I can't imagine enjoying such spectacular sunsets every night."

"Well, tonight's wasn't much," John said.

"Oh, but it was," Mary disagreed. "The clouds parted just as we drove up your drive. It was magnificent."

"We are blessed," Maria admitted. "When John first invited me over for a barbeque with my sister Izzy a few years back, I knew immediately that I was going to live here."

"Mind you, it was our first date," John teased, "so imagine my surprise when both women rolled their suitcases up to the porch!" He kissed the back of his wife's hand.

"Had Mary known how incredible the view is, she would have brought hers," Jimmy said.

"Well, we have two spare bedrooms tonight, if you'd like to stay," Maria said. "Our children—Jackie and Sam—are at John's folks' for the night."

"Aww. I would have liked to meet them," Mary said.

"Next time," Maria replied. "Our menu couldn't compete with their granddad's famous stuffed cheeseburgers."

"Well," Jimmy said, "I'll eat just about anything, so bring it on."

"Oh, we will," John said, laughing.

"So, Mary," Maria said, "are you writing a second book? I loved your first."

"Let's just say it's in the planning stages."

"Do tell," Maria prompted.

"No, I don't think we'll talk about it tonight. It might spoil our good time. Instead, tell me about yourself."

Maria laughed. "There's not much to tell. I'm a wife, stepmom, and a part-time interior designer. My various hats keep me as busy as I want to be, although the kids do seem to need me less and less all the time."

"Would you ever consider expanding your design business?" Mary asked. "I've been in homes you've decorated, and they're all so unique. I don't know how you do it."

"Thank you, Mary. I try hard to give each home a distinctive look, though sometimes it's hard when so many owners want the same thing, thanks in part to HGTV. But yes, if the right opportunity arises, I might consider taking on a broader client base."

"Where are you from, Maria?" Jimmy jumped in. "That's not a Southern accent I detect."

"No, I'm from a small town north of Philadelphia. Doylestown."

Mary looked to Jimmy, and their eyes widened. "No way," Mary exclaimed. "I'm from Doylestown. I still consider it my home."

"What a small world," John chimed in.

"What school did you go to?" Maria asked.

"CB West. You?"

"Archbishop Wood, way back when it was all girls."

"I'm probably right behind you," Mary said. "I bet we know a lot of the same people."

As the two women talked, John beckoned for Jimmy to follow him into the house. "You girls talk," he said, "while Jimmy and I tend to dinner."

Hours later, as Jimmy negotiated the winding back roads leading from the Franklins' home, Mary said, "I like her a lot. I'd never suspect what she's been through."

"The same could be said about you, Mary. You remind me of each other."

"That's nice to say, Jimmy. You and John are a lot alike, too. We'll have them to our house for a cookout this summer."

"I think that's a great idea."

Mary closed her eyes and dozed for the rest of the drive home. Waking when they turned onto their street, she flashed back to the cold night they'd come home from dinner at Bella Cucina to find their neighbor on the front porch, waiting to warn them of an intruder on the property. Since that horrific night, Jimmy had taken it upon himself to go inside first whenever they'd been out after dark. She shivered involuntarily, thinking, *no wonder Maria Franklin sold her home in town after she was brutally attacked there.* As she trailed Jimmy into the mudroom, she wondered if she'd ever again feel one hundred percent safe in her own home. Really safe. *Maybe tomorrow,* she thought hopefully.

MONKEY

MONKEY DROVE through Southport's narrow, oak-lined streets to get his bearings. He found the Seaside Siren easily enough, but its darkened windows and the *Closed* sign hanging on the door stopped him from getting out of the truck. Good thing, too, as a marked police vehicle rolled past while he idled in front of the two-story building. Nodding to the officer, he proceeded to the intersection and turned left. Following the signs to the marina, he parked at the rear of the lot and shut off his engine.

The drive over the mountains had been nerve-racking, with torrential downpours threatening to sweep his tires off the road on more than one occasion. He flexed his fingers to loosen the joints, stiff from gripping the wheel. He laid back his head and closed his eyes. The steady beat of raindrops pelting the roof lulled him to sleep.

MAMA WAS real sick and couldn't catch her breath. Monkey shook her inhaler, listening for the slosh of liquid. It might be enough for a few more sprays. Before heading out to the repair shop, he implored Ina Rose to pick up a new canister at the pharmacy when she went into town later.

By the time he came in for dinner, Mama had taken on a sickly, gray pallor and was sucking air like a fish out of water.

"Oh, she's been fine all day," Ina Rose told him, shaking her head at Monkey's panicked expression. "She only started doing that when she heard you come in. Just get her to drink some hot tea with honey to break up all that phlegm. I tried a little bit ago, but she knocked the cup right out of my hand." She held out her arm, pointing to a barely visible pink mark.

"You know she can't be without her medicine, Ina Rose," he whispered angrily. "You shoulda fetched me if you wasn't gonna get it, and I woulda." He patted Mama's sunken cheeks, then lifted her chin to dribble in a few drops of water.

Primping her hair in the dressing table mirror, Ina Rose said, "I know, baby, but I didn't even think about bothering you. By the time I was done at the beauty parlor, all I thought of was hurrying back to fix Mama's dinner. Besides, the sky was about to let loose, and if I'd stayed out any longer, the rain woulda ruined my do."

Mama wasn't fine, and after twenty minutes of Ina Rose begging him to wait a while longer for the spell to pass, Monkey picked up Mama and carried her to his truck in the worst of the tempest. Lightning lit up the sky as deafening thunder boomed down the hillside. He tossed her body, just skin and bones in the threadbare nightie, onto the seat of his truck, then fishtailed it down to the center of town. The pharmacy's neon sign flickered like a beacon in the storm, and his rear tires spun out as he braked at the front door. He jumped from the cab and slammed headlong into the pharmacy. With one glance at his stricken face, Mr. Booker grabbed Mama's inhaler from the prescription bin, then followed him out to the truck.

But it was too late. Mama hadn't been faking the attack, and no amount of medicine sprayed down her throat could revive her ravaged lungs. A few days later, they buried her in the plot behind the house, side-by-side with Daddy for all eternity.

Ina Rose was guilt-ridden, and after three weeks, Monkey had about all he could take of her groveling, and he forgave her. He missed Mama something terrible, but the emphysema would have gotten her sooner or later. If Ina Rose was partly to blame for how early she'd been called home to the Lord, so be it.

Life gradually returned to normal, and before long, Ina Rose was badgering Monkey to take her to California.

"You promised me that when Mama was gone, we'd go. She ain't holding us back no more, Monkey, so why are you?"

Monkey was torn, especially with both his folks planted out back. Who would want to buy the old place anyway? No one, that's who. Leaving didn't make no sense to him, and he refused to talk about it.

One evening, the spring after Mama died, he came home to a dark house. Thinking Ina Rose had maybe gone to town and lost track of time, he went to lie down til she came home. Entering the bedroom, he noticed that all her makeup and hair products were gone from the top of the dresser. He threw open the closet, but only his shirts hung inside. Ina Rose's clothes and shoes were gone. Panicked, he ran to the kitchen, where he found her note on the table, slipped beneath the salt and pepper shakers:

MONKEY, honey, I love you and I'm so, so sorry, but I gotta go. It's now or never for me. I don't want to die in this house and be buried out back like them. I can't. You'll be fine on your own, so don't come looking for me. Stay here where you belong.

I will love you forever.
Your wife,
Ina Rose

BELOW HER CHILDLIKE SIGNATURE, she had drawn two halves of a broken heart. Her dime-store wedding band was taped atop the heart's jagged split.

Monkey sat for hours, spinning the sheet of paper round and round. Each time it stopped, he closed his eyes and prayed, *Lord, let the words be different this time.* But the words never changed. Ina Rose was gone.

A BOOM of thunder startled Monkey awake in the cab of his truck. His cheeks were wet with tears, and he rubbed at his face. Mama's death and Ina Rose's betrayal slowly slipped away, leaving only a familiar, haunting pain.

Dusk was settling in, and he needed to find a place to stay for the night. He recalled a chain hotel on the outskirts of town, but when he spotted the quaint River Oaks Inn, its low white buildings nestled under a canopy of ancient oak trees, he turned in.

The manager was real sweet, and after handing him the key card to room number six, she offered him an umbrella. "This storm's due to settle in on top of us for the next twenty-four hours. It's a shame you won't be seeing the best of our little town, but at least this will keep you dry."

"No worries, ma'am," Monkey said. "Rain's never hurt me none before."

"Well, if I can take care of anything for you, restaurant reservations or directions, just call the office."

"Will do. Thanks, ma'am." He tipped his cap and turned up the collar of his rain jacket before pushing out the door.

After finding his room, he lay on the comfy bed and stared up at the ceiling. As rain hammered the roof, his thoughts turned to his plans for tomorrow. The rain might prevent him from experiencing the best Southport had to offer, but he hadn't come all this way to sightsee.

35

DIANA

DIANA WAVED at the departing ferry, and when Roger disappeared inside the cabin, she dropped her arm to her side. She opened the umbrella and wandered back to the parking lot, hesitating when she approached the row of parked carts. They all looked the same to her. Fortunately, she quickly spied the Flyers flag, then the vanity plate *HT#39*, in the exact spot she'd left it. The vanity tag had confused her at first, but Roger explained its meaning: H for *Hat*, T for *Trick* and #39 for his team number.

"And a hat trick is what?" she asked.

"My specialty," he answered, beaming. "Three scores in a single game."

She leaned into him and sighed. "My hero."

He snorted and kissed her head. "Yeah, well, I'm glad you think so, but I'm nothing but a has-been these days."

"Hush. You're no has-been to me, you're a..." She hesitated, grasping for the right word.

"A what?" he asked, his eyebrows arched.

"I'll come up with it," she teased him. "Trust me."

AS SHE STARTED THE CART, a niggling worry popped into her head. Bobby. Days ago, she had texted that she'd be in touch once she returned to Southport, but he hadn't been appeased.

How long will you be gone?

American Fish has a live band Friday. Will you be back by then?

Nabbed a grouper from today's catch. Fix you dinner?

And lastly, *Miss you, Diana.*

Funny thing was, she missed him, too.

Roger had suggested she stay at the house until he returned—by week's end at the latest, he assured her. The idea was tempting, but there was too much to do at the shop, which was true, and if he let her know when he'd be back, she'd have dinner waiting for him.

She powered on her phone, and the dings sounded one after the other. She scrolled through to the most recent text from Mary, then replied: *Catching the ferry later this afternoon. See you tomorrow?*

She then composed a message to Bobby: *Be home tonight. Stop over at 8?*

Shifting into reverse, she backed from the parking spot and sped through the lot. A dog walker held up his arm and shot her an evil look when she braked abruptly at a crosswalk.

"Slow down, lady," the Sperry-shod man snarled. He

proceeded to stop directly in front of the cart, allowing— encouraging, really—Fido to slurp at a puddle. The tiny dog, a breed Diana couldn't identify, was dressed in a bright yellow slicker and hat that matched those worn by his owner.

Diana couldn't help herself. The laugh started in her belly, spreading upward until it exploded from her mouth. The man, clearly perturbed, muttered, "I hate tourists." In no hurry to get out of the way, he bent to adjust the dog's ridiculous hat.

"Get a life," Diana replied dismissively. Spinning the cart's wheel, she floored the accelerator and swerved around the coordinated duo. Rainwater sprayed everywhere, and the irate man screeched like a little girl. With a quick glance behind her, she saw him clutch the sopping wet pup to his chest. The look on his face was absolutely priceless. She made a mental note to kiss Roger for getting his friend to remove the cart's speed-regulating governor.

36

MARY

MARY TURNED THE KEY, then pushed into the darkened interior of the Seaside Siren. She flicked one of the light switches inside the door, and a single overhead chandelier flickered on, casting an eerie glow across the cool, damp space.

Smelling mustiness in the air, she went in search of a scented candle, finding instead a half-burned stick of incense resting in a narrow wooden bowl at the register. She brought it to her nose, inhaling the earthy scent of patchouli, Diana's signature fragrance. She struck a match and held it to the burnt end of the stick until tendrils of smoke curled upward into the air.

The incoming delivery was due to arrive shortly, and looking back out on the torrent streaming down the front window, she hoped the driver would be willing to help her get the boxes inside rather than dropping them on the sidewalk.

In the office, she hung her jacket on the back of the door, then transferred her revolver into the waistband of her jeans. She heated the water in the coffee maker, selecting a pod of peppermint tea. As she closed the lid, the bell on the front door chimed.

"Hello," Mary called out, pushing through the beaded curtain. "Are you here with my delivery?"

"No, ma'am," the man replied, his voice hushed.

Silhouetted as he was in the dreary light, it took a moment for Mary to realize he wasn't holding any cartons, and instead of a uniform, he wore baggy jeans, a drab rain jacket, and a ball cap pulled low on his forehead.

"Sorry, I thought you were a courier. The store's not open today."

"You sure?" the man questioned. "Door was unlocked."

Mary detected a hint of challenge in his voice, and she took a step toward the register, focusing on the cold steel nestled in the small of her back. "Be that as it may, we're closed, and you'll have to leave." She hoped her voice sounded strong.

"You're not the owner," the man said.

"No," Mary replied, "but I do work for her, and I'm asking you again to leave."

"Where is she?"

"She's not here," Mary said, more calmly than she felt.

"When will she be back?" he asked, stepping closer.

Mary stood her ground. "Sir, if you give me your name, I'll be more than happy to tell the owner you stopped by."

"Are you nervous?" he asked. "I ain't trying to make you nervous." He fingered the sleeve of a plush cotton bathrobe hanging from a carousel near the front window.

"Please don't fondle the merchandise," Mary said as she moved behind the counter.

He raised the robe's sleeve to his nose and inhaled deeply. "Patchouli," he whispered, his voice barely audible.

Mary cleared her throat impatiently, and he dropped the sleeve. Tapping the bill of his cap, he said, "Thank you for your time, ma'am. I'll come back later. No need to tell the owner I stopped by." He took one last look around the room, then pushed out the door into a booming clap of thunder.

Mary rushed to lock the door, chastising herself for not doing so when she arrived. She searched the street for the stranger, but he'd already disappeared. Who was he? Definitely not a local, or at least no one she'd met before.

She returned to the office and pressed the brew button on the coffee maker. Her heartbeat slowed as she waited for the steaming tea to fill the mug, and when it did, she carried it gingerly to the desk. She sat for a few moments while it cooled, picking up the invoice for the incoming shipment.

She found the business credit card hidden in the secret compartment beneath Diana's desk, then dialed the vendor. After reading the card number to the customer service agent, she waited on hold while the transaction processed. As music played in her ear, she mulled over how she'd describe the stranger to Diana, but she was hard-pressed to come up with anything—other than *slight* and *wet*—that might positively identify him. As for his voice, she might have detected a slight twang, but she couldn't be sure of that, either.

"Miss Forrester?" the agent said, coming back on the line.

"No, I work for Miss Forrester, and she's authorized me to use the store card," Mary replied.

"Well, here's the thing," the woman said. "The card you gave me was denied. Is there another one you can use?"

"Oh my gosh, give me a second." Mary set down the phone to search the hidden cubby. "I can't put my hands on one just now," she told the woman, "but will you take my personal card?"

"Sure, I don't see why not."

After disconnecting the call, Mary wrote a note to Diana explaining what had happened. She'd surely be reimbursed, but she couldn't help wondering why the store's card was rejected. She made a copy of the invoice, then slipped it into the pocket of her jacket.

A loud bang at the door caused her to flinch. She reached for her gun, stopping when she spotted the brown-clad delivery driver huddled with his hand truck beneath the blue-and-white striped awning. She rushed to door to let him in.

JIMMY

JIMMY SWIPED OPEN HIS PHONE. "Hey, George, what's up?"

"Man, am I glad you answered."

"Uh-oh. What's wrong?"

"I just got off the phone with a PI out of Philly by the name of Rafe Samms. He tells me he was hired by Vanessa Michaud a few months before she died."

"To do what?" Jimmy asked, watching out the front window as Mary's sleek white Audi pulled into the drive-way, its windshield wipers furiously beating off the incessant deluge.

"To look into who and where her husband was plunging his dipstick. He says he turned in his final report a week before Vanessa was killed. Turns out the cops found it when they searched the house after her murder."

"Incriminating stuff?" Jimmy asked, waving as Mary paused in the doorway.

"Lots and lots of incriminating stuff," George said.

"Hey, George," Mary greeted. "Sorry I didn't pick up, but it's raining so hard, I needed to keep my eyes on the road."

"No problem, Mary. I'll fill you in."

"Okay, give me a sec."

While they waited for Mary, the two men chatted about spring training and the Nats' chances for repeating last season's winning record. Returning to the study with a towel draped across her shoulders, Mary said, "Go on, George. I'll catch up."

"Sure. I was just telling Jim how a search of the Michaud house turned up a PI report commissioned by Vanessa. I talked to the PI, and he confirmed the report's existence."

"What's in it?" Mary asked.

"Photos of Roger with women not his wife, along with names, dates, times, and places."

"Uh-oh. Could be a motive," Mary said.

"But whose?" Jimmy asked.

"Can't say at this point," George said. "What's certain is that Mr. Hockey has a very busy extracurricular life. Any one of the women in the photos could have motive to kill Vanessa. Which, by the way, Mary, includes your friend."

Jimmy watched Mary fidget uncomfortably. "So the police know about Diana?" she asked, tousling her wet hair.

"Yep. They now know about Diana and the other women, both in and out of the country. In addition to his trip to Costa Rica two weeks ago, Rafe—he's the PI, Mary—trailed him to the Bahamas last fall. Seems he's quite the dog wherever he travels."

"Dang," Jimmy said, shaking his head. "Way I see it is Vanessa Michaud gets the photos, calls hubby out on his infidelities, and threatens to take him to the cleaners. Hubby kills her before he leaves the country, or he hires someone to do it while he's gone. Either way, he's guilty of murder one, alibi or no alibi."

"Man, if it were only that easy," George said. "Seems Michaud couldn't have done the deed himself. His alibi is solid. He didn't land back in the States until late the night the cops were called to the house."

"How long had she been dead by then?" Mary asked.

"Coroner puts death at forty-eight to sixty hours prior."

"Did Samms say if Vanessa wanted the photos as grounds for divorce?" Jimmy asked.

"No, just the opposite, actually. She told him they were her guarantee that she would remain Mrs. Roger Michaud til death do them part."

"Tell me she didn't use those words," Jimmy said.

"Nah, that's just my little joke. The report was her assurance that she'd hold onto the money, the house—or houses—and her standing as Mrs. Roger Michaud."

Mary said, "Smart girl."

Jimmy gave her a sideways glance. "But then again, Mary, she's dead."

"Smart girl or not," George said, "she couldn't keep King Slap Shot happy at home. Getting back to those photos, on one particular night, Rafe followed the horny bastard to the homes of two women, one right after the other."

"Yuck," Mary said, cringing visibly.

"I expect the cops will take a good look at all the women, including Diana," Jimmy mused. "Did he seem to favor one over the others?"

"Yes, all in all, he spent a greater percentage of his time in North Carolina with Diana. As for up here, I think I actually met his favorite at the memorial service. Remember, Mary, I mentioned one who got all pissy before I could ask her a single question?"

"Is she the girl who gave you the finger?"

"That's her. Darla Smalls is her name. Rafe said when Michaud's in town, they've been hooking up twice a week."

"I have an unsettling thought," Jimmy said. "If this Darla Smalls, or another of Roger's lovers, killed Vanessa, is she done?"

Mary looked perplexed. "Done what?"

"You could be right," George responded. "If she's serious about purging the competition, why stop with the wife? Mary, I'd warn your friend to watch her back."

"I've already done that. But you two don't understand how stubborn she is."

"Then if I were you, I'd keep my distance until the real murderer is behind bars. You don't want to become collateral damage."

"George," Jimmy said, "I've been trying to get Mary to stay away from the woman since the day she first invited her into our home."

"Good luck to both of you, then," George teased. "I'm outta here."

38

DIANA

THE FERRY back to Southport was rocking and rolling, and by the time it reached the terminal, Diana was lightheaded and her legs wobbled beneath her. When she hefted her carry-on bag over her shoulder, it felt as though it weighed twice as much as when she'd boarded forty minutes earlier.

As she drove into town, the thought of Bobby put a smile on her face and eased her wooziness. Sure, he was much younger than she, but the age difference had never been a problem for either of them. She always managed to keep pace with his high energy, whether drinking at the bar, dancing to the music of a local band, or making love. Especially when making love.

A flutter of desire passed through her, but with it came an irksome dose of guilt. How was it possible that her body and mind shifted so effortlessly from one man to the other?

Her stay on the island had been magical, and just last night Roger had jokingly asked her to "go steady," offering to bring back his high school letter jacket for her to wear. She'd laughed—he'd been quite drunk at the time—but wasn't that exactly what she'd been hoping for?

Letter jacket or not, there was no question Roger offered more than Bobby ever could, but sadly, a future with Roger meant a goodbye to her young Adonis.

A flash of lightning lit the sky as she turned onto Howe Street, and after pulling into the alley behind her building, she waited in the car until the downpour subsided. When it did, the prospect of a hot shower, a glass of Merlot, and a quick power nap began to quell her nagging doubts. After all, until the dust settled from Vanessa's murder, Roger was in no position to make good on his hint of a future together.

As she stepped from the car, her phone dinged. It was a text from Roger: *Arrived safely. Call you after meeting with DA. Miss you already.*

"Uh-oh," she said, biting her lip. She responded with a simple *xoxo* and a kissy-face emoji. If luck was on her side, he'd call before Bobby showed up.

She bypassed the store and ran straight up to her apartment, stripping off her damp clothes as she let herself in. She poured that glass of Merlot, then headed to the bathroom. In the shower, she allowed the hot water to wash her doubts and guilt down the drain. Tonight, she would give in to her yearning for Bobby's sweet, young body. There would be plenty of time to think about Roger, about her future with him, tomorrow.

39

MARY

"AND HOW WAS YOUR DAY, DEAR?" Jimmy asked, coming up behind Mary as she prepared a large salad at the kitchen island. He reached around her and grabbed a candied pecan from the bowl, popping it into his mouth.

Mary turned and swatted him with the tongs. "Hey, wait for dinner!"

"Okay, okay." He held his hands up in surrender, startling when a deep rumble of thunder shook the house. "That was close," he said, glancing out the back window.

"It hasn't let up all day," Mary said. "Downtown was deserted."

"I'm not surprised. Did you get everything unboxed at the store?"

Mary placed the salad on the table and lit the two candles nestled in the centerpiece. "I did, but I also ran into a couple of unanticipated hitches."

Jimmy, pouring himself a glass of wine, looked up. "Really? What happened?"

Mary hesitated. "Let's eat first, and then I'll tell you about them."

After the dinner dishes had been cleared and the kitchen was again spotless, Jimmy and Mary settled into the sofa to catch the end of *Jeopardy!*.

"You never did tell me about your day," Jimmy prompted.

"Oh," Mary replied with a frown. "A weird one, is all."

"How so?"

"I wasn't going to confess this, but I ended up covering the delivery with my own credit card."

"You what? Mary, for God's sake. We can't afford to buy inventory for that store! You'll be reimbursed, right?"

"Of course I will," Mary replied. "Diana's back tomorrow, and I left her a note. In her defense, I think she got today's delivery mixed up with a purchase she made in Atlanta last week. Today's order was made months ago."

"Don't excuse her sloppy bookkeeping, Mary," Jimmy chastised. "She either knows what she's doing, or she doesn't. Just how much are we talking?"

"A little over five hundred," Mary admitted.

"Geez," Jimmy said, rubbing his hands over his close-cropped hair.

"She'll pay me back, Jimmy. Don't worry."

"I'm not worrying, but if you don't get the money this week, I'll go in there and get it myself."

Mary shook her head. "Whatever."

"What else?" Jimmy asked.

Mary turned to face him. "I'm almost afraid to tell you now."

"Spill it," he ordered, taking her hand.

When she finished telling him about the man who'd come into the store, he asked, "And you're sure you haven't seen him before?"

"No, but I got the impression he's not from around here."

"Can you be a trifle more specific?" he asked.

"Believe it or not, there's not much I can tell. He was soaking wet and drowning in an oversized rain jacket and ball cap, but it was too dim and dreary to make out any defining features."

"So, what about him raised the alarm?"

Mary scrunched her nose. "It wasn't what he said, so much, as how he acted. How he laughed. Menacing, like he enjoyed giving me the willies. But then again, I might have overreacted. I'd just gotten there, and it was storming, and I hadn't even had a chance to turn on all the lights yet. He startled me is all."

"Where have I heard that before?" Jimmy asked, and Mary flushed.

"Okay, I messed up. Again. I'm sorry. I should have locked the door behind me."

"You'll remember next time," Jimmy said. "Did you leave Hippie Chick a note about him, too?"

"Yes, but I'll tell her more when I see her tomorrow."

"What time will that be?"

"If this rain stops, I'm going to morning yoga on the dock, so probably not til after."

"Good, I'll go with you."

"You'll do what?" Mary asked, her eyes wide.

"I think I'll go check out the pretty scarves we bought." He pretended to wrap one around his neck.

"No, you will not," Mary countered. "I'm perfectly capable of handling this by myself."

"And you will, but I'll be your reinforcement, as needed."

"Jimmy, it's Diana, for God's sake. I hardly need backup to talk to my best friend."

Jimmy shook his head and started to say something else, but Mary didn't give him the chance. She stood and headed for the stairs.

40

ROGER

ROGER DODGED behind a concrete pillar until the cameraman lowered his head to adjust the settings on his tripod-mounted video recorder. With a newspaper shielding his face, he dashed from his hiding spot and pushed through the tinted glass doors. At the elevator, he pressed the button for the top floor offices of Leonard and Associates, PA.

"Where the hell have you been?" Wallace Leonard boomed when his assistant ushered Roger into the expansive office. "I expected you first thing this morning."

"I agreed to be here, Leonard, and here I am," Roger retorted. "Least you could do is pretend you're glad to see me."

"Don't be a smart ass, Roger. You've pissed off a lot of people, especially the DA, and unless we play our cards right, she'll revoke your bail and send you somewhere a lot less cozy than that oceanfront shack of yours."

"I won't go back to jail, Leonard. I told you that on the phone. I didn't kill Vanessa, and I won't be treated like I did."

"Maybe not, but you'd be wise to adopt a show of humility until the allegations against you are put to bed. Now sit down. We have a lot to cover before she gets here."

DESPITE LEONARD'S claim that Roger misunderstood the terms of his release and had returned voluntarily from his home in North Carolina, the DA was not inclined to extend him any mercy. She didn't buy his excuses or care where he'd been. Instead, she threatened to return him to lockup before the dinner hour. Upon hearing that, Roger jumped to his feet with fists clenched. Fortunately, before he managed to spit out an expletive-laced protest, or worse, Leonard grabbed his arm and yanked him into his seat.

"Mr. Michaud," the woman said, her voice haughty, "I suggest you follow your attorney's directive. I'm not certain of, nor do I wish to know, your intent with that little display, but be aware, sir, that threatening a prosecutor is a felony."

Leonard squeezed Roger's arm, and Roger turned his gaze out the window. "Madam District Attorney, please accept my client's apologies. Despite Mr. Michaud's recent questionable behavior, history proves him to be an upstanding citizen with an unblemished record."

"I heard all this over a week ago, Mr. Leonard, but I'm afraid I now differ with you on those points. Additionally, inculpatory evidence has come to light that further exacerbates Mrs. Michaud's vicious murder and your client's possible involvement therein."

"What evidence?" Roger asked before Leonard could do so himself.

"Yes, what is this new evidence?" Leonard repeated.

"You'll know when the coroner releases his official report. Until then, I'm keeping the details close to my vest," the woman said, a glint in her eye. "As such, I am rescinding all offers of bail."

"That's not fair," Roger groaned and looked to his attorney for back up. "How am I supposed to defend myself if I don't even know what I'm up against?"

"Mr. Michaud," the DA said, "why don't you tell me what, exactly, you feel the need to defend yourself against? Then we'll compare notes."

This time Leonard spoke first. "There will be time for comparing notes post discovery. Until then, my client remains innocent in the murder of his wife. Period. We, therefore, request that he be granted pre-trial release with supervision."

"I'm afraid I can't do that. He jumped bail once, and he'll do it again."

"We're willing to consent to supervision with house detention."

"And an ankle monitor," the DA finished, smiling smugly at Roger.

"We accept," Leonard said.

Roger did no such thing, but he knew he was beat. He closed his eyes and concentrated on his breathing. It was too late now, but he should never have flown back for this meeting. He should have stayed on Bald Head with Diana. Better yet, he should have borrowed Josh Mason's cruiser and taken off for the Bahamas. A thought popped into his head. *If I can't get back to Diana, maybe she can come to me.* He would call her once he was alone again.

The DA had come prepared, and after a deputy secured the electronic bracelet to Roger's right ankle, she quickly departed.

"I've arranged for a forensic cleaning crew to put your house to order, but in the meantime, you'll stay at the condo," Leonard told him.

"How long will all this take?" Roger asked.

"The cleaners can be done in two days, tops. As for the detention itself, it will likely be in effect for the duration of a trial, if it goes to that. I wouldn't count on returning to North Carolina anytime."

Roger growled. "Maybe I need to find myself another attorney."

"Another attorney, Roger, and you'd be wearing an orange jumpsuit instead of that." He motioned to the tracking device visible below the hem of Roger's slacks. "And by the way, I'll need an increase in my retainer. Please wire an additional twenty thousand to my account by Wednesday."

"What the hell? That's forty-five grand, and you haven't done squat for me."

"Are you wearing orange?" Leonard asked, not waiting for a reply.Roger threw up his hands. "Whatever. I'll need to arrange the transfer from an offshore account."

"However you wish to handle it is fine with me." Leonard buzzed his assistant to provide Roger with wiring instructions. "Shall we leave you alone to make the arrangements?"

"No, I'll do it tonight." He stood and shook out his leg, cursing under his breath. The damn thing pinched.

"Very well. I'll have my driver take you to the condo."

"Thanks, but no thanks. I'll get an Uber," Roger said, limping toward the door.

"That won't be possible. The terms of your current release require that I, or an authorized employee of my firm, transport you at all times and to all places. My limo is waiting downstairs."

Roger slammed his palm against the door, startling Leonard. He had no doubt Vanessa was laughing at him from wherever she was.

41

VANESSA

DESPITE THE POURING RAIN, Vanessa made it back from the beach in record time. She hadn't wanted to leave, but her time there left her rejuvenated her in body and spirit, and she was ready to face reality.

As she let herself in through the garage, she shivered. This house was so different from the cozy cottage in Bethany. But she loved each in its own way, and so long as she could hold onto them, she would be perfectly happy.

She had spent much of her time at the beach struggling with decisions that would ensure just that. But as pressing as those decisions were, she hadn't allowed them to mar her good time, especially not while entertaining Carlos, the waiter from Rehoboth, or Patrick, the Dewey Beach life-guard. She smiled now remembering the hot, young men. Carlos had been so much fun, she promised to call him the next time she was down. As for Patrick, she knew where to find his beach stand when the mood for his particular talents struck again. Sadly, Bart's appearance had thrown cold water on their heated night, and after he stormed off, she kicked Patrick out. He protested, of course, but her ardor had been thoroughly doused.

She deposited her suitcase in the laundry room, then stopped in the kitchen to fix a mug of hot tea. There were still two nights before Roger returned from Costa Rica, and she wanted to make the most of them. First up was a relaxing bath, followed by an evening of dress up. She knew just the gown, too. Not the Badgley Mischka from Sasha's—there hadn't been time to replace the ruined shoes—but a bright sapphire number from an up-and-coming designer who sold through his fledgling website. Fed Ex had delivered it the morning she'd left for the beach, and she could hardly wait to try it on.

She carried the mug up to the third floor, setting it on the bathroom vanity. Turning on the faucet, she waited for the water to heat up, then plugged the drain and dropped in two lavender bath bombs. While the tub filled, she unboxed the new gown and hung it outside her closet. It was every bit as sumptuous as the designer had promised.

Returning to the bathroom, she heard the distant melody of her cell phone. She'd left it on the kitchen counter and was tempted to ignore the incoming call. There was no one she wanted to talk to, anyway. But unable to resist, she checked the water level before bounding down the back staircase.

Swiping open the phone, she saw the call had come from Bart. After his visit to the cottage, she promised herself she wouldn't let him get to her anymore. As far as she was concerned, they were done. She never wanted to see him again. But this call, and his earlier texts, told her he wasn't taking her seriously.

Sure, her marriage was loveless, a bit of a nightmare even, but her life wasn't. No, her life was actually full of promise. More so now than ever before. Maybe it wasn't exactly what she'd initially planned for, but promising, nonetheless.

"Sorry, Bart," she muttered. With only a minor twinge of guilt, she blocked his number, then switched the phone to silent.

The hot, scented water instantly soothed her body and mind, and she allowed her thoughts to drift to the gorgeous gown waiting outside the bathroom. She envisioned how it, like most of the gowns she brought home, would transform her into a fairy princess. A cherished and precious fairy princess.

On the cusp of sleep, she jerked at the sound of a crash below her. Shaking as she stood, she slipped into the bath tray. The mug tumbled into the water, and tea splattered everywhere. Careful to avoid the now-broken shards of ceramic, she stepped gingerly onto the bathmat.

Panicked, she couldn't think what to do. Should she leave the bathroom to check out the noise or lock the door and hide? And where was her phone? Looking into the tub, her eyes widened with dread. She reached beneath the bubbles, her fingers creeping along the tub floor until they settled on the unmistakable object. She lifted the dripping phone and attempted to power it back on. Nothing happened.

Not bothering to towel off, she reached for her robe and threw it over her shoulders. She inched open the door and peeked out, sucking in her breath when a cool draft prickled her wet skin with gooseflesh. Her eyes darted right and left.

Not seeing anything, she nudged the door wider, then crept out onto the deeply padded carpeting. Moving quickly toward the hallway, her heart seized in her chest at the sight of the elegant blue gown twirling on its padded hanger in front of the floor-to-ceiling mirrors. Like an animated princess brought to life, the gown waltzed in an unseen breeze, lit from above by thousands of iridescent prisms.

A shadowy figure stood in the doorway to her closet. Vanessa opened her mouth to scream, but nothing came out. When the shadow moved toward her, she turned back to the safety of the bathroom. She took one step, then felt her body falling, her arms helpless to stop the collision with the floor. Her final thought was that she'd never again dress up in a beautiful princess gown.

42

ROGER

"HEY, BABE."

"Hey, yourself," Diana replied. "I miss you already. How soon are you coming back?"

Roger sucked air between his teeth. "Not anytime soon, I'm afraid. This DA has a hard-on for me."

"How so?" Diana asked.

"According to her, I violated my release by flying down to be with you," he said. He was lying on the too-small sofa in the too-small condo, flicking through the channels on the muted TV.

"That's not fair. You're innocent and shouldn't even need bail, or bond, or whatever they call it."

"I know, I know. But I've been thinking. Since I'm stuck up here, and horny as ever, why don't you fly up for a few days, and we'll pick up where we left off."

Diana giggled. "Tempting, but I have the shop to think about. And since I was away with you, I'm way behind."

"I thought your friend Mary was giving you a hand. Did she cut out on you?"

"No," Diana replied. "She handled the delivery today, but I can't keep asking her to help, and I really can't afford to pay my part-time girl with business so slow. Especially when I need to order more spring and summer inventory, not to mention cover my rent. I'm stretched super thin right now."

Roger sat up. "Why didn't you tell me? I can give you money."

"I can't ask you to do that," Diana insisted.

"You're not. I'm offering to make an investment in your business. I've been looking for just that type of opportunity. And think of it, once you're back on track, you can hire someone to take over while you travel the world with me."

Diana snorted. "That would be lovely. Really."

"Good. How's fifty sound?"

"Fifty what?" Diana asked breathlessly.

"Fifty thousand. Is that enough to entice you to get your sweet ass on a plane?"

"Roger, I can't."

"You can't what?"

"I can't be in debt to you for that much."

"You won't be. It'll be an investment, not a loan."

"Still," she said.

"Baby, let me explain it in the simplest of terms. I need somewhere to put my money, and you need money."

"But what if I can't pay you back? Or it takes me a real long time."

"That's the beauty of this. I don't need to be paid back."

"I don't know," Diana said quietly. "I've always gotten by without anyone's help."

"That's why I'm here." His doorbell buzzed, and he walked to the door and pressed the release button. "Consider it done. Listen, my pizza's here, but I'll call you in the morning to get your bank details."

"Oh my God, Roger, how can I ever thank you?"

"I'll come up with some inventive ideas on that," he joked. "Rest up, and we'll try them out as soon as we're together again."

"Thank you," Diana whispered.

"You're welcome, baby. Remember, it's just you and me now."

As he disconnected the call, a knock sounded at the door. Opening it, he greeted the petite redhead, "Well, hello, gorgeous."

She grinned up at him. "You've been a naughty boy, I hear."

"Darla, dear, you've got me all wrong."

"You can tell me about it later," she said, stepping into his arms. "After you've shown me the bedroom."

43

DIANA

DIANA HUNG up the phone and fell back against the sofa cushions. Fifty thousand dollars! Enough to pay off all her debts and put a decent down payment on the building. She had never owned real estate before, but it had been her dream to buy her apartment and the Seaside Siren rather than continuing to pay rent to Mr. Baxter. He was a nice enough old man, always willing to fix things as needed, but she was tired of giving someone else her hard-earned money.

Barely able to contain her excitement, she downed the last of her wine, then danced to the kitchen to select a second bottle. She was more than a little tipsy, but with so much to celebrate, why not get more so?

She poured the wine into one of her 'special occasion' Waterford glasses, then carried it into the bedroom. Folding back the bedspread, she plumped the pillows and fanned the sheets, then went about lighting the many candles scattered throughout the room. When finished, she dimmed the overhead chandelier. The effect was both erotic and romantic, the exact mood she wanted to set.

Back in the living room, she put a Billie Holiday album on the turntable, setting the volume to low. Swaying to the iconic singer's enchanting voice, she smiled when the doorbell buzzed.

"That you, Bobby?" she asked into the intercom.

"Yes, it is, darlin'."

She waited at the top of the stairs, and when he reached her, she jumped into his arms and wrapped her legs around his hips. He pressed her against the wall, kissing her deep and hard. His mouth was hungry, and he tasted of mouthwash and bourbon. When they separated, she purred, "Mm, you taste good."

"So do you." He carried her inside to the sofa and sat down with her on his lap. "Damn, girl, I was afraid you up and left town for good."

"Hardly," she replied with a laugh. "Just a quick trip to take care of some business."

"Another gift show?"

She ran her fingers through his curls. "Doesn't matter now. What matters is that I'm back."

"You're right there," he said, moving his hands over her silky caftan. "And as my daddy always says, 'Absence makes the heart grow fonder.'"

"Your daddy's a smart man, Bobby, but it's not your growing heart I'm interested in at the moment." She kissed him again, then shifted off his lap. Taking him by the hand, she led him to the bedroom.

. . .

SHE KICKED him out before dawn, pleading that she desperately needed a few hours of sleep before a very busy day.

"No. I want to stay," he protested with a yawn. "It's so warm here. I promise not to touch you again, even if you beg me."

She pushed against him. "You can come back tonight, I promise, and we'll both be stronger for it."

"Okay," he said, pouting as he disentangled himself from the sheets. The sight of his early morning erection tempted her to change her mind. To allow him stay longer. His body was certainly an addictive substance, but she'd be the strong one. She watched as he stumbled toward the bathroom, scratching his wild head of curls with one hand and his gorgeous ass with the other. When the shower started up, she rolled over and was asleep before he let himself out.

THREE HOURS LATER, she sat hunched at her desk. "Shit," she cursed after reading Mary's note about the credit card. She should never have put her friend in such an uncomfortable position.

She pulled out the accounting ledger. She had told Roger the truth about not having extra cash to pay for help. The Seaside Siren was in deep financial trouble. Diana was in deep financial trouble. She wasn't proud of herself, but Roger's money was her only salvation. As soon as it hit her bank account, she would pay Mary back.

Picking up the second note about the man who had stopped by the store looking for her, a shiver raced up her spine. *Please don't let it be a repo man*, she prayed. Like so many other bills, she was way behind on her car payments.

She rushed to the rear window and looked out. Her car was parked where she'd left it yesterday afternoon.

In an effort to calm herself, she prepared a cup of cannabis-infused tea, adding a dollop of local elderberry honey. Yawning as she sipped the brew at her desk, her jaw popped loudly. Her TMJ was acting up big time. It always did when she was stressed. On more than one occasion, it had locked in an open position, causing both intense pain and embarrassment. The best and quickest remedy, she knew, was to religiously wear her orthodontic headpiece while she slept. Sadly, the contraption gave her the appearance of either an awkward teenager, something she had never been, or Hannibal Lecter from *Silence of the Lambs*. With Roger or Bobby in her bed most every night, just how was she supposed to get away with that?

44

IVY BLUE

ALEJANDRO'S PUNCH connected with Ivy's left jawbone, snapping her head back and bouncing it off the headboard. The pain was instantaneous and blinding, her jaw most likely dislocated. Oddly enough, her immediate concern was how she would hide the inevitable damage. She had become quite adept at camouflaging the recurrent bruising to her arms and legs, but he had never struck her in the face before.

"I thought I told you to brush your damn teeth before you come to bed!"

"I did, Alejandro, I swear," Ivy mumbled. It hurt like hell to talk. "I'll gargle and come right back." Covering her mouth with a trembling hand, she slid off the mattress.

He smacked her hard on her bare ass and laughed. "And no more of Saul's cooking for you. Too much garlic and onions. Plus, you could stand to lose a few pounds."

She hurried from the room before Alejandro noticed the tears welling in her eyes. She knew all too well what his prescribed diet consisted of. Nothing but distilled water, lettuce, and desiccated chicken for breakfast, lunch, and dinner—if she could still chew with a dislocated jaw, that is —until the scale registered what he deemed to be her ideal weight.

The last time he ordered her to "lose a few pounds," she became so weak and light-headed that she passed out in the middle of a rehearsal. By that point, her stringent caloric intake, coupled with daily rehearsals and twice-nightly performances, had shaved eighteen pounds off her already trim body.

Gargling at the sink, she was overcome by a feeling of suffocation. She spit out the mouthwash, then inhaled deeply. Looking at herself in the mirror, she was saddened by the dull, lifeless eyes staring back. Gone was the beautiful, playful girl she had once been. If she didn't escape soon, Alejandro would snuff that girl out completely.

IT WAS her second night dancing in the glitzy casino on the strip. During a particularly difficult routine, her concentration faltered when she spotted a man ogling her from backstage. Discomfited by the unmistakable mix of lust and danger darkening his deep brown eyes, she stumbled. Humiliated, she quickly caught up to the other dancers. When she dared another glance in the man's direction, he was gone.

When he showed up outside the dressing room later, hugging and kissing the showgirls as they hurried to the exit, she attempted to pass him without being noticed.

"*Mi ángel*," he said, grabbing her arm. "Who are you?"

She pulled her arm away and replied with a curt, "Ivy Blue."

Despite her obvious annoyance, he was not discouraged. He seized her hand and brought it to his lips. "Pleasure to meet you, Ivy Blue. I am Alejandro, and you, my dear, are exquisite."

His dreamy accent sent tremors through her tired body, and his unwavering gaze was mesmerizing.

Unable to resist the flattery, she managed, "I am?"

"Sí," he replied. He grinned then, his teeth perfectly straight and blindingly white. "And, if you do all things as perfectly as you dance, I will keep you forever happy."

"What things are you talking about?" she asked nervously.

He pulled her close and ran his hands down her firm backside and hips. He was strong and insistent, and despite a nagging voice warning her to tread carefully, she allowed him to kiss her on the mouth. Hard. When they parted, he whispered, "That, *mi ángel*, is a most excellent beginning."

"HURRY THE HELL UP, *PUTA*," Alejandro yelled from the bedroom.

Ivy pasted on a painful smile. *Only a few more nights*, she thought. *Just hang in there a few more nights.*

45

JIMMY

JIMMY PICKED Mary up at the Yoga Dock in his F-250, securing her bike in the covered bed. After parking in front of the Dosher Hospital Thrift Shop, they crossed at the corner to grab lattes at Moore Street Market before walking over to the Seaside Siren.

"You'll be nice, right?" she asked as they meandered toward Howe Street.

"So long as she's nice to you," he answered.

"She'll probably be mortified. I know I would be. And having you there isn't going to help."

"It won't hurt."

"It just might, Jim, and the last thing I want is to humiliate her more than she already is. We all make mistakes."

"She needs to accept responsibility for the difficult position she put you in."

"It wasn't difficult," Mary objected with a shake of her

head. "Why don't you just wait outside, and I'll come get you if I need you." She grabbed his arm. "Please?"

Jimmy took a swig of his coffee, then looked up to the sky. He loved his wife more than himself, but she repeatedly frustrated his attempts to take care of her. That fierce streak of independence was one of the reasons he had fallen so hard for her in the very beginning. But, dammit, he almost lost her, and he wasn't prepared to risk it again.

"Okay, okay," he said in resignation, "but I'll be right outside the front door, and if you're not out in ten minutes tops, I'm coming in after you."

"Deal," she said with a big smile. She took his hand and squeezed.

AS HE WAITED on a bench outside the shop, Jimmy poked at his phone. "Hey, man, what's up?" he asked when George picked up.

"On a mission today," the PI replied.

"Do tell," Jimmy said.

"I'm heading into the Delaware Slap Shots to talk to Bart Nixon, Michaud's business partner."

"You think he's got any solid info?"

"Not sure, but a few weeks ago, Samms snapped a photo of him arguing with Michaud outside the store. Before Vanessa was killed. Rafe wasn't within earshot, but it looked at one point like they might come to blows. *Quite animated*, were his exact words."

"Interesting."

"Yep, and it backs up what Nixon's son, Ben, told me the day of the memorial service. But where the kid thought their arguments were over money, Samms's hunch is that they were fighting over something—or someone—else entirely."

"Vanessa?"

"Exactly. She was the kid's nanny prior to meeting Roger, but maybe she was more than that to his dad?"

"If that's the case, could he be her killer?"

"Your guess is as good as mine, but I figure asking him straight up is a solid start."

"Sounds like fun. You sure you don't want some help? Mary seems to think she doesn't need me to watch out for her, so I might as well come on up."

"I'll let you know, buddy," George said before the call ended.

Jimmy checked the time. Mary had been inside for twelve minutes, two over her allotted time. He walked to the front door and yanked on the handle. Locked. "Dammit," he swore. He thumbed a quick text to Mary: *You are in deep shit if you don't come out of there in thirty seconds.*

He peered through the window into the darkened interior. Light shone from a room at the back of the showroom. He figured it was Diana's office, but since he'd never set foot in the shop, he couldn't be sure. He was sure, however, that Mary had outsmarted him. Despite his anger, he had to give her credit.

The silhouette of a woman appeared in the doorway, waving in his direction. He waved back, then, feeling ridiculous, he returned to the bench to ruminate. Joe Vickers's Ford Explorer pulled up at the curb, and the police chief rolled down the passenger-side window.

"Hey, Jim. Out for a stroll?" the man asked.

"Waiting on Mary," Jimmy replied, walking over to the

SUV's open window. "She's inside talking to Diana Forrester."

"I take it you're not interested in perusing the Seaside Siren's wares?" Joe asked.

"Don't know what's in there, and don't care. Don't care for her much either, to be honest."

Joe laughed. "She's different, that's for sure."

"Know anything about her? Mary likes her, even considers her a friend, but I find her way too nonconformist for my liking."

"How so?" Joe asked, shutting off his engine.

"Well, for one, it's the company she keeps. You heard about the murder of Roger Michaud's wife, right?"

"Yes. We're aware, but seeing as he's out on the island and not in Southport, there's not much we can do. He and Miss Forrester are friends, from what I've been told."

"Closer than friends," Jimmy corrected. "Not that her sex life is my concern, per se, but when Mary's pulled into their drama, it becomes my business."

"I can appreciate that, Jim. Especially after all you two have been through. What can I do?"

"Any way you can dig a little into her background? I'd sure rest easier if I knew more about her."

"I've got no real grounds to do that, but if she concerns you that much, I suppose I could make a fraternal exception."

"Thanks. And while I'm thinking about it, Mary was in there by herself yesterday," he nodded toward the shop, "when a strange dude came by looking for Forrester. He gave Mary the willies, to use her word."

Joe frowned. "What he look like?"

"Sadly, all she could tell me was that he was slight and wore wet, baggy clothes and a ball cap."

The chief laughed. "I think most of us fit that bill yesterday."

"Yeah, sorry. I was hoping for more, too. I thought I trained her better."

"That's all right, Jim. Let me first see what I can uncover on Miss Forrester. Beyond that, can't you just ask Mary to stay clear of her and her shop? You would think she'd want to shy away from further drama, criminal or otherwise. God knows I sure do."

"I agree," Jimmy said, shaking his head. "But the success of her first book garnered a lot of buzz in the publishing world, and she's being pressured to follow it with an even better story. Not to mention, Mary seems drawn to drama like a moth to a flame."

"Better your wife than..." His radio crackled, and Joe picked it up. "Vickers."

"Chief, gotta multi-vehicle on River Road at Jabbertown."

"On my way," Vickers responded, firing up his engine. "Jim, I'll see what I can find out and get back to you. Keep Mary out of trouble til then, 'kay?"

"I'll do my best."

The chief's vehicle was rounding the corner as Mary joined Jimmy on the sidewalk. "What were you two talking about?" she asked.

Taking Mary by her elbows, he pulled her close. "Damn you, Mary Margaret," he snarled, before planting a kiss soundly on her lips.

When they parted, she eyed him suspiciously. "That was nice. Guess I'm not in deep doo-doo, after all."

"I haven't made up my mind yet," Jimmy said. "So?"

"So, like I said, your kiss was nice."

Mary turned to walk away, and Jimmy stopped her. "No, Mary, what's the story with our money?"

"We'll have it by the end of the week."

"You sure?" Jimmy asked, looking at the darkened storefront.

"Yes, I'm sure. Now come on. I'm starving."

46

BART

BART CHECKED off the contents of each pallet as it was unloaded from the semi, directing his warehouse staff on which bay to stack it. When the truck was empty, he signed the manifest and wiped a hand across his sweaty brow. The temperature-controlled facility was a comfortable and constant seventy-two degrees, but last night's way-too-many double Scotches were now leaching from his pores. He could smell the booze on his skin and breath, and he hoped no one else could.

Of course, on their way in this morning, Ben had complained that he reeked, but he was still pissed about not being allowed to go to a movie last night with a friend. In hindsight, Bart should have given his okay, then he wouldn't have been around to witness his spectacle of a father.

"Bart Nixon, you have a visitor on two," the overhead speaker announced.

Bart swore quietly as his intestines gurgled angrily. Whoever it was had better be quick. He had needed to take a shit all morning but hadn't had the chance.

As he crossed the catwalk toward his office, the sour contents of his stomach pushed into his throat. No dinner, an entire bottle of Famous Grouse, and too little sleep were wreaking havoc at both ends. He swallowed back the foul-tasting bile and swore to never touch another drop of Scotch. *Just let me get through this day*, he pleaded to a god he no longer believed in.

He had little recollection of yesterday, and nothing whatsoever after four o'clock or so. He still couldn't pin his stupidity on any single event, but it must have been a doozie to get him so incredibly hammered.

Pushing through the steel-enforced safety door, he stopped when he spotted his visitor, the bald, Black reporter.

"Mr. Nixon," the man said, grinning as he held out his hand. "George Purnell. We met last week."

"I remember," Bart snapped. "What do you want?"

"For starters, I thought we could sit down for a few minutes. Talk about Mr. and Mrs. Michaud, may she rest in peace."

Bart felt his intestines convulse. Of course. Memories of Vanessa had set in motion yesterday's drinking binge. Wallowing in misery, he had reread every single text she ever sent him. They were all saved on his phone, beginning with the first eleven years ago—*I'd be happy to sit for Ben Saturday nite*—and ending with her last—*No!*—in response to his begging to see her when she returned from Bethany. It had been sent the very day she died.

"I have no interest in discussing Mr. or Mrs. Michaud."

"Okay," Purnell agreed amiably. "But—" He pulled a

photo from his inside pocket and held it discreetly against his chest for Bart to see. "Maybe you want to tell me why Mr. Michaud had you in a chokehold outside this very building just weeks before his wife's murder?"

Bart was seized by a pain in his chest, and he turned his head to cough into the crook of his elbow. His lungs burned with the effort. Despite knowing he'd likely regret it, he motioned for the man to follow him into his office.

He took a seat behind his desk but didn't ask the unwelcome visitor to sit. Glancing at his watch, he said, "You have exactly five minutes."

"I won't even need that long," the man said. "Question one. Did you and Michaud fight over his wife? Is that what's going on in this photo?" He set the photo on the desk facing Bart.

"No comment."

"It looks like he's about to whoop your butt here. Whatever the reason, you had to be ticked off big time, huh? Which brings me to question two. Were you ticked off enough to kill his wife as payback for all the abuse he piled on you over the years? Did you finally have it with being treated like dirt, going way back to your days with the Flyers?"

Bart blanched, and his insides churned. He felt his face redden as his blood pressure skyrocketed, but he held his tongue.

"No? Then here's question three. Did you kill Vanessa Michaud because she rejected you?"

Bart shoved out of his chair. "What slimy media outlet do you work for? The *National Enquirer*?"

"I don't work for a media outlet," Purnell said with a laugh, "slimy or otherwise. I'm a private investigator."

Confused, Bart said. "Let me see your ID." He glanced at the man's license, then demanded, "Who hired you?"

"I'm not at liberty to say."

"Well, if it was Michaud, you can tell him that if he's hoping to frame me for Vanessa's murder, he's shooting at the wrong net. Like always."

The PI shrugged his broad shoulders, and his jacket rode up on his hip, revealing the Glock strapped to his belt. Seeing it, Bart threatened, "Leave now, or I'll have you arrested for bringing a loaded firearm into this store."

"I have a permit," Purnell said, "want to see it?"

"No, just get the hell out of my office and this building."

"No problem," the big man said as he turned for the door. When he reached for the handle, he snapped his fingers and turned around.

"What?" Bart demanded.

"One final question. Were you aware Vanessa Michaud was pregnant at the time of her murder?"

47

MARY

JIMMY POURED himself a glass of Zinfandel and motioned to Mary. "Having one tonight?"

"I don't think so, but thanks."

"More for me," he replied as he corked the bottle. He pulled out a stool at the island and sat down. They'd spent the afternoon touring three potential venues for his conceal carry classes, and now, as Mary prepared dinner, he was trying to narrow the choices to one.

Mary glanced at him from the sink, where she stood peeling shrimp. "I think I know which one will work best. How 'bout you?"

Jimmy held up the contract from the hunting club in Bolivia. "I'm liking this one. It has the perfect setup, ample space, reasonable rent, and it's centrally located."

Mary smiled. "That's my choice, too. Not that the

others wouldn't work, but I think the club has the best potential."

"I agree," Jimmy said. "I'd like to sign a short-term contract to get started."

"Good idea," Mary said. "After six months or so, maybe you can renegotiate based on how many clients go on to become club members."

"Great idea," Jimmy agreed, nodding. "I could incentivize that in a number of ways, like coupons for trial hunting days, merchandise discounts, or a percentage off the initiation fee. Maybe the club would even consider doing the same in reverse. It'd be a win-win."

"Absolutely," she agreed.

Jimmy set the contract aside and sipped his wine. "Can I help?"

"Nah, I've got everything under control. But let me ask you something." She leaned her elbows on the island's granite top.

Jimmy grinned. "Shoot."

"I heard you on the phone with Joe Vickers. You mentioned Diana. What's going on?"

Jimmy averted his eyes and ran his index finger around the rim of his wineglass. He cleared his throat, then said, "I wasn't going to say anything until I had more details."

"About?"

"I asked Joe—" he began, then paused to swipe open his ringing cell. "Hey, George." Mary could barely hear the PI, so she walked around the island to stand at Jimmy's shoulder. "If it's okay with you, let me put you on speaker so Mary can hear this, too."

"Hey, Mary," George said.

"Evening, George," she replied.

"I'm calling with some noteworthy facts I learned after I hung up with you this morning, Jim."

"Do tell," Mary said.

"Just so you understand, this is all hush-hush until the yet-to-be-released coroner's report comes out. I was read from a purloined copy, along with a few choice pages from the murder book."

"Nice to have inside sources." Jimmy said. "What did it cost you?"

"I ain't saying," George replied.

"Got you," Jimmy said. "So?"

"Topping the list," George said, simulating the sound of a drumroll, "Vanessa Michaud was twelve weeks pregnant, give or take, at the time of her death."

Mary's mouth opened wide. "Oof, I didn't expect that."

"Nor I," George said. "Not that I considered the possibility one way or another, but given that they were married for ten years with no children, and the marriage wasn't all that secure, I'm surprised she let it happen."

"She could've been planning to use the child as a pawn in her quest to remain Mrs. Michaud," Jimmy suggested.

"That's harsh, Jimmy," Mary scolded.

"Only because you would never do it yourself," George chimed in. "I've seen it before, Mary. Kids used as nothing more than high-stakes poker chips."

"Was her pregnancy a well-known secret?" Jimmy asked, simulating quote marks with his fingers.

"I didn't hear it from anyone else, but then she was a tiny thing and might not have been showing yet. Unless she confided in someone, her condition wouldn't have been evident to the casual observer."

"Do you think Roger knew?" Mary asked, thinking immediately of Diana.

"If he didn't, he does now."

"Could have been yet another motive for killing her," Mary suggested.

"Maybe, but whose motive?" Jimmy asked.

Mary slumped onto a stool beside Jimmy and put her head on his shoulder.

"Again, a good question, but there's more," George continued. "It's theorized she was attacked from behind, as evidenced by a glancing wound to her upper back. Once she fell, the killer went for her throat. The death blow, if you will, came when her carotid artery was slashed wide open, almost to the point of decapitation. As she bled out, she was stabbed one final time through the umbilicus. The only defensive wound was to her right hand, which the coroner concluded, came shortly before she succumbed. Mary, this is going to upset you, but it's likely she died covering her abdomen in an effort to protect the baby."

Mary's stomach turned. "That's unspeakable. Whoever killed her had to know about the baby."

"A classic crime of passion," Jimmy said.

"I agree with both of you," George said. "The body appeared to have been repositioned after death with hands crossed over her heart. According to the profile from the murder book, this shows some remorse on the part of the killer."

"Too little, too late," Mary said.

"Well, anyway, I learned all this right before I talked to Bart Nixon, and I wonder if I might have blundered by spilling the news about her pregnancy."

"Did he act as if he already knew?" Jimmy asked.

"If I go by the stricken look on his face, he did not."

"Did you ask if the baby was his?"

"He didn't give me a chance. He nearly knocked me

over as he ran out of his office. I hope he made it to the head in time. Daddy or not, he definitely had a thing for her. I got the strong sense that's why he and Michaud came to fisticuffs."

Mary reached over and picked up Jimmy's half-full glass of wine, downing what remained. She closed her eyes as the warmth spread swiftly to her belly. Jimmy got up to fetch the bottle and a second glass.

"Okay, you two. I'll leave you to ponder these juicy tidbits, and I'll check back in when I know more."

As Jimmy poured the wine, Mary disconnected the call.

"Diana's going to be heartbroken," she said, accepting the glass.

"About?"

"The baby. What else? It means Roger was sleeping with his wife even though he told Diana he wasn't."

"Maybe he wasn't," Jimmy suggested, "and the baby wasn't his. I'm sure the coroner is comparing their DNA. Regardless, if he knows Vanessa was pregnant, he's probably told Diana already."

"She would have told me," Mary insisted, frowning. "Oh, Jimmy. I'm so worried about her. I'm afraid her feelings are far deeper than she's prepared to admit, and if so, she'll ignore any warning signs. She's sure to end up hurt, either emotionally or physically."

"God, Mary, I don't want to talk about Hippie Chick's feelings."

"Fine," she grumbled. "Let's eat."

AFTER DINNER, they sat at the table enjoying the final tracks of Simply Red's *Home* album. When the music ended, Mary grew quiet, staring into her wine.

"What's troubling you now?" Jimmy asked, reaching for her hand.

"You won't care," she said, sighing.

"Maybe not, but tell me anyway."

"Okay. You already know I'm worried that Roger will hurt Diana. Maybe even physically."

"Yeah, you've said."

"What you don't know is that she's been making other questionable choices that could easily cause her greater harm. At least emotionally."

Jimmy grimaced. "Ok, I'll bite."

Mary blew out a breath. "Well, besides her affair with Roger, which has been going on for a couple years now, she's sleeping with another man. Has been the whole time. He's much younger and is truly smitten with her."

"Smitten?"

"Yes, smitten. Despite what you may think of her, Diana's a loving woman with a big heart. Men are naturally drawn to her. It was all fun and games when it started, you know, just carefree sex with no strings attached. I fear, though, that she's become her own worst enemy."

"What?" Jimmy said loudly. "I can't hear you."

Mary gave him a curious look, grinning when she realized he'd stuck his index fingers into his ears. "I know, I know. Too much information."

"You got that right."

"Is it too early for bed?" she asked, leaning into him.

"Depends on whether we're sleeping or..."

She looked up at him. "*Or* sounds good to me."

He grinned. "Go on up, and I'll set the alarm."

48

MONKEY

MONKEY'S PLAN was to show up at the Seaside Siren as soon as it opened, but when he approached the building from the north, the woman he'd encountered yesterday was walking through the door. He crossed the street and sat under the gazebo behind Southport Market to wait for her to leave. The woman stayed inside for over twenty minutes —damn clucking hens—and by the time she came out, the whole town was crawling with shoppers and tourists out enjoying the sunshine after thirty-six hours of merciless rain.

There was also a man outside the store who appeared to be waiting for the woman. He was likely her husband. Had she complained to him about Monkey? Whatever. What neither of them knew was that he'd tailed her little white sports car after she left the shop yesterday. He followed her to a big house in a classy neighborhood, but hard as it was raining, he was sure she hadn't noticed his truck.

Figuring it was best to return later after the tourists thinned out and the sidewalks rolled up, Monkey returned to the motel. He watched an old episode of *Law and Order*, this one about a man raped by a group of drunk women. When it ended, he shut off the TV and closed his eyes. He was tired, but apparently not tired enough to sleep. When his stomach growled, he got up and reached into his duffel bag. He pulled out a plastic jar of peanut butter pretzels and unscrewed the lid. The jar was almost empty, and he made a mental note to pick up another the next time he went to the grocery store. With his belly happy, he rolled over and closed his eyes.

WILL HAD DONE A RUNNER, most likely with his mangy tail between his cowardly legs, so Monkey decided to go right to the source. When he arrived at senior's home on the hoity-toity Main Line shortly after eleven p.m., the bluish glow from a television was visible in a first-floor rear window. Stepping down from his truck, he cinched the hood of his sweatshirt tightly about his head, then tiptoed to the window and peered inside. An old man was lying in a recliner, eyes closed and snoring loud enough to be heard through the panes of glass. Monkey watched the chest rise and fall, frowning when he realized the man was still wearing a starched white shirt and tie. With a sudden sense of empathy, he shook his head. Senior was every bit the uptight douche Will claimed him to be.

Monkey crept around back, stopping at a rear door and jiggling the knob. It was flimsy but locked. Pulling out his knife, he inserted the blade into the keyhole, twisting it back and forth. The lock released with little effort, and he let himself into a well-stocked pantry. The door leading into the kitchen stood open, and the light above the gas stovetop was enough for him to make out bags and boxes of dry goods lining the pantry shelves. His stomach gurgled at the sight of a large plastic jar filled with peanut butter–stuffed pretzels. *Later*, he told himself, moving quietly toward the bluish glow.

At the doorway to a paneled den, Monkey took a moment to gather his wits before moving quickly to the recliner. He covered senior's mouth with one hand and pressed the blade to his throat with the other. Howard Raskins opened his eyes but knew enough to hold perfectly still.

"That's right, old man," Monkey whispered. "Don't make any sudden moves, and I won't have to kill you."

Raskins nodded, and Monkey continued. "Your no-good son owes me a lot of money, and I've come to collect. Now I'm gonna uncover your mouth so you can talk, but if you scream like a pussy, I'll cut your throat." The trembling man bobbed his chin.

Monkey's hand moved from Raskins's mouth to his tie, yanking it hard. His head jerked sideways, and the freshly sharpened blade nicked the stubbled skin of his throat. The man squeaked as a bead of blood bloomed on his collar. Monkey snickered. "That'll need dry cleaning. Now show me where the money is, and I promise that's the only blood I'll draw."

The man's eyes widened, and he attempted to shake his head. "There's no cash in the house," he whispered, his voice raspy with fear.

Monkey released the tie long enough to slap the man

hard across the cheek. "Let's try that again. Where's the money?"

"There isn't any. I swear. Take my credit cards. They're in my pants pocket."

"I don't want your damn credit cards," Monkey said, elongating every word. "Will told me there's cash in a safe, and I ain't leaving til I get it." He held the knife to the man's right eyeball, and Raskins slammed his eyes shut, whimpering.

"Sniveling won't save you, senior. Or your wife. She upstairs in bed?" He ran the steel point down the man's cheek, tracing the trail left by a tear.

"B-b-behind the painting," the man stuttered. He pointed to an elaborately framed canvas of George Washington crossing the Delaware River.

"Good," Monkey said calmly. In reality, his heart was racing a mile a minute, and he prayed his fear didn't show. "Now get up." The man struggled to his feet, and Monkey pushed him toward the wall where the painting hung above a demilune cabinet. "Open it," he ordered.

Raskins tugged the right side of the frame, and it swung toward him, revealing a safe set into the wall. With trembling fingers, he fumbled with the cylinder dial. When the iron door popped open, Monkey whistled at the stacks of hundred-dollar bills lining the interior.

"Kneel," he told the man, "and take off your shirt." The man loosened his tie, then began undoing the buttons. His fingers were shaking so hard, he only managed the top two before Monkey ordered, "Over your head, dammit." Again, the man did as he was told. "Now lay on your belly and lace your fingers behind your head." When the man did, Monkey gagged him with his tie, then immobilized him using zip ties he pulled from his pocket.

Spreading the shirt on the small table, Monkey stacked the bundles of bills in the center of the fabric, noticing for the first time its pale blue stripe. Eight stacks in total for a cool forty grand. For good measure, he reached back into the safe and felt around. When his hand brushed over something hidden beneath the felt bottom, he peeled it back. Pulling out a clasped yellow envelope, he said, "What do we have here?"

Raskins twisted his head to look over his shoulder. Seeing the envelope in Monkey's hands, he began to squirm and protest as loudly as the muzzle would allow. Monkey stepped on his back, and without looking inside the envelope, he added it to the pile of cash. Then like a hobo of old, he gathered the shirt together, creating a tidy bundle. Without another word, he walked calmly from the room and closed the door behind him. He returned to the pantry, grabbed the jar of pretzels, then exited the house where he'd entered.

THAT HAD BEEN A GOOD NIGHT. Tonight would be a better one.

He napped off and on through the afternoon, leaving the motel again just after seven p.m. He parked his truck in front of the library, then took up a position across from the Seaside Siren. As he watched a boisterous group of diners walk by the store, he caught sight of a woman in the window. She stood there for several minutes before disappearing into the darkened interior. He had to restrain himself from racing across the street and busting through the door. It almost hurt to lose sight of her, but he'd waited this long, another hour or so wouldn't kill him.

He headed toward what the motel manager had called the Yacht Basin. A few cars and golf carts were parked outside one restaurant, a turquoise joint called Fishy Fishy, but it didn't appear to be overly crowded. Avoiding the hostess, he settled himself on a stool at the bar and ducked his head into a menu. After ordering a cheeseburger and basket of onion rings, he turned his attention to the basketball game playing on the corner TV. No one seemed interested in chatting him up, which was perfectly fine with him.

The greasy food hit the spot, as did two pints of IPA, but as he paid the bartender, his intestines groaned in distress. Figuring it was best to get back to his motel room to take care of business, he rushed to his truck.

49

DIANA

ROGER CALLED at ten a.m. for Diana's banking information, assuring her that the fifty grand would hit her account by the next day. When Mary came by a short time later, Diana apologized profusely for troubling her with the delivery of scarves. She promised to reimburse her, with interest, within a few days. Mary hadn't seemed at all worried, but no doubt Jimmy, who was hovering impatiently on the sidewalk outside while she and Mary talked, was peeved, to put it mildly.

Mary's hunky husband was usually civil to Diana, but he sure had a knack for making her feel inadequate. Perhaps he didn't find her attractive. Or maybe he did but went out of his way to hide it by acting unaffected by her charms. Whatever his issues with her were, since the unfortunate pot-smoking incident, she tried hard to be on her very best behavior around him. Thankfully, that wasn't very often.

As for the mysterious visitor, Mary reported that the man was physically unremarkable. She hadn't even detected an accent or dialect, not that he said all that much. Diana pressed her for more details, but all Mary could say for sure was that he seemed *menacing*, and that Diana should keep her doors locked. If he had been a repo agent, she prayed he would be called off as soon as she settled her past-due car payments.

She spent the rest of the day rearranging the showroom. She dragged tables and carousels back and forth, sweeping and dusting as she went. Her sparse inventory made it a challenge, but she did what she could to jazz up the place. As soon as she had Roger's money, she would place lots of orders for new merchandise.

By the time she had the showroom looking presentable, the streetlights were flickering on. With a final nod of approval, she shut off the overhead lights, then stood at the darkened display window. The western sky was alive with color as it transformed itself from deep gold to a vibrant purplish pink.

"Red sky at night, sailor's delight," she whispered.

A group of rowdy tourists, no doubt heading to dinner at one of the nearby restaurants, passed by, and she waved. One of the women paused to peer in the window, mouthing that she would return tomorrow. Diana gave her a thumbs up, and the woman ran to catch up with her friends. As Diana turned to head up to her apartment, a lone figure across the street caught her attention. It—she couldn't tell if it was a man or woman—stood motionless outside the Southport Market. Diana's skin crawled when the headlights from a turning car captured the silhouette of a man sporting a billed cap. She stepped back from the window, then double-checked the locks before racing upstairs.

As the hot water massaged her aching neck and shoulders, the man across the street niggled at her. Did he fit the description of Mary's visitor?

A quiet rustle outside the shower sent a jolt through her body, but a quick swipe of the shower glass had her chastising herself to "chill out, Diana!" The towel hanging on the hook behind the door had simply dropped to the floor.

After towel-drying her hair, she weaved it into a loose plait, then dabbed perfume behind her ears and on her belly. Coco, with its notes of jasmine tinged with patchouli, was her favorite from way back. The small, boxy bottle was nearly empty after years of rationing, and she often thought of buying the less expensive eau de toilette. Maybe she would splurge once she had the cash to do so.

She slipped an emerald-green caftan over her naked body. The silky fabric draped her full, firm breasts and swished across her hips and bottom. Tonight, she and Bobby would be staying in, and when they came up for air, they would order sushi from Thai Peppers around the corner.

With a glance at the time, she pulled a beer mug from the cupboard and placed it in the freezer. Pouring the remains of the bottle of wine she'd opened before her shower, she contemplated opening a second. As tired as she was, she feared she'd surely pass out if she drank much more on an empty stomach, so she dashed off a quick text asking Bobby to pick up food on his way over. Just as she hit *send*, the doorbell buzzed. Shrugging, she headed downstairs in her bare feet to let in her ravenous young lover.

50

IVY BLUE

"IT'S RAINING, IT'S POURING." Ivy sang the childhood refrain to the beat of the slapping windshield wipers. She had been navigating through the torrent since the glow of the Vegas Strip disappeared in her rearview mirror. With sunrise still hours away, there was no telling where, or when, the storm clouds would disperse. Fortunately, the new-to-her minivan was quite alone on this stretch of highway, and she hadn't been blinded by oncoming headlights in over an hour.

Her plan was to drive until exhaustion forced her to check into a motel, but at the moment, her energy level remained high. The thermos of black coffee wedged between the seat and center console was taking care of that. She had pulled over to pee a while back, not bothering with a gas station or rest stop. Men did it all the time, so why couldn't she? She had gotten quite soaked, but it hadn't bothered her in the least.

Her upper back and shoulders ached some from the strain of pushing Alejandro's lifeless body off her, but her sense of relief far outweighed her discomfort. She was free, and no amount of pain or deluge of rain could dampen the joy of freedom.

Glancing in the back seat, she could just make out the outline of her one small suitcase. It contained everything she wanted from her past, and everything she needed to start over—once again. She reviewed the contents in her head: a photo of Mama taken the summer before she passed away; Mama's Bible and rosary wrapped tenderly in tissue paper; a week's worth of clean underwear; a faded pair of jeans; black leggings; several tops; dancing shoes and tights; Mama's treasured ballet slippers—too small since puberty; and the three-carat monstrosity Alejandro had forced upon her when he told her they would marry. That, she would be sure to pawn at the first opportunity.

She had tucked a few other bits and pieces into the bag's corners and pockets: toiletries and makeup, a stuffed monkey picked up in the casino gift shop, and fifteen thousand dollars in cash.

She had been stashing away the cash a little at a time. Ever since Alejandro pummeled her into unconsciousness the first time. She couldn't quite remember what set him off then. She wasn't even sure the next day when she awoke in the bathtub drained of water but streaked with blood. Her blood, her baby's blood.

Ivy gulped down the bile that burned her throat. An unbidden sob signaled a renewed eruption of grief and guilt. "No!" she shouted. She swiped at an escaped tear and cleared her throat. She took a swallow of coffee, thankfully still warm. A new life was ahead of her, the old ones behind. Behind and dead, gone and unforgotten.

She forced a smile and checked her reflection in the mirror. If the lighting were better, she might not recognize herself, but in the van's shadowy interior, she saw a young and vibrant woman, a woman still hopeful for her future self. She lifted her hand to her scalp, grimacing a little as the newly shorn hairs grazed her palm. "You'll grow back," she said in way of apology to her previously long, golden tresses. The buzz cut might be hideous, but it provided a perfect disguise.

She wasn't yet settled on a new name. Or a final destination, for that matter. Those answers would come in time. It had been enough to figure a way out. More than enough. What she knew for certain was that tonight, in the dark and rain and desert, she was driving east toward freedom. Ivy Blue, headline diva and wife of casino magnate Alejandro Vila, was no more.

HOURS LATER, long past dawn, Ivy pulled into a two-story motel on the outskirts of Amarillo, Texas. Stepping down from the van, her body trembled from the fatigue of sitting for so long. She bent at the waist and laid her palms against the blacktop. It felt wonderful to stretch out the contracted muscles running from her head to her heels. When she righted herself, she glanced through the parking lot, assessing the caliber of guests. It was filled predominantly with older vehicles, but the property was neatly maintained. A blinking vacancy sign beckoned from beneath a carport, and she headed that way.

"Hello?" she called out in the empty, glass-fronted office.

"Just a sec," came a voice from a room behind the counter.

While she waited, Ivy picked up a brochure from a rack by the door. It was for the Cadillac Ranch, and she smiled at the photos of psychedelically painted vehicles.

"Afternoon," a heavyset woman greeted her. "Need a room?"

"Yes, ma'am," Ivy said. "With a bathtub if you have one."

"I just might," the woman replied. "You're a tad early for check-in, but I think there might be a clean room just about ready."

"That'd be great," Ivy said with a smile. "I drove all the way cross state through that storm, and I could sure use a hot bath and some shut-eye."

"Staying with us long?" the woman asked.

"Not sure yet," Ivy answered. "Never been to Amarillo before, so I may take a day or two to look around. You need to know that now?"

"No, ma'am. Room's yours as long as you pay me every day before noon. We're easy like that in Amarillo."

"Glad to hear it," Ivy said with a grin. She pulled the cash from her bag and handed it to the woman.

The woman slid a key across the counter. It was a real metal key, clipped to a ring the shape of Texas. "You let me know if you need anything."

"I will. Thank you."

IVY HEADED out late the next morning to do a little exploring. She stopped for breakfast at a roadside diner, then followed the colorful tourist map to Palo Duro Canyon. After sitting for so long yesterday, she looked forward to stretching her legs with a good, long hike. Fortunately, she had thought to grab her hiking boots before she left Vegas, tossing them into the rear of the van.

The canyon was breathtaking, especially the views from the visitor overlook. She spent three glorious hours exploring, and everyone she encountered along the trails was friendly and helpful. When she returned to her van, she was fatigued, but in a good way. She could definitely see herself adding regular hiking trips to her daily dancing routine. Just because she was no longer a professional, she had no intention of losing her hard-earned body.

As she drove from the lot, she counted the cars with Nevada plates—five out of twelve. With sadness, she realized she hadn't yet gone quite far enough. She would need to find a town that wasn't situated on such a direct route to and from Las Vegas. Wherever she settled, though, she would make sure the folks were kind, like those here in Amarillo. But not too nosy, she amended.

Along with a new name for herself, she would need to come up with a fresh and interesting past. Like she had done when she left Tennessee, but far more convincing. Not a history that someone could easily unravel. She had left far too much mayhem in her wake for that to happen. Again. Alejandro had discovered who she really was, who she'd been in Tennessee, not long after she moved in with him. He had used that knowledge against her time and time again. Typically, with his fists.

Rested and energized after a second night's stay, Ivy checked out of the room and pointed the van east towards Oklahoma. Wide open pastures, many of them dotted with oil pumpjacks, bordered the highway as far as the eye could see. She rolled down the windows and allowed the breeze to wash over her. She hadn't felt so carefree in years, and she made a vow then and there to never relinquish her freedom to anyone, man or woman.

As she approached the Arkansas state line, an overhead sign forced her to choose her next route. She could merge east onto 40, but that would take her into Tennessee, a state she swore never to step foot in again. North or south would lead to unfamiliar territory where no one knew her, and she knew no one. Her hands gripped the wheel, and after a moment's indecision, she activated her turn signal.

51

ROGER

"PREGNANT?" Roger was stunned. He sagged in the chair and closed his eyes as a myriad of questions and doubts ricocheted through his brain.

"Around three months," Leonard said. "I take it you didn't know?"

Roger swallowed hard. "No, she never said anything."

"Was it yours?"

Roger felt his face twist with the stab of uncertainty. When had he last made love to Vanessa? "That, I don't know."

"Well, we'll know one way or the other once the fetus's DNA results come back."

"Is that really necessary?" Roger asked as the jagged knife sunk itself deeper into his heart. "The DNA test, I mean. Both Vanessa and the baby are dead. What difference does it make who the father was?" The coffee he had finished a short while ago seared as it percolated into his esophagus.

"The DA already ordered it. Paternity is an important consideration in the case against you."

"But what if it wasn't mine? What if—" He stopped himself from finishing the sentence. He knew *what if*.

"Yep, if you're not the father, it's a better case for her, a worse one for you. Goes to motive."

Roger swore under his breath. "But if it wasn't mine, the real father could just as easily be the killer."

"Yes, but unless we discover who else she was sleeping with, that might very well remain a mystery. Think hard, Roger."

"About what?" Roger asked, feeling himself come apart.

"Who Vanessa might have been intimate with, assuming she was and the child's not yours."

"I don't have a clue. I never even considered the possibility until this moment." He hadn't cared, either. He stood to pace the room.

"No one comes to mind?" Leonard asked. "Your landscaper, the pool boy?"

Roger gave him an angry look. "Just who do you think she was? Some bored and horny housewife?"

"I don't know, Roger. You tell me."

Roger walked to the window and stared out at the endless blue sky. Losing his wife was one thing. It was a blessing, really, and he had already come to terms with it. He was moving on. But a child? His child?

"There are rumors, you know," Leonard said, inserting himself into Roger's anguish. "That she and your partner, Bart Nixon, were extremely close."

"Bart?" Roger said, not bothering to look at his attorney.

"That was years ago. He's such a loser now, she would never leave me for him."

"I didn't say she was leaving you, Roger. Only that there was something alleged to be going on between the two."

"Before me, maybe, but no way recently. He's not her type." Roger sat back down. "Vanessa babysat his kid after his psycho wife killed herself. She was young and impressionable and saw herself as a replacement mother." He shrugged.

"Before you were in the picture, right?"

"Yeah, like I told you. She quit working for Nixon, both at the store and watching his kid, when we hooked up, and she never looked back."

"You absolutely sure of that? Rumors do occasionally prove true."

"I'm sure." His mind flashed to the argument with Bart a few weeks back. He had accused him of telling Vanessa about his fling with Darla. And the others. Bart had denied it, but someone had told her.

"Were you jealous of their friendship?"

"Hell, no." He was, at one time, but not in years. Should he have been? "Nixon had a thing for her still. I knew that, but I'm one hundred percent certain she didn't return his feelings. Hell, lots of men found her attractive. She might have been bat-shit crazy, but she was also crazy-hot."

"Did all that attention make you crazy, too?"

"What are you insinuating?"

"Just playing devil's advocate in light of this new information. I told you I don't want to know if you killed her, but the DA sure does. The pregnancy makes her care even more. I wouldn't put it past her to charge you with a second count of murder."

"Well, you tell her this. I may have been a lousy

husband, but I didn't kill my wife, and I could never kill her baby, even if it wasn't mine. That's just sick. She needs to dig elsewhere."

"Stick to that story, Roger. In the meantime, as far as the DA is concerned, she's got her man, and it's not in her interest to dig elsewhere."

"Fuck her."

"Stay on point, Roger. Who did Vanessa encounter on a regular basis? And I'm serious about the pool boy or gardener." He slid a pad of paper and a pen across his desk. "I want at least five possibilities. When you're done, we leave the rest to my investigator."

Roger snorted. "Fine, but there's no way Nixon makes my list. I'm just telling you."

Leonard shook his head, looking amused. Refocusing on his laptop, he said, "There's an additional discovery that reinforces the urgency of that list."

Roger's sphincter clenched. "What's more unsettling than someone stabbing my wife and her unborn child to death?"

Leonard hesitated, looking at Roger with renewed sympathy. "There was evidence that Vanessa had recently engaged in, to put it as politely as I can, violent sexual activity."

Roger pushed out of the chair and leaned across the desk to read the report himself. "She was raped?"

"Maybe, maybe not." Leonard tilted the screen away from Roger. "Sit down and I'll read it to you. *Vagina and rectum bruised. Bruises in early stage of healing. Minor tearing to labia and anus, also in early stage of healing. Absence of semen on body. Minor abrasions on knees, mostly healed. Findings consistent with forced intercourse of inde-*

terminate consensuality. Sexual activity occurring twenty-four hours to seven days prior to exsanguination."

Roger blew out an exasperated breath. "Ex what?"

"She bled to death."

"And that bit about the sex being consensual? You're telling me Vanessa was a two-bit whore?"

Leonard raised his eyebrows. "That is not what the findings say. And neither should you, especially within hearing range of anyone who could use it against you. Frankly, I prefer that you not talk to anyone whosoever about this report. Especially not someone who could be called to testify for the prosecution, regardless of who or what *she* might be to you."

The point hit its mark, but it also brought Diana to mind.

"You understand me?" Leonard asked.

"Yes." He took a sip of water. "For how long?"

"My advice is that you keep to yourself and deny the DA any further ammunition until such time as another suspect is named, arrested, tried, and convicted for the murder of your wife and child."

Roger frowned. There it was again. Child. They had never discussed having a baby. He figured she didn't want to ruin her perfect body. She had even laughed at how fat one of their neighbors had gotten when pregnant with twins. For nearly a year after, too. If Roger was honest with himself, he hadn't wanted her to get fat, either—baby or no baby. He was proud of how fit and toned she was and had gladly paid for those fake boobs when she complained hers were too small. Not that he'd found them lacking; more than a mouthful, and all that. Up until she started whining about them, their mere outline would give him a rock-solid woody every single time. He had to admit, though, the fake ones were amazing. He'd loved those tits.

When had he stopped hungering for them? For her? He couldn't recall the exact moment, but one day, he looked up and saw only a skinny woman with enormous boobs. The gorgeous bombshell she'd become after they married, the one he lusted after so desperately, had all but disappeared. In her place was a frigid, gold-digging shopaholic.

He dropped his head into his hands. "There is someone I need to call."

"Who?" Leonard asked.

"A friend in North Carolina. She'll be expecting to hear from me, and I want to be the one to tell her about the baby."

"Who is she to you?"

He cleared his throat. "Just someone I care about."

"Well, call her now while I'm listening," Leonard said, nodding at Roger's cell phone. "And when you're done talking, give me your phone for safekeeping."

Roger dialed Diana's number. It rang four times before switching over to voicemail. He didn't leave a message.

"She's not picking up. Can I keep my phone until I reach her?"

"You have til the morning," Leonard replied. "But tell me her name so I'm not blindsided when the DA drops her in my lap."

52

BOBBY

DIANA WAS a sight for sore eyes, and she jumped into his arms before the outside door was even shut. He carried her up the stairs, her legs wrapped tightly around his waist.

"I missed you today," she said breathlessly.

"I can tell," he said, setting her down inside the apartment.

"You haven't seen nothin' yet," she said, batting her long eyelashes.

"Well, ma'am, before we get started tonight, how 'bout a beer for a parched mariner?"

"Long day?" she asked, reaching into the freezer for a mug.

"Heavy-duty deck cleaning."

"I did some heavy-duty cleaning of my own," she said, handing him the beer. "I'll rub your back later if you rub mine."

"It's a deal." He grinned, then took a deep pull from the frosty mug.

He watched as Diana grabbed an unopened bottle of wine and twisted off the cap. She took a clean glass from the drainboard, then filled it to the brim, air-toasting him before gulping down half of it.

As he followed her into the bedroom, she swayed unsteadily and fell back against him. The mug of beer spilled all over his shirt.

"I guess you started drinking without me," he said. "Are you okay?"

"I will be once we lie down."

"Then allow me, ma'am," he said, leading her to the bed. "Now, you lay right here, and I'll be back in a flash." In the bathroom, he hung his shirt in the shower and turned on the cold water to rinse out the beer. He just bought the darn thing at Ocean Outfitters, and it cost him nearly a whole day's wages.

When he came out of the bathroom, Diana was lying in the center of the bed, stark-naked. She appeared to be sleeping, but when he knelt on the mattress, she opened her eyes.

"Look at that," she said, slurring her words slightly as she pointed to his erection. "You are beautiful, Bobby."

"You are, too," he said, leaning down to kiss her.

"Not yet," she said pushing him away. "Pose for me." She grabbed her phone off the nightstand and pointed it at him.

Laughing, Bobby flexed his toned biceps and pecs while Diana snapped a series of photos.

"Now, turn around," she ordered. He did, clenching the chiseled muscles of his back and butt.

"That's enough," she said, lying on her back. "Now come to mama."

Bobby grinned and dove onto the mattress.

HOURS LATER, Bobby pulled himself from the bed. He was in dire need of something to quench his incredible thirst. He was famished, too, and intended to raid the fridge. An hour earlier, after round two or three, Diana had begged him to run for takeout. By then, she'd finished off nearly the entire bottle of wine, and he was rather drunk himself. Thankfully, all restaurants in town were closed, and neither of them was fit to drive to one that might still be open. When he told her as much, she was ticked but passed out shortly afterward anyway.

As he headed to the fridge, he noticed her phone on the coffee table. It was lit up and vibrating with an incoming call. He read the caller ID. It was the old guy from last summer, Roger something-or-other. Without thinking, he swiped the screen and held the phone to his ear.

"Diana. Thank God," Roger said.

Bobby bit his tongue and kept silent. The man spoke again. "Hello. Diana? You there?"

Bobby pressed *end call*. Scrolling through the phone, he was surprised by an uncomfortable jolt of jealousy. The dude had called repeatedly, leaving two voicemails and four text messages. Diana's voicemail was password protected, but the texts said much the same thing: *I miss your body. Can't wait to spend another week alone with just you. Call me.*

"What the hell?"

He stomped into the bedroom and shook Diana, but she was dead to the world. In an uncharacteristic fit of petulance, he tweaked her nipple. "Wake up!" he demanded. She moaned, but her eyes remained shut.

Spying her glass of wine, still half full on the nightstand, he picked it up. Tilting it, the red liquid spilled onto her face, settling in her eyes, nose, and ears. Diana sputtered, and she batted at Bobby's arm, knocking the glass from his hand. It dropped to the floor and shattered.

"What are you doing?" she cried, now fully awake.

"Waking you, that's what. Paybacks are a bitch, aren't they?" He stepped back from the bed, and his foot landed on a shard of glass. "Ouch!" he cried, hopping on the other foot. He yanked a nice-size chunk from his instep, and blood seeped from the wound. Pissed, he threw the shard onto the mattress. It bounced up and struck her arm.

"Hey," she yelped. "What's gotten into you?"

"Why don't you ask lover boy," he replied, turning angrily and limping out of the room.

"Who?" she yelled after him.

Seconds later, he returned, tracking blood across the floor with every step. "Roger the dodger," he said. "That's who." He tossed her phone onto the bed.

"You looked at my phone?" she asked, incredulity crossing her face. "I can't believe you spied on me." She rose and headed toward the bathroom, phone in hand.

Bobby grabbed her by the arm and forced her into the chair. "I didn't spy on you. It was ringing, so I answered it."

Diana's eyes widened, and she glanced at her phone, then back at him.

"You lied to me, Diana."

"I didn't lie to you," Diana insisted. "We may be sleeping together, Bobby Moore, but that doesn't give you the right to know where I am every waking minute. Or dictate what I do and who I do it with."

He jabbed his finger in her face. "Never said I wanted to, but the truth matters, Diana."

"I know it does," she said, "but I give you all I have to give."

Bobby smirked. "Then you turn right around and give it to Roger. And from what I gather, he's been getting way more than you give me."

"You talked to him?"

"No, but his texts tell me all I need to know." He grabbed the phone out of her hand and hobbled into the bathroom, slamming and locking the door behind him.

He heard her jiggle the handle. "Bobby, come on, open the door. You know you can't stay mad at me. You love me."

When Bobby didn't reply, she added, "And I love you. You've got to know that. Now let me in. Please."

"Does Roger know? Or should I call him back and tell him?"

"No! Don't!" she shouted, her voice high-pitched. "You'll ruin everything."

Bobby turned on the water to drown out her voice.

Diana pounded on the door, pleading, "Open the door, Bobby. Don't be mad. Come back to bed, and let me make it up to you."

He heard the desperation in her voice, but he couldn't help himself. He was mad. And hurt. He sat on the toilet, debating what to do, and after a minute, she became real quiet. Sitting there, he felt the tiny room spin, and he had to admit that he was still quite drunk. Maybe the alcohol was messing with his head. It sure seemed like he was being stroppier than the situation called for. But then again, she was too. He stood and lifted the toilet lid, then dropped the phone. It splashed when it hit, and he smiled. *Serves them both right*, he thought as he opened the door.

Diana was no longer in the bedroom, and he found her

standing at the kitchen sink. Her back was to him, and her shoulders were trembling.

Dammit, he thought, *I've gone and made her cry.* He'd never seen her cry before. "I'm sorry, Diana," he said, reaching out to knead her shoulders. "Please don't cry. We're both drunk, so let's just go back to bed."

She nodded but didn't turn around. "Go on ahead. I'll be in in a minute."

Bobby returned to the bedroom and crawled under the covers. Closing his eyes, he fell asleep.

53

ROGER

FRUSTRATED, Roger dropped his cell phone onto the sofa and sighed moodily. His call to Diana had gone to voicemail, but after already leaving two messages, he didn't leave another.

His stomach growled, and he picked the phone back up to order a pizza. His second night of doing so. He knew he would regret the greasy cheese and empty carbs, but since he wasn't permitted to leave the townhouse on his own, what else could he do? While he waited, he dropped to the floor with the intent to crank out twenty-five pushups. He barely made it to twenty before his biceps and shoulders screamed in revolt, and he dropped to his belly. After resting a few seconds, he rolled onto his back, counting off fifty agonizing crunches. With a sense of self-loathing, he groaned and picked himself up off the floor.

Chugging a bottle of water, he tried to remember the

last time he had worked out hard. With deep shame, he realized it was before he'd traveled to Costa Rica, nearly a month ago. He sure as hell needed to hit the gym again, and soon. He didn't know if there was one in this complex, but tomorrow he would insist that Leonard find one for him until he was allowed back in his house.

When the pizza arrived, he sat watching ESPN—an early NCAA match that meant next to nothing to him. The kids playing today were talented, but they had nothing on him in his prime. He had been an incredible specimen then. Still could be if he laid off the carbs.

When nothing but crust remained, he picked up his phone and dialed Diana's number again. For a moment, he thought she picked up, but the call ended abruptly, and he was again sent to voicemail.

Realizing he didn't actually enjoy being alone, he considered calling Darla, but he couldn't muster the energy. Besides, not being able to reach Diana made him miss everything about her. Even her Southern drawl, so soothing and sexy at the same time. It was more of a turn-on than Darla could ever hope to be.

With a start, it occurred to him that Diana sounded a lot like Vanessa when he'd first met her. Unlike Diana, though, his wife had worked hard to lose all traces of her accent, even going so far as to repeatedly watch *A Philadelphia Story* in an effort to sound like Katharine Hepburn's character.

The two women were similar in other ways, too. Both blond, both lithe, both great in the sack. Or at least Vanessa was before becoming a cold fish. Leonard had asked him earlier when they'd last had sex. He still couldn't recall. It must have been on their last anniversary—right? What husband doesn't make love to his wife on their anniversary?

For a panicked moment, he couldn't pull the date from the recesses of his brain. *Shit*, he thought, *maybe I'm getting Alzheimer's*. When their wedding date popped into his head, he relaxed. To be sure, he said it aloud, following it with the date of his first wedding, to Veronica.

That had been a big one. Fresh off his final season with the Flyers, he was living the high life, making regular appearances on TV and radio, and hawking every product put in front of him so long as he was paid the hefty fee dictated by his agent.

He and Veronica had been dating for almost six years by then, and while he never pretended to be faithful, she gleefully accepted his two-carat diamond. Five hundred guests were invited to the Philadelphia Art Museum for an elaborate, formal dinner, with entertainment provided by a twelve-piece swing band and a violin trio that played during the band's breaks. Talk about *A Philadelphia Story*. The night was written up as the toniest event in Phil-adelphia in a generation, with the small exception of a Kate Smith impersonator who belted out *God Bless America* just as the emcee announced the new Mr. and Mrs. Roger Michaud.

That wedding was indeed dramatic, but the fireworks set off over the art museum as the couple departed for the Ritz Carlton honeymoon suite were the only fireworks in their union. And when Vanessa came into his life, Roger quietly divorced Veronica, granting her an enormous settle-ment with no attempt to deprive her of anything her attorney demanded. It had set him back substantially, but he recovered that and more in the years that followed.

With his belly full, Roger lay on the sofa and closed his eyes. If only he could rewind the past twenty years and start all over again. He imagined meeting Diana first and marrying her instead of Veronica or Vanessa. No other women to sidetrack the attention of his heart or his dick.

"Shit!" he cursed, sitting up in frustration. He went to the kitchen and fixed himself a stiff vodka martini. Back in the living room, he flicked through the channels, settling once again on the basketball game. What he'd give to be rewatching his final hockey match. Whatever had transpired in all the years since then, reliving those final moments, the incredible rush of thousands of hats being thrown onto the ice, never failed to settle him down.

With dread, he found himself thinking of the night he discovered Vanessa's body. He hated reliving that horror, which was yet another reason he should have stayed in North Carolina. Diana had known how to expertly sweep away those memories. As his anxiety blossomed, he downed the vodka and shuffled to the kitchen to pour himself another. Carrying the tumbler and bottle into the bedroom, he lay on the mattress, staring at the ceiling.

VANESSA'S CAR was in the garage, and he cursed. He'd been hoping she was still in Bethany Beach. *Whatever*, he told himself. He wouldn't let her get to him tonight. The trip to Costa Rica had been a blast, the weather perfect. He and his buddies had fished every single day, catching more than fifty sailfish and marlin over the course of the week.

Nights had been just as memorable, with delicious local food, ample alcohol, and a delightful bevy of young, nubile women. There was one, in particular, he enjoyed more than the others. A beauty by the name of Rosita. He laughed at how she pronounced it, the *R* rolling seductively off her tongue. Mistaking his laugh for teasing, she pouted, and he begged her forgiveness by covering her ripe, plump lips with his own. He took to calling her Rosita Lolita, and while he romped with a few of the other girls, Rosita was his chosen favorite. She performed this one trick with her teeth that repeatedly drove him to the brink of insanity, and he couldn't wait to coach Diana and Darla on how it was done.

He dropped his bags in the mudroom, then headed to the kitchen. The first of two flights had left early that morning, and at eleven p.m. East Coast time, he was long past tired. All he wanted was a glass of wine, a hot shower, and his own bed. As he moved to the living room, he felt a cool breeze blowing through the room.

"Vanessa?" he called out. There was no answer.

At the rear of the room, the sheers covering the French doors were billowing ever so slightly. It would be just like his crazy wife to come in from the veranda and forget to close the doors. After all, she didn't have to pay the heating bill.

When he pushed aside the sheers, he saw the doors were, in fact, shut, but a pane of glass near the handle was shattered. The deadbolt was in the unlocked position, and on closer inspection, he noticed shards of glass scattered at his feet. Fear crept up his neck, and he turned around quickly.

"Vanessa!" he shouted again. "Where are you?"

He pulled out his phone and dialed her number. It went straight to voicemail. Forgetting his wine, he moved to the staircase and bounded up to the second floor. The master bedroom door was open, the bedside lights turned on, but she wasn't there. Their bed appeared undisturbed.

"Vanessa," he called. "Where are you?" Again, no answer.

He searched their bathroom and closet, then moved

down the long hallway toward the gym and a second master suite, the one no one ever slept in. *Huh*, he thought, with a smile of satisfaction. *The princess has finally moved out of our bedroom.* Honestly, he'd been waiting for this moment, and he couldn't be happier that she chose tonight to make the move.

There was no response to his soft knock, so he turned the handle and nudged the door. It was snug against the jamb, and he had to exert pressure with his shoulder to force it open. The smell of stale air was the first thing he noticed, and when he flicked on the overhead light, this bed was also empty.

Puzzled, he looked up at the ceiling. Maybe she had taken over one of the third-floor bedrooms. He couldn't remember the last time he'd ventured up there, but perhaps the idea of sleeping farther away appealed to her as much as it did him. He started up the steps. An obnoxious odor filled his nostrils the higher he climbed. *Damn*, he thought, *we really need to air out these rooms more often.*

At the top of the stairs, he groped for the light switch, but it wasn't where he remembered. As his eyes adjusted, he shook his head in confusion. Sure, he was exhausted, but he could swear there were three doors up here, two for the bedrooms and one for the attic. Instead, a set of French doors was centered on the wall directly in front of him. Beyond the doors, a shimmering glow of light beckoned. A memory of the disco ball above the dance floor at his senior prom came to mind, and then, unbidden, his thoughts pivoted to the prom scene from *Carrie*. To the bucket of blood above that dance floor.

With a shiver, he recognized the putrid smell, sickeningly stronger from where he now stood. Blood-red hamburger meat left too long in the sun.

IT WAS A LATE SUMMER AFTERNOON, shortly after
he and Vanessa had married, and he was doing his very best
to impress his new wife with his grilling talents. He finally
got the gas grill lit—a first for him—and he called through
the open doors for the burgers. When he turned to accept
the platter, he stopped mid-reach. His beautiful bride was
naked except for an apron tied at her waist.

When they returned to the terrace two hours later, the
gray blobs of meat were oozing under a swarm of green-eyed
flies. Vanessa gagged and ran back into the house, and
Roger was left to carry the foul-smelling meat down the hillside, gagging himself before tossing the entire tray into the
woods.

THAT'S EXACTLY what he smelled now, and the hairs on
his neck bristled as he stepped into the room. He noticed
the lights first, radiating not from a disco ball but a massive
crystal chandelier hanging from the ceiling of a room he had
never before been in. Suddenly dizzy, he imagined himself
somehow transported to an alternate time and universe.

The room was enormous, with floor-to-ceiling mirrors
lining one entire wall. A four-poster canopied bed covered
in luxurious linens was situated atop a platform built into
an alcove on the opposite wall. As his bewildered gaze travelled across the plush carpeting, the chicken sandwich he
had wolfed down on the drive from the airport erupted from
his mouth before he could even form the thought to swallow
it back down.

54

MONKEY

AFTER HIS DUMP, Monkey trudged through the vacant
lot behind the motel, muddy earth sucking loudly at his
sneakers. He came out on a residential street of small but
tidy, older homes. Nothing like the ritzy neighborhood he'd
been in yesterday. It was quiet here, and he stayed in the
shadows of the trees as he headed toward the water, grateful
that he knew the lay of the land a little better this time out.

Across from the Seaside Siren, he took up his position
behind the general store. Despite the slow walk from the
motel, he was sweating. *Calm down*, he told himself. *It's not
like a first date, for God's sake!* To center himself, he closed
his eyes and counted to ten, a technique he'd learned in the
joint to help block out the hushed voices and furtive
couplings of nearby inmates.

On the floor above the shop, lights flickered in the
window overlooking the street. Was that her bedroom? He

smiled as he imagined her getting ready for bed. She would slip a nightie over her head, then lean forward to brush out her impossibly tangled hair. One hundred strokes exactly. Done counting, she would straighten, her flushed face encircled by a sea of golden waves. His grief caught him by surprise, and he pressed his forehead against the building's cool brick exterior.

HE FOUND her bent at the waist, the light from the dresser lamp revealing the dark outline of nipples beneath her sheer cotton shift. Overcome with desire, he moved behind her and grasped her hips, grinding himself against her firm, inviting derriere. It was more than a month since they'd last made love, and he was ravenous for the heat of her.

She pressed back against him but continued counting aloud each brushstroke. When she reached one hundred, she righted herself and backed away from him. In her eyes, instead of desire, he saw only regret. He was confused and reached for her.

"What's wrong, baby?" he asked. "Here, let me hold you."

She shook her head and slipped by him, heading down the hall.

He followed her and stood outside the closed bathroom door, listening as she cleaned her teeth. When the water shut off, he waited. After five minutes of silence, his impatience was beginning to bubble to the surface. Hadn't he made it clear that he forgave her? Her refusing him now wasn't right.

"Honey, come to bed."

The light beneath the door went out, and the knob turned. He couldn't see her face in the dim hallway, but when he pulled her close and kissed her mouth, her cheeks were wet. At the time, he assumed it was from washing her face, but later, after she left him, he understood she'd been crying.

THE MEMORY BROUGHT BACK a feeling of defenselessness, one Monkey thought he had banished for good with his release from prison. He closed his eyes again, and after ten seconds, he moved out from the shadows.

When he reached the curb, a young man rounded the corner and headed his direction. He was whistling a happy tune, a little off-key, but when he noticed Monkey, he stopped.

"Hey," the man said in a friendly drawl. "Nice evening, huh?"

Monkey nodded.

The man resumed his tune as he crossed the street. He stopped at the steel door adjacent to the Seaside Siren and pressed the doorbell. Monkey felt sick. That was her apartment.

When the door opened, the man disappeared inside.

Monkey was befuddled, unsure of what to do. He stepped into the market's outdoor gazebo and lay down on a bench. *One step forward, two steps back*, he thought. The pathetic tale of his entire pathetic life. He was done with it, and come hell or high water, tonight he would take back what rightly belonged to him. He just had to fine-tune his plan a little.

He hadn't counted on falling asleep, and when he jolted

awake, he was unsure at first where he was. The hard surface pressing against his spine reminded him. Checking his phone, he realized he'd been out for nearly two hours. It was long past time to make his move.

He pushed to his feet and crossed the street. As he approached the steel door, he saw that it was slightly ajar. It must not have closed tightly when the whistler went inside. Or maybe the kid had left while Monkey was sleeping. Pulling on the handle, the door swung toward him. He stepped inside and found himself in a dark vestibule that opened to a narrow staircase leading to a second floor.

Swallowing hard, Monkey took his first step up. A second later, he paused mid-stride as loud voices drifted down from above. Listening intently, he made out two distinct voices, one hers, the other the kid's. He couldn't make out what was being said, but he could tell they were angry. Second-guessing himself yet again, Monkey thought, *maybe now isn't the best time after all.* A door slammed above him, followed by repeated banging, then quiet. Monkey waited a beat longer, then with a deep breath of resolve, he resumed his ascent.

55

BART

BART DIMMED his headlights when he turned into the high-dollar community of higher-dollar mansions. He recalled being surprised on his first visit that there wasn't a security gate to keep out the riff-raff. *Like me*, he thought now.

He drove unhurriedly past the massive house, nearly invisible in the starless night. No light shone from the windows, but he wouldn't need it. Every detail of the layout was imprinted on his brain from the last night he'd come here.

In the cul-de-sac, he turned his truck around, then drove slowly by the house again. Turning right out of the neighborhood, he followed the winding road to the nearby state park. A sign warned that it was off limits from dusk to dawn, but he proceeded to the first parking lot anyway, backing into a spot at the edge of the forest. When he stepped down from the cab onto the dirt and gravel surface, his thick-soled boots crunched loudly. Using his cell phone as a guide, he climbed into the truck bed, where he pulled a flashlight and a crowbar from the diamond-plated saddle box. With the flick of a finger, a powerful shaft of light bounced off the seemingly solid wall of trees. After getting his bearings, he jumped down and trailed the beam into the dark woods.

As he trudged along a narrow deer path, he again questioned his sanity. There was so much shit coming at him right now, he had to be certifiably insane to purposefully bury himself any deeper. But as hard as he tried to ignore the crushing despair gnawing at his soul, it just wouldn't go away. Every time he came up for air, it pulled him back under. The only thing he had come up with that might stop him from drowning was to relive their last night together. As soon as the idea had formed, it quickly became an obsession. An obsession to return to the very spot his love for Vanessa had been most promising.

If he had only known she was pregnant, she would still be alive. He was convinced of it. He would have saved her. Saved their baby. He had already done the calculation. New Year's Eve was fourteen weeks ago. The baby was most definitely his. Why had she kept it from him?

His heartbeat quickening with every step, he picked up his pace.

AFTER VANESSA'S call on New Year's Eve, he showered quickly, then drove way too fast, arriving at the Radnor house around ten. She was waiting for him in the open garage where she motioned for him to pull his truck into the empty bay.

He had been to the house for a summer gathering years earlier when Roger was married to Veronica. It looked very much the same tonight. Vanessa led him to the den, where an open bottle of Cabernet Sauvignon and two crystal goblets sat on the cocktail table.

His hands were slick as he poured the deep red wine. He carefully handed her a glass, then downed a big gulp of his own. As the warm liquid hit his belly, his shoulders relaxed. He settled into the opposite end of the sofa, watching as she swirled the wine, quietly contemplating the dancing flames. He wanted so badly to touch her.

"Vanessa?" he whispered.

She looked up. A fresh application of makeup and her low-cut dress, gold and shimmering in the glow from the fireplace, did a fair job of distracting attention from her red and puffy eyes.

"I'm glad you're here," she said.

"I am, too." He moved a little closer.

She tensed and looked away. He stayed where he was for what seemed like an hour but was probably only minutes. He finished his wine, then reached for the bottle, filling his glass first, then offering more to her.

"Thank you," she said, holding out her glass.

"You're welcome. Are you okay?"

She nodded, then set her wine down. Standing, she moved to the ornate cabinet situated to the right of the room's French doors. The sheers dressing the doors were closed against the night, but Bart recalled how the doors opened onto a stone terrace. He remembered thinking how the pristine lawn, sloping gently downward toward a dense forest, would be ideal for sledding. He'd said as much to

Roger, hoping to finagle an invitation for Ben and him to do just that some snowy winter day, but the invite never came.

Vanessa opened a cabinet door and punched a button on the stereo. When the score from *Phantom of the Opera* filled the room, she turned toward him and smiled.

He stood and held out his hand. After a moment's hesitation, she walked into his embrace. They swayed in each other's arms until the first track ended. Then, with an expression somewhere between desire and resignation, she took him by the hand, leading him up the wide staircase to the third floor.

He made love to her over and over throughout the night. Tender at times, passionate at others, her intense sensuality was everything he had longed for, and far more than he ever imagined. He reached heights of ecstasy he never thought possible, and he was convinced that she had, too.

It was only the need to relieve himself that woke him just before dawn from a brief but sound sleep. Slipping from the bed, he knelt by her side. She was lying on her back, so peaceful, so angelic. He kissed her softly on the lips, and she smiled sleepily, wrapping her arms around his neck. She clung to him for a few seconds of shared warmth, then relaxed again.

"Go back to sleep," he whispered, then moved to the adjoining bathroom. After pulling on his slacks, he tip-toed from the room and headed down the staircase to investigate Roger Michaud's house.

He wandered through the first floor, imagining himself living there with Vanessa. What more could a man ask for? In the kitchen, he grabbed a bottle of water to slake his thirst, guzzling the cold liquid as he walked leisurely through the living room. They had left the fireplace burning when they'd gone upstairs, and, after finding the remote behind a sofa cushion, he shut it off.

In the study, its walls covered with a mix of antique wood paneling and saddle brown leather, he sat behind the desk. The aroma here reminded him of the horse stables at the Brandywine Polo Club. Rich, earthy, and redolent of old money. Just who did Roger think he was?

In the fully equipped gym, he stepped onto a treadmill, likely misappropriated from Slap Shots, and checked out his physique in the wall of mirrors. Shirtless and barefoot, he looked paunchy and pale. That would change if he lived here. Working out with Vanessa, he would whip himself into peak shape, with her as both motivation and reward.

Across the hall was the media room. Bart had been in here before, again at that summer party. Roger had called his guests in, ten at a time, throughout the afternoon, forcing them to suffer through a video of his final, season-winning hat trick. He never once acknowledged the teammate who had flawlessly fed him that last, perfect puck. Humiliated, Bart kept his mouth shut. No one cared that he was the player who made each and every one of Roger's goals possible. What a farce.

Opening the door to the second-floor master bedroom, a queasy feeling came over him. The bed here, bigger than the one upstairs, was where his true love slept beside his nemesis. He quickly closed the door without stepping into the room.

Back in Vanessa's suite, he stood at the foot of the bed, memorizing every detail of her perfect body, her perfect face. If only he didn't have to leave to pick up Ben. If only he didn't have Ben's welfare to consider for the remainder of his life. He guiltily banished those thoughts and finished dressing. Before leaving, he leaned over her once again. "I'll be back very soon," he whispered, then kissed the tip of her perfect nose.

Downstairs, he scribbled a note, leaving it tucked beneath the coffee brewer: *Happy New Year, My Love.* As he drove home, the sky turned from a deep purple to pink, then gold. It was the dawn of a new year and a new life with Vanessa.

56

GEORGE

GEORGE SIPPED lukewarm coffee from a thermos as the black truck drove slowly past the Michaud house. When it returned moments later from the opposite direction, exiting right at the stop sign, he briefly debated following, but his instincts told him to stay put.

Yesterday, when he leaked Vanessa Michaud's pregnancy to Bart Nixon, something in the man's eyes warned him to stay watchful. Tonight, he arrived at the Delaware store shortly before closing. He watched Nixon climb into his truck, then trailed him onto Route 1 and I-95 North. He quickly guessed the man's destination, so when Nixon diverted into a rest area just north of the Pennsylvania line, George continued on.

He parked his SUV around the corner from the Michaud house, out of sight of nosy neighbors and passers-by. The position afforded him a one-hundred-eighty-degree view of the property. He waited only twelve minutes for his hunch to play out.

Setting the thermos back in the cupholder, George shifted his position, leaning his back against the door. His view was now of the rear of the house and sloping lawn. Again, his wait was short. In the forest beyond the property, he glimpsed a stream of light bouncing off tree trunks and branches. He blinked to clear his vision, and when he reopened his eyes, a shadowy figure darted from the cover of trees.

From George's position, it was impossible to ID the figure, but odds were good it was Nixon. As George himself had done earlier, the man had likely trekked over from the state park. George holstered his firearm and slipped down from his vehicle. He cleared the post and rail fence, then sprinted to the side of the house, pressing against a broad brick chimney while he caught his breath. Seconds later, he stepped quietly to the rear of the house, stopping short when the sound of splintering wood echoed through the quiet darkness.

Reconsidering his decision to go it alone, he swiped open his phone and tapped out a quick text to Mike Molino with the Radnor Police. *Intruder breaking into Michaud house. Going in. Send backup.* He didn't wait for a response before rounding the corner and climbing the terrace steps.

Sheer fabric billowed eerily onto the terrace through an open doorway. When George approached, he could see the glass-paned door hanging crookedly from its hinges.

His phone vibrated in his shirt pocket, but he didn't bother to pull it out. It was no doubt Molino advising him to wait for backup. He led with his gun as he crossed the threshold, allowing the curtains to hide him until he could case the room.

Nixon was nowhere to be seen. George slipped into the room; his ears perked. The sound of a door creaking overhead led him to a sweeping staircase, and he moved quietly up the carpeted treads. Again, his phone buzzed, but again, he ignored it.

On the second floor, all doors were shut to the hallway. He stopped outside the nearest one, pressing his ear to the paneled wood before moving on. When a floorboard groaned above him, he found his way back to the staircase.

On the next landing, he noticed light shining from beneath a set of double doors. Recalling details from the filched murder book, George realized this had to be the room where Vanessa's body was found. Where she had been murdered. Listening at the door, he could just make out the muffled sounds of a man sobbing. He wasn't going anywhere soon.

George retreated to the first floor to wait for that backup. He was sitting in a chaise on the veranda when a gun-toting man rounded the corner from the driveway. George stood and held up his hands, announcing, "I'm George Purnell. I reported the break-in. Are you Molino?"

"I am. Where's this intruder?"

"Inside, third floor. I didn't see him up close, but I suspect it's Bart Nixon, Michaud's business partner."

"I know who he is," the detective said, shaking his head. "So, you went in by yourself, after all."

"I had to be sure," George said unapologetically. "I knew you wouldn't want him to get away."

Seconds later, four additional officers showed up, and the five policemen moved to the stairs. They found Nixon on the third floor, in Vanessa's enormous private suite. He had stripped off his dark clothing and was lying in the center of the bed, naked and bawling like a baby.

The officers forcefully re-dressed him, then cuffed his hands behind his back. He sobbed the whole way down the stairs and out the back door. In the driveway, he jerked to a stop when he recognized George. "This is all your fault," he cried. "You and Roger did this to me."

57

JIMMY

JOE VICKERS SAT at the counter of Local's Family Diner, waiting for his plate of eggs and bacon, toast and jam. The waitress refilled his coffee, then grinned at Jimmy as he took the adjacent stool.

"Morning, Jim," Joe greeted, not bothering to look up.

"Joe," Jimmy replied as he turned up his mug.

"What can I get you?" the waitress asked as she poured his coffee.

"Just the coffee for now," he replied, then addressed Vickers. "You have something for me?"

"I do at that," Joe said. "Left it in my truck, but if you're in a hurry, I can go fetch it for you."

"Nah, I've got time. Anything you want to share now?"

"Rather not. Big ears at these tables." He gestured behind him.

"Everywhere," Jimmy agreed.

Vickers's radio crackled. "Chief, we got ourselves a situation at a residence downtown."

"Hold on," he replied, swiveling off the stool and heading out the back door. A moment later, he returned, telling Jimmy, "Come with me." He waved an apology to the waitress.

Jimmy quickly drained his coffee and followed the chief out.

BY THE TIME the EMTs brought out the black body bag, a growing crowd was gathered across the street. Jimmy stood among them, Mary at his side.

When he and Joe had left the diner, they didn't know much of anything. Only that a body had been found in Diana Forrester's apartment above the Seaside Siren. Someone had called 9-1-1, but they'd hung up before giving the operator any information. The police were summoned to investigate, and once they gained access to the building, they discovered the victim.

Jim had called Mary after Joe disappeared inside the building.

"Hey," she answered. "You done with breakfast already?"

"No. I need you to come down to the Seaside Siren."

"Why?" she asked, sounding worried. "What's wrong?"

"I don't know for sure," he said, choosing his words carefully, "but you'll want to be here."

Mary gulped, and the call ended.

She arrived minutes later to find the street blocked with police and emergency vehicles. Tears rolled down her face now as the stretcher was lifted into the coroner's wagon.

She clenched a rosary of blue beads, pressing them to her mouth.

Jimmy hugged her tightly and kissed the top of her head. "We don't know, Mary."

He spotted Vickers exiting the building, and when Joe noticed them in the crowd, he beckoned them over.

"Joe?" Mary said, her eyes pleading. "Tell us what's happened."

Vickers looked pained. Turning his back to the crowd of onlookers, he said quietly, "The decedent they just brought out has been identified as one Robert Moore."

Mary shook her head and sucked in a breath. "So, it's not Diana. Thank God."

"No," Vickers said.

"Who is he?" Jimmy asked.

"A local kid. Goes by Bobby. Works on the shrimp docks."

Mary's legs buckled, and Jimmy caught her before she collapsed. "You know him?"

She nodded. "I mentioned him to you just last night." To Joe, she asked, "What happened to him? Was Diana hurt?"

Vickers looked up to the second-story window, then back to Mary. "To answer your first question, we haven't determined that yet, and we won't until we can get Miss Forrester to talk to us, and we conduct a thorough investigation."

"Why isn't she talking?" Jimmy asked.

Vickers shook his head. "Could be she's suffering from shock. To answer your second question, Mary, she has no obvious physical injuries, but the EMTs are with her now. She'll be transported to Dosher Hospital, and if I had to guess, they'll admit her for observation. Once the docs do their thing and give the okay, I'll get my opportunity to ask questions." He shrugged, adding, "There's not a damn thing more I can tell you right now."

"Thanks, Joe," Jimmy said. "You've got your hands full, so we'll let you get to it. If there's anything you need from us, call."

"Will do." He stepped toward the building, then paused. Turning back, he said, "We still need to notify Moore's next-of-kin, so keep his ID to yourselves for the time being."

"You got it," Jimmy agreed, then added, "About that report, when you have a second, I'd still like to take a look at it."

"Oh, that's right," Vickers said. "I all but forgot about it." Vickers crossed the street to his SUV and retrieved a file from the backseat. Bringing it over to Jimmy, he said, "Let's talk this afternoon. I'll call you when I finish up here."

"I'll be waiting," Jimmy replied. He grabbed Mary's hand, but she resisted.

"I should go to the hospital with Diana," she said.

"No, you shouldn't," he objected. "Let them do their job, and you can see her later. Now, where'd you park? I need you to drop me at the diner for my truck."

At the intersection of Moore and Howe, they pushed through a throng of curious onlookers. When Mary tensed, stopping abruptly in the middle of the crosswalk, Jimmy was tempted to throw her across his shoulder to get her to the car.

"Let's go, Mary."

She looked up at him, her eyes a mix of fear and agitation.

"What?" he asked, now wary and alert himself.

"That's him." She pointed discreetly to a man milling at the edge of the congregation.

Jimmy tracked her finger to a man wearing baggy jeans, an oversized gray sweatshirt, and muddy sneakers. A ball cap was pulled low over his eyes. "The guy from the store? The one who creeped you out?"

Mary nodded, squeezing Jimmy's forearm hard enough to leave dents. He led her to the sidewalk, then pulled out his cell while keeping his eyes on the man. As he tapped out a text, the man glanced in their direction. As if sensing he was being watched, he lowered his head and wound his way toward the waterfront.

"We need to follow him," Mary said, her voice rising.

"Let Joe handle it."

Just then, the police chief stepped onto the sidewalk, tapping at his phone. Jim's phone buzzed, and he typed a brief response. Vickers pulled aside one of his officers and whispered in his ear. He then moved north while the officer headed south.

Jimmy heard Mary's breath catch as they watched the take-down unfold, and if Jimmy were honest with himself, he longed to be part of the action, minimal as it turned out to be. The man offered no resistance when the two officers approached him, and he willingly fished his identification from his back pocket. They were too far away to hear what was being said, but Jimmy imagined how the conversation was playing out:

"Mind if we ask you a few questions?"

"About what?"

"We can go into details at the station, if you'll come with us."

"Don't have to, do I?"

"No, but it'd sure be a big help if you did. Unless there's somewhere better you need to be."

Jimmy watched the man's posture deflate as Joe led him by the elbow to a nearby police cruiser. Once he was patted down, Joe opened the rear passenger door, and the man crumpled onto the seat.

Nearby onlookers, sensing something big was going down, became quite animated. As they pushed against each other to get a better view of the police activity, Mary and Jimmy hurriedly left the scene.

58

ROGER

A PERSISTENT RINGING woke Roger from a sweat-drenching sleep. His brain drummed inside his skull, and when he opened his eyes, they threatened to pop out of their sockets. He fumbled with his phone. "Diana?"

"No. Wallace Leonard."

"Shit, Leonard. What time is it?" His mouth felt like it was crammed with cotton balls.

"Nine. Time for you to wake up and listen to me."

"It's too early," he said, and disconnected the call.

An hour later, the townhouse doorbell buzzed, waking Roger once again. Wishing for it to be Diana, he stumbled out of bed.

"Yes?" he answered, stopping the relentless buzzing.

"Invite me up, Roger." It was Leonard.

Great, he thought as he pressed the release button. He propped the door open with a shoe, then headed to the bathroom. Twenty minutes later, he found Leonard sitting at the counter.

"Rough night?" he asked, handing him a fresh cup of coffee.

"I don't remember."

"I take it you didn't get ahold of Miss Forrester?"

"Like I said, I don't remember." He pulled his phone from his pocket and scrolled. "No, but I'll try her again now."

"I wouldn't bother just yet. You'll have more to tell her after you listen to me."

"Why? What's happened?"

"Sit down, and I'll tell you."

A SHORT TIME LATER, Roger asked, "Then I'm free to go wherever I want?"

"The DA still wants you to notify her office if and when you leave the state."

"Why? If Nixon's been arrested, she shouldn't care."

"Don't fight this, Roger," Leonard cautioned. "The more cooperative you are, the better it'll be in the long run."

Roger shook his head. "Whatever. Hey, can you take me home? It'll only take me a few minutes to gather my things."

"Ah, that," Leonard said. "Seems Nixon took a crowbar to your rear doors. You'll need to have them repaired or replaced."

"Shit. Screw it then. I'm taking the first flight back to North Carolina."

"Take my advice, Roger, and stay put for another day or two. Let this all sort itself out before you take off again. Miss Forrester will wait."

Roger wasn't so sure.

Leonard stood and extended his hand. "It's been a pleasure."

"For you, maybe," Roger said. As he walked the attorney out, he added, "By the way, I want back what's left of my retainer."

"You'll get it," Leonard said. "Unless you think you'll need me again sometime soon."

"Not a chance," Roger said, slamming the door in the man's face.

59

DIANA

THE IV ALARM woke Diana from a dream about Alejandro. The synchronized bleeps sounded much like the metronome he would set while she practiced her dance routines in their basement studio. Every morning except Sunday, he forced her downstairs, resetting the thing repeatedly from his chair in the corner.

"Alejandro, I've got it," she'd protest, dropping to the floor in exhaustion.

"No, you don't!" he'd scream. "You missed that sequence entirely. Now start from the top."

Again, and again, and again. At some point, he'd throw up his arms in frustration and allow her to stop. If she was lucky, she'd have time to grab a shower and a bite to eat before heading to the casino for more rehearsals with the entire troupe.

. . .

A NURSE ENTERED the room and shut off the alarm. "Sorry 'bout that," she said.

"Not a problem," Diana said, attempting to sit up. "I need to get out of here, anyway."

"Not yet, you don't," the kindly woman said. "Dr. Sopher will be in shortly, and he'll decide when you can leave."

Diana lay back down and looked out the window. To be truthful, she didn't have the energy to go anywhere. If this Dr. Sopher would let her, she'd hide out here for the rest of her life, or at least until last night's events became a faint, distant memory. For her and everyone else.

The nurse checked her blood pressure and pulse, then brushed the hair back from her face. "I'm sorry about Bobby," she said. "He was a good kid."

Diana's shoulders quavered, and tears filled her eyes. "Yes, he was," she managed.

"Don't worry," the nurse continued, handing Diana a box of tissues. "I won't let the cops in until you're ready to talk. Chief Vickers can wait til hell freezes over, for all I care." She leaned down to give Diana a quick hug, then pulled a blanket around her shoulders before raising the side rail. "I'll see about getting you another sedative so you can rest a bit easier." She turned and left the room.

Diana yawned and closed her eyes. Pulling the blanket over her head, she rolled onto her side. A sharp jab zinged the inside of her right elbow, and she gasped, more tears slipping down her cheek.

It took a few moments before she settled into a some-what restful position, but no sooner had she started to drift off that she realized she needed to use the bathroom. Resigned, she pushed herself up, then wiggled to the foot of the bed. She was careful not to yank the IV as she squeezed between the side railing and footboard. Dropping to the ugly green linoleum, she saw that her feet were adorned with floppy yellow socks dotted with tiny rubber dog paws. An equally fashionable cotton gown hung loosely on her body. She shook her head, then shuffled across the room with the IV trolley trailing behind her.

Sitting on the toilet, she was struck by a surge of nausea. Just how much had she had to drink last night? She'd lost track sometime after Bobby arrived at her apartment. She heard the nurse re-enter the room, followed quickly by a soft knock on the bathroom door.

"You okay in there?"

"Yes," Diana replied. "but I need a few more minutes."

"Take your time and come out when you're ready."

Which will be never, Diana wanted to tell her.

Moments later, the nurse knocked again, and Diana stood and flushed the toilet. The whoosh of water was annoyingly loud in her ears, and a wave of vertigo had her holding onto the sink. She turned on the faucet and splashed her face. The water was cold, and she filled her hands to drink some. It felt wonderful on her parched throat.

She dried her face with a white hand towel, then dared to check her reflection in the mirror. Dark, puffy circles beneath sunken eyes gave her a zombie-like appearance. Her blond curls were wild and tangled, and she ran her fingers through to tame them. They came away sticky. Examining herself in the mirror, she saw the deep red blotches dotting her head and throat. The gluey substance in her hair was blood. Bobby's blood.

"Oh, my God," she cried out, dropping to her knees.

The nurse yanked open the door and pulled the emergency cord hanging from the wall beside the toilet.

"No, no, no," Diana sobbed.

"Shh," the woman in scrubs whispered, rocking Diana in her arms.

Diana felt herself being lifted, then carried back to bed. Within minutes, a warm sensation spread through her arm, traveling from her elbow to her fingertips. The voices above her dimmed, then everything went black.

BART

BART WAS PERMITTED one call when he arrived at the police station, and he dialed Ben.

"Can't talk, Dad," the young man answered. "Sammy and I are playing *Hitman 3*. I'm kicking his butt."

"That's good, Ben," Bart said sadly. "Have fun, and I'll see you tomorrow."

IT WAS TOMORROW NOW, and he was still in the same drab room, waiting. For what, he wasn't sure, but he prayed they would release him soon. Other than the officer who brought him breakfast an hour ago, he hadn't seen or spoken to anyone since being processed and fingerprinted.

He sat up, and the cot creaked loudly under him. The damn room—was it a cell?—was hot. Stifling even, as if the thermostat was purposely set to make him sweat. He stripped off his long-sleeved shirt and used it to wipe his face. It smelled sour with a mix of sweat and vomit. He didn't remember throwing up, and he had a sudden thought that maybe the puke wasn't his. He walked over to the commode and looked in. A vague memory surfaced of his kneeling on the floor in front of it. Maybe it was his.

Keys jangled outside the door, and the detective from last night, a short, stocky Italian guy, pushed into the room. "Put your shirt back on and come with me," he ordered. Bart followed him into the dim hallway. He wasn't cuffed now, though he was last night. He rubbed the raw skin on his wrists.

"When can I talk to a lawyer?" he asked, but the man didn't reply.

He was led to a bigger room, with a square table and four chairs. "Sit," the detective ordered, and Bart did. " My name is Detective Mike Molino." He flashed his badge. "I was at the Michaud house last night, but since you went kind of bonkers, you might not remember me. A court-appointed attorney is on his way over, but I thought you and I could talk a little before he gets here. That okay with you?"

Bart nodded. He knew he was in trouble for breaking into Vanessa's house, but he'd had no choice. He had to be there. Surely, Molino would understand.

"So, Mr. Nixon—can I call you Bart?"

Bart nodded again.

"I'm a big fan of yours. If you ask me, you were the best winger that ever played for the Flyers."

Bart smiled weakly.

"Too bad for you, though, Michaud was on the same team. Am I right? It's like you and every other player were hosers in the eyes of the press. He was all show, though, grabbing all the glory while the damn sports writers lapped him up."

Bart stiffened, and he felt a sudden urge to pummel the detective.

"I knew, though," Molino continued. "Me and my friends from South Philly knew the score. We thought Michaud was good, sure, but he was too much of a pretty-boy for us. Too pretty for his own good, ask me. You and the right winger—what was his name—"

"Stein," Bart said. "Scottie Stein."

"Yeah, that's right," Molino said, grinning. "Now I remember. You and Stein made Michaud look good. Your combined talent's what made him a star."

Bart sat up straighter. *See*, he told himself.

"Is that why you did it?" the detective asked, his voice lower, conspiratorial. "You can tell me."

"Why I did what?" Bart replied, puzzled.

"Is that why you killed Vanessa? Because Roger glommed all your fame and fortune? You can't *still* be envious. Not after all these years."

Bart shook his head, confused. "No! I didn't kill her. He did!"

"Who? Michaud? He wasn't even in town that night," Molino said.

"I know, but he must've arranged it. I'm sure of it. He was the jealous one. Vanessa loved me, not him. She was pregnant with my baby, for God's sake!"

"Ah, now we're getting somewhere," Molino said. "You and Vanessa were sneaking around behind hubby's back. But then you went and knocked her up, and she told you to take a hike. It was fun while it lasted, but she was staying with Michaud in her big fancy house. She didn't need you anymore. For a lover or a baby daddy. Am I right?"

"No!" Bart shouted, slamming his fist on the table. "I didn't even know she was pregnant."

"But you just told me the baby was yours. How can you be so sure if she didn't even tell you she was expecting?"

Bart hung his head, and his heart stuttered in his chest. He didn't know. He wasn't sure.

"That's what I thought."

A knock sounded at the door, and a uniformed officer stuck his head in. "Court attorney's here, Detective."

Molino stood, knocking over his chair. Bart startled. "We'll chat again soon, Mr. Nixon." He strode from the room as fresh tears filled Bart's eyes.

61

JOE

JOE VICKERS WAS in his office, biding his time. Like so often in police work, he was at a standstill. Firstly, the man they'd brought in a short while ago, Michael Parker, was cooling his heels in an interrogation room down the hall while they waited to hear from authorities in Tennessee. No sense talking to him until they knew exactly who he was and where he came from.

Secondly, the Brunswick County forensics team had yet to complete their work in Miss Forrester's apartment. If a smoking gun—or knife, as likely applied in this case—was found, there was no sense in Joe's wasting valuable time spinning alternative scenarios.

And finally, Miss Forrester herself remained under observation at Dosher Hospital and had yet to be cleared for visitors, official or otherwise. Until she was, and until Joe had the opportunity to interview her, he wouldn't know if she held any clues about what happened to Bobby Moore.

Joe pulled a thin sheaf of papers across the desk. It was the dossier his deputy had pulled together on Diana Forrester. He had read it last night but didn't glean anything suspicious or unsettling from the sparse information. But with Bobby Moore's murder less than twenty-four hours after Branson had asked him to look into her, he would take the time now to read the findings more carefully.

Diana Forrester arrived in Southport a decade ago, moving into the apartment above the old pharmacy. Mort Baxter, the pharmacist, retired the following year, which was when Forrester rented out the first floor and opened her shop, the Seaside Siren. Baxter still owned the building, and according to him, his tenant never missed a single rental installment. She had, however, been late a few times, most recently just last month.

Forrester and the Seaside Siren were well-liked and respected in the community. The only complaint filed against the business was when she started selling CBD products a few years back. Vickers personally talked to her at the time, but as she wasn't trading in anything illegal, there was nothing he could do or say to stop her.

In addition to the CBD products, the shop sold essential oils, incense, and scented candles—*all woo-woo*, Joe thought —women's clothing, jewelry, accessories, paper goods, and coastal home accents.

Joe turned the page and read on. Personally, there were no citations or arrests against her, but it was well-known that she frequented the local bars and restaurants, especially those in the Yacht Basin. *No crime there*, Joe though. *She's hardly alone in those pursuits.*

Setting the papers aside, he leaned back in his chair and

stared up at the ceiling. He was tired and worried. For such a small, seemingly bucolic town, Southport had experienced more than its fair share of crime and tragedy. And Joe had only been on the job a few short years. He sure hoped this latest murder wasn't a harbinger of more to come. If it was, citizens and elected officials alike would be up in arms, threatening to again fire the town's entire police force. Joe's head, he knew, would be the first on the chopping block.

With his morning coffee burning a hole in his belly, he righted himself and picked up his phone.

62

JIMMY

"JOE," Jimmy said, answering his phone. "What's going on at your end?"

"Our new guest—one Michael Parker—is busy making himself at home, giving me the opportunity to reread the report on Diana Forrester. You look it over?"

"I did. There's nothing there that concerns me, but then it really doesn't tell us

much. What do you think?"

"I agree on both points. Mind you, we didn't delve too deeply yesterday, but given what's happened, we'll start over and dig deep. Any idea where we might begin?"

"No, I don't, but maybe Mary does."

"That's what I'm hoping. Is she available?"

"She can be," Jimmy said. "Should we come to the station?"

"Nah, sit tight, and I'll come to you. Give me ten minutes."

JIMMY OPENED the door and led Joe into his study. "Mary'll be down in a minute. She was lying down when you called and then hopped in the shower."

"That's fine," Joe said. "I'm in no hurry to get back to our Mr. Parker. The longer he marinates, the more forthcoming he's likely to be."

"You get any background on him yet?" Jimmy asked.

"No, but we will soon enough." He pulled out the file on Diana and laid it on the desk. Jimmy did the same with his copy.

"But as for Miss Forrester, my biggest question for Mary is what she knows of her past. Before she graced Southport with her presence."

"Hippie Chick was here years before us."

Joe raised his eyebrows. "Hippie Chick?"

"Yeah. That's what I took to calling her after she lit a joint at my dinner table."

"You didn't tell me that."

"I know I didn't. Rest assured it's not because I condone it. It was a couple years ago, and she's been on her best behavior since. At least around me. Last night, though, Mary confided that Forrester was carrying on with both Bobby Moore and Roger Michaud. 'Course I didn't realize it was our victim until this morning."

"What do you think happened in that apartment?" Joe asked.

"If you're asking me to speculate—" He glanced toward the door. "Never mind. Here's Mary now."

"Good to see you again, Joe. You wanted to talk to me?"

Her eyes were red-rimmed but glinted with a steely deter-
mination.

"About Diana," Jimmy said.

"How is she?" Mary asked.

"Last I heard," Joe replied, "she's sedated, and it might
be tomorrow before I can talk to her. While I wait, I figured
you might be able to answer a few burning questions."

"I'll do my best."

Jimmy leaned back in his chair and let Vickers take the
lead. While the two talked, he watched his wife. She was
unmistakably tired, and shaken. *But safe*, he added quickly.
He made a mental note to call Cathy later, to ask her to fly
down for the weekend. They hadn't seen Mary's daughter
since her Christmas break. Far too long for both women,
and for him, too. He loved Cathy like his own, and being so
far away was the only regret he had about relocating from
Pennsylvania.

"Well, Mary," Joe said, pocketing his Moleskin notebook. "I'm not sure if what you've told me has any bearing
on Bobby Moore's murder, but I thank you for answering
my questions."

"Of course," Mary said with a forlorn smile. "If I think
of anything else, I'll call."

"You do that, and I'll be sure to let you know when Miss
Forrester can have visitors or is released from the hospital."

"Speaking of that," Jimmy said, coming around his desk
as Mary and Joe stood. "Seeing as her apartment is a crime
scene, she'll need a place to stay. If it's okay with Mary, I'm
prepared to put her in one of our guest rooms."

An expression of disbelief crossed Mary's face, and she
grinned up at Jimmy. "Are you sure?"

"Yes," he said. "I doubt she'll bring any illegals into the

house," he gave Joe a knowing look, "so why not? A few days won't kill me."

"That's actually a great idea," Vickers said, glancing at his watch. "Until we know if and how this Parker fellow figures into Moore's death, I need to make sure Miss Forrester doesn't suffer the same fate.

Jimmy nodded. "We'll take good care of her, won't we, Mary?"

63

MONKEY

AFTER HE WAS ESCORTED to the patrol vehicle, Monkey watched from the backseat as the looky-loos swarmed into the street. At one point, the officer blasted his siren to disperse the crowd. Some of them looked real angry. Thankfully, the darkened rear window prevented them from seeing in.

Moments later, he found himself inside police head-quarters, a two-story white structure on the north end of town. A young officer, Zellers, his name tag read, led him to a sparsely furnished, windowless room.

"Have a seat, Parker, and the chief will be in to talk to you. Want something to drink in the meantime?"

"No," Monkey replied. When the door clicked shut, he plopped down in one of the bolted-to-the-floor chairs and sighed heavily. He was beyond exhaustion after his late night and the early morning, sirens-blaring wakeup call.

He laid his head on his hands and closed his eyes. *What a ginormous step backward*, he thought. After so many months of preparation, he was at another unanticipated roadblock. As if last night's fiasco hadn't been bad enough, here he was locked up yet again.

AFTER DEBATING what to do next, Monkey crept to the top of the stairs and put his ear to the apartment door. No more angry voices, no more slamming doors. He jiggled the handle, but it was locked. He pulled out his trusty credit card and slipped it between the strike plate and bolt. His breath quickened with the whispered release, and he slowly turned the knob. He nudged the door open slowly until it was stopped by a hotel-style swing bar. Monkey cursed silently, hoping the metallic tap hadn't been detected.

He peered through the two-inch crack, and an electric current shot through his veins. There she was, at last. She stood with her back to the door. The curly-haired whistler was behind her, his hands on her shoulders. "I'm sorry, Diana. Please don't cry. We're both drunk, so let's just go back to bed."

Monkey's heart sank. *Back to bed*. She had already let him violate her. *Of course, she had*. What else would they be doing up here all night? He had an urge to break down the door, strangle the kid with his bare hands, and grab her. He would throw her in his truck and drive right on out of this town. He closed his eyes and drew in a silent breath.

When he dared to look again, she had turned around. She was so pretty in the dim lighting, and Monkey felt his body stir. He wanted her so, so bad. How could she not feel him this near? He watched her for the briefest of moments, and then she moved out of his line of vision. The sudden sense of loss was like a thousand-pound weight settling on his chest.

He sank to the floor to ponder his limited options. What he needed was a knife to pry off the lock's faceplate, but after the trip to Philadelphia, he got rid of his.

He considered returning to the sidewalk and ringing the outside buzzer, posing as a cop like originally planned. She would come down to let him in, and he would whisk her away then. But what if lover boy came to the door instead? The kid sounded sloshed just now, his words slurred, but if he still managed to overpower Monkey, the gig would be up.

Impassioned noises came from inside the apartment, and he tugged the door shut to silence them. Rocking himself, he covered his ears and began to hum. The last thing he needed was to hear her screwing another man; his imagination was already more than his heart could handle.

NO, he corrected himself now, the last thing he needed was to be sitting in a police interrogation room. He had been here for what seemed like hours. His butt was numb from the cold metal chair, and he needed to take a leak something fierce. He walked to the door and banged. "Hey, let me out!"

He heard a brush on the outside of the door, and then it swung inward, smacking him on the forehead. "Ouch," he cried, stumbling back into the room.

"Sorry 'bout that, Mr. Parker," the tall, uniformed officer said. "Should we call a medic to check that out?"

"No!" Monkey replied angrily as he rubbed the lump forming above his left brow. "I've gotta take a leak."

"Sure thing, but this won't take long, so sit yourself back down." The man lowered himself into one of the chairs, then said, "In case you've forgotten, I'm Southport's police chief, Joe Vickers."

"Yeah, so?" Monkey remarked. "Tell me why I'm here!"

"Well, for starters, a very heinous crime has been committed against a citizen of my town, and you, sir, are a stranger in my town."

"Seems to me there are a lot of strangers here. Town's crawling with them."

"Very true. But most of our visitors don't go about frightening people—or worse—like I understand you specialize in."

"I didn't do nothing."

"In that case, why don't you tell me where you were between, say, eight p.m. and eight a.m. this morning."

"In my motel room."

"At the River Oaks Inn—right?"

Monkey snorted. "CIA's got nothin' on you."

"That's right. I also know you weren't in your room the entire night. You were seen going in and out at all hours."

"So, I stepped out. No crime in that."

"Where'd you go when you stepped out?"

Monkey looked at the ceiling and smiled. "Lemme see. I grabbed some grub at a joint on the water. Sat at the bar and ordered a burger and a beer."

"Which joint?"

Monkey tapped his finger to his upper lip. "The name escapes me, but it was painted bluish-green, or some such color."

"Fishy Fishy?"

"Sounds right."

"Alone?"

"Yes."

"What time was that?"

"I dunno. Seven, maybe."

"Where'd you go after?"

Monkey laughed. "I hightailed it back to the room to take a massive dump."

Vickers nodded. "I can appreciate that. But you still weren't yet ready to call it a night, were you? Where'd you head to next?"

"I ain't exactly sure."

A knock sounded at the door.

"Keep trying," Vickers said, stepping toward the door. He spoke quietly to an officer outside, then turned to Monkey. "Officer Zellers here will escort you to the men's room, then we'll pick up where we left off."

Back in the windowless room, Monkey's stomach grumbled. He hadn't eaten a thing since last night's burger, and he was feeling a little peaked. He also didn't remember if he took his meds this morning, given all the hoopla. When he last filled his prescription, the pharmacist warned him that he couldn't afford to miss a single dose. He knew that without being told. Those pills were the only thing keeping his demons at bay. Someone would need to bring them from the motel if Vickers had plans to hold him for long.

When Vickers returned, he was carrying a sheet of paper, which he laid face up on the table. Glancing at it, Monkey's heart sank.

"You've lived a troublesome life, Mr. Parker. Or should I call you *Monkey*?"

Monkey looked away, staring into the wide mirror covering the opposite wall.

The chief picked up the sheet of paper. "Let's see here. Possession with intent to distribute, burglary, armed robbery, assault with a deadly weapon. Hmm. Troublesome indeed. There's more. Shall I go on?"

"I know what I did, but I done my time."

"I see that, too. Fourteen years, five months. A good long time. Must've been tough being away from your family for that long. This here says you were married when you went in. Did your wife run out on you while you were inside?"

Monkey shoved out of his chair and limped to the mirror. His bum leg was aching worse with every minute he spent locked in the damn room. The man staring back at him looked tired—whacked, even. Purplish-black bags dipped beneath bloodshot eyes. *Is that me*, he wondered.

Vickers walked up behind him. "There's a reason you left Tennessee and came all this way, son. I'm not exactly sure what it is, but you need to know that we don't cotton to ne'er-do-wells around here, less of course they're our own. You being from a small town, I figure you understand that."

Monkey ignored him.

"How about this," the police chief said. "You and I both know how this is supposed to work. You're gonna get it off your chest sooner or later, so why not sit yourself back down and talk to me. You'll feel better, and if it's true what you say, that you've done nothing wrong, I'll personally escort you all the way to the Carolina-Tennessee state line."

Monkey closed his eyes, counting backward to center himself. He felt the man breathing down his neck, but he wouldn't be hurried. After a full minute of what his shrink had called mindful breathing, he opened his eyes. "I'm hungry. Bring me a turkey sandwich and a bag of chips. And a can of Coke. I'll talk when I'm done eatin'."

64

DIANA

IF SHE COULD HAVE STAYED comatose forever, Diana would have gladly done so. But this morning's nurse, too chipper by far, yanked open the blinds and announced, "Time to get up and out of here, Miss Diana."

Diana shielded her eyes from the sun's glare and moaned. "Why?"

"The doctor says there's no reason to keep you any longer. I removed your IV while you were still asleep, so there's nothing keeping you drowsy."

Diana checked her inner elbow. Sure enough, the needle and tube were gone, replaced by a smiley-face bandage covering a small square of gauze.

"And," the woman continued without stopping for air, "Chief Vickers has been parked outside your room for the last twenty minutes. He's itching to talk to you."

"I can't talk to anyone yet," Diana said, feeling the panic rise in her chest.

"Nonsense. You're talking to me, aren't you? And the chief's not the only one lighting up our switchboard. Miss Mary Branson called this morning, and a man named Roger called a short while ago. He sounds real nice, by the way. He told me to tell you he's catching a flight out of Philadelphia sometime today—I think that's what he said—and he'll see you this afternoon."

Diana closed her eyes and smiled. Roger was coming for her.

"You'll feel better once you're up, so, let's get to it." The nurse dropped the side rail and swept away the sheets covering Diana's legs. "A quick shower and some clean clothes—scrubs, mind you—and you'll be good as new."

A shower did sound good. Late yesterday, with the nurse's help, she managed a sponge bath, but it hadn't taken care of the sticky blood matted in her hair. She swore she could smell it on her. In resignation, she allowed the cheerful woman to help her out of bed and into the bathroom.

"Need me to help?" the nurse asked after starting the water.

"No, I think I can manage on my own."

"I'll be standing right outside if you need me."

As Diana allowed the warm, albeit meager, flow of water to wash over her, she felt herself slowly coming awake. Whatever drugs they had given her yesterday, she'd love to get her hands on some. She'd been lost in a dreamless sleep for hours and hours. Sadly, that sleep was no longer sheltering her, and with Chief Vickers chomping at the bit to talk to her, she needed to clear her head.

When the water turned cold, she shut it off and stepped

carefully onto the bathmat. Once dry, she pulled on the cotton drawstring pants and top hanging from a hook behind the door. The get-up was too big, but cinched tightly, it fit the bill. As soon as Vickers left, she would call Mary and ask her to bring over something more fashionable. The two women were about the same size, and anyway, it would only be until she got back to her apartment.

"Miss Diana, you good to come out?"

Diana opened the door. "I need to dry my hair."

The nurse stepped past her and retrieved a small comb from the plastic toiletry bin. "The hospital doesn't provide blow-dryers—sorry 'bout that. But why don't I comb it out for you, then we'll tie it back." She led Diana to the bed and stood behind her as she worked on the mess of the wet tangles.

Diana's shoulders sagged as the woman teased the comb through her hair. It was soothing, like Mama's loving touch.

"There you go," the nurse said. "Now go sit in that chair over there, and I'll let the chief in."

Diana hesitated, then moved to the mustard yellow chair tucked under the window. The vinyl cushion squeaked as she sat down, and a shiver travelled from her scalp to her toes.

"Miss Forrester, hello," Chief Vickers greeted as he entered the room. "How're you feeling this morning?"

"Alright, I guess." Her voice wavered.

"That's good to hear. I, um, I'm sorry about Mr. Moore. Bobby. He was a good man, and the entire Southport community is in mourning."

Diana felt her insides clench. She attempted a thank-you, but the words wouldn't come. She nodded instead and blinked back tears.

The chief glanced around the room, then held up his

finger. "Hold on just a sec." He hurried from the room, and a few moments later, he rolled in a black desk chair, closing the door behind him. After situating himself in front of Diana, he opened a small leather-bound notebook.

"Let's try again. I realize this has been an especially traumatizing time for you, but I think it's best to get right to the point. What happened in your apartment Tuesday night into Wednesday morning?"

"I don't—" Diana started, then shook her head. "You know, do you think I could get a cup of tea? Or coffee, maybe? My head's a little fuzzy, from all the drugs, you know, and maybe some caffeine would help me."

"Sure," Vickers said, a pained look on his face. "Let me ask the charge nurse. I'll be right back."

When he left the room, Diana squirmed in the uncomfortable chair. She felt a draft from the window, cool against her wet head. She got up and grabbed the blanket from the bed. Back in the chair, she curled her legs beneath her.

The chief returned with a Styrofoam cup. He handed it to Diana, then sat back down.

"Thank you," she whispered, taking a careful sip.

"So, where was I?" he asked, flipping open the notebook. "That's right. You were about to tell me what you remember from the other night."

"Chief, I've tried, but I can't much of anything. It's, it's like the whole night's stuck inside my head and won't come out." She tapped the fingers of her free hand against her forehead. "Like when you wake up from a dream, and you try to remember the details, but they're gone."

"That happens to me all the time," the chief said. "It can be frustrating, I know. Why don't we try this. As painful as it might be, I want you to think about Bobby. Focus on something he might've said or done that night, and maybe the rest will come back to you."

Diana dropped her chin to her chest. After a few moments, she looked up, shaking her head. "I must have had way too much to drink because I don' remember a thing. Not even what he was wearing. But I do, kind of, remember parts of the next morning. Wednesday."

"Then, start there. We can always work our way backward."

"I'll try." She took another sip from the cup, then closed her eyes. "Okay. I woke up in bed, and it wasn't light out yet. Bobby was lying beside me, and I thought he was sleeping. My head hurt so bad, and I rolled over to spoon against him. That usually helps me relax enough to fall back to sleep." Her voice faltered.

"I know this is tough," the chief said, "but you're doing good. Keep going."

"When I touched him, he was cold, which was strange. He's usually so hot-blooded. You've probably seen him around town wearing shorts and flip flops when it's thirty degrees out—right? Anyway, I didn't think much of it, but I reached down to the bottom of the bed and pulled up the blanket. I tucked it around him, and after a while, I must have fallen asleep. When I woke the second time, it was light out. That's when I saw it." She shuddered.

"What did you see, Miss Forrester?"

"Blood. Everywhere. I tried to wake up Bobby. I shook him real hard, but he didn't move, and he didn't open his eyes. He must have already..." A sob escaped her throat.

"Already what?" Vickers prompted, taking the tea from her shaking hands.

"Already died."

Tears streamed down her face, and Vickers handed her

a box of tissues from the bedside tray. She blew her nose and swiped away the tears. Once she composed herself, he scooted forward in the chair, his face inches from hers. When their eyes met, he asked, "Diana, what happened to Bobby?"

She looked away, twisting the tissue in her hands. "I don't know," she said. "Believe me, I wish I did."

The chief took her hand to still it. "Who else was in your apartment that night?"

She shook her head. "I don't know that, either. There had to be someone, but I can't remember who it was or how he got in." She pulled her hand away and covered her mouth.

"You need to try real hard to remember."

"I want to help. I really do."

"I know you do. Maybe the best thing is to get you out of this hospital. Have you rest up somewhere quiet where you're not being poked and prodded every waking minute."

"Rest? Chief, do you really think I can rest when there's a murderer on the loose?"

"Maybe not, but there is a chance he's no longer on the loose."

"What do you mean? Have you arrested someone?"

Vickers nodded. "We do have someone in custody. He's currently being housed at the Brunswick County Detention Center."

"Then why all the questions for me?"

"I wouldn't be doing my job, Miss Forrester, if I didn't investigate every possible angle. And of course, our suspect insists he didn't do kill Bobby. If we're going to find justice, we'll need your testimony. In court. You're our only witness. Bobby's only witness."

Diana swallowed hard. "Can I ask who he is? The suspect?"

"I'll tell you, but bear in mind that he is innocent, as he claims, until proven guilty."

"I understand."

"His name is Michael Parker. He's an ex-con from Tennessee."

Diana felt the blood drain from her face, and a deafening roar sounded in her ears.

"Are you all right, Miss Forrester?" Vickers reached out to her. "Should I call the nurse?"

Diana felt like she'd just been dropped into a deep pit. "Oh, my God. I don't believe it."

"Believe what? Do you know this Parker?"

She nodded. "If it's who I think it is, yes. At least I used to."

"Care to tell me?" Vickers prompted as he pocketed his notebook.

"He's my husband," she whispered.

65

ROGER

ROGER'S PLANE TOUCHED DOWN, and he reached under the seat in front of him to pull his leather bag onto his lap. While they taxied to the terminal, he stared blindly out the window, but instead of the marsh grasses bordering the tarmac, the events of the last thirty-six hours played out before him.

Bart Nixon was under arrest for Vanessa's murder. His motive was still in question, but Roger suspected that Vanessa had spurned his advances, and he snapped. The man had always been unstable, even claiming at one point that he was responsible for Roger's stellar career, which, of course, was a bunch of hooey. In hindsight, he should never have brought him on as a business partner. Sure, he was good with the employees, and a whiz with the books, but any HR person or bookkeeper worth his salt would have proved better in the long run.

With Nixon behind bars, the frigging DA had sent a deputy to remove Roger's ankle monitor. The uniformed man brought a release form for his signature, and once that was taken care of, all charges, including the earlier parole violation, were rendered null and void. He was a free man.

His first order of business was to find Diana, to tell her the good news. As soon as the deputy left, he tried again to reach her, but she didn't pick up. Something had to be wrong, and he considered hopping on the next plane out, but Leonard had convinced him to wait. He continued to try her cell phone throughout the afternoon, and by the time he dialed the Southport PD to request a welfare check, he was out of his mind with worry. It was then that he learned she was in the hospital. The desk sergeant couldn't give him any details, and when he called the hospital, they refused to tell him anything either. He kicked himself for not leaving earlier.

After spending a sleepless night, he was on his way to the airport in the back seat of an Uber when he answered a call from the Southport chief of police, a man by the name of Vickers.

"Mr. Michaud," the cop said, "I'm wondering if you have a moment to answer a few questions?"

"Is this about Diana?" Roger asked. "How is she?"

The chief ignored his question, asking instead, "Where are you?"

Confused, he replied, "At this very moment, I'm heading to the Philadelphia airport."

"Any chance you're flying down our way?"

"Yes," Roger confirmed.

"In that case, rather than talk over the phone, would you be kind enough to come by the station when you get here?"

"Frankly, Chief Vickers, I've had my fill of law enforcement these past two weeks, so unless it's a matter of life or death, I'd rather not."

"I can understand that," Vickers said, "but I'm going to insist."

Roger pulled the phone away from his ear and stared at it. *WTF?* "Then, Chief Vickers, you need to tell me what's so godawful important that you're my first stop instead of the hospital to see my girlfriend."

He heard Vickers clear his throat. "I appreciate your concern for Miss Forrester, but I'm afraid my matter takes precedence."

"I doubt that very much," Roger said.

"Let me explain something," Vickers said. "A local man has been murdered in Southport, and I'm looking to you to provide some insight as why that happened."

A murder in Southport? This is getting more bizarre by the minute. "Who was it?" Roger asked. "Someone I know?"

"Possibly."

A sudden, sickening thought occurred to him. "Does this have to do with Diana being in the hospital? Tell me, dammit!"

"HIPPA laws prevent the release of that information, Mr. Michaud," Vickers explained, "but, the sooner we talk, the sooner you can visit her."

After ending the call with Chief Vickers, Roger phoned the hospital. He left a message for Diana that he was on his way, feeling like a knight in shining armor charging to the rescue of his damsel in distress.

While he waited in the airline's VIP lounge, he searched the internet for details of the murder, but it wasn't mentioned in any of the major media outlets. When he departed Philadelphia, he still had no clue of who the murder victim was or why Diana was in the hospital.

By the time the plane taxied up to the arrival gate, Roger's insides were coiled so tightly that he felt as if his lungs and heart were being squeezed with every breath. When the flight attendant bid him a pleasant afternoon, he barely acknowledged her flirtatious tone.

66

MARY

MARY WALKED into the hospital room to find Diana sitting at the window, staring out at nothing.

"Diana?" she said quietly.

Seeing her friend, tears sprang to Diana's eyes, and she cried, "Oh, Mary, Bobby's gone."

"I know, I know," was all Mary could say without choking on her own tears.

After a few moments, Diana allowed Mary to help her change out of the hospital scrubs into the black leggings and flowing top Mary had brought. *Black for mourning*, Mary thought but didn't say.

At the house, Mary led Diana to the first-floor guest room, insisting that she lie down.

"Mary, I've been sleeping for two solid days. I need to do something other than lie down."

"Fine," Mary said, tucking a faux fur throw around her friend's lap. "Can I get you a cup of tea?"

"Honestly? I'd rather have a glass of wine."

Mary paused. "Think that's wise with all those sedatives in your system?"

"I don't care," Diana admitted. "If I fall down, I won't fall far."

Mary smiled. "Okay. I'll bring one in. In the meantime, here's the remote. Make yourself comfortable."

Jimmy met her in the kitchen. "How is she?"

"Okay, I guess. Likely cried out at this point." She reached into the cabinet for a wineglass, and Jimmy gave her a questioning look.

"Not for me. Diana asked for some."

Jimmy shook his head. "I should probably go get more, then. If she's drinking and here longer than a day or two, our stock will be gone in no time."

"I suppose, but before you go, let's decide on dinner."

"I'll figure something out when I'm at Food Lion. You okay here by yourself with her?"

"Yes, dear," Mary said. "Take your time, and maybe give Joe a call to see if there's anything new to report."

Mary carried the wine and a small plate of cheese and crackers down the back hallway, past the sunroom that served as their home gym. She found Diana staring mindlessly at a rerun of *Gilmore Girls*. She set the tray on the ottoman, then said, "This was always one of Cathy's favorite shows."

Diana started to say something but stopped herself.

"What is it, honey? Do you want to talk?"

"Not really."

"I understand, but I'm here when you're ready."

"I know, and I thank you," Diana said, downing the wine in one long swallow. She held out her glass. "I could use more wine, though, if you don't mind."

"Of course," Mary said, taking the empty glass.

She returned a few minutes later to find Diana's eyes closed. She moved the tray of wine and crackers to the dresser, muted the TV, then stepped from the room, closing the door.

When Jimmy came in, she put her finger to her lips, following him out to the garage to collect the wine and groceries. When everything was put away, she trailed him to his study.

"Did you talk to Joe?" she asked, taking a seat.

"Yep. Michael Parker maintains his innocence, but given the circumstances, the judge denied bail."

"I'm sick thinking how close I let him get to me," Mary said, feeling nauseous.

"Me too, honey." He squeezed her shoulder, then sat down across the desk. "He confirmed to Joe that he came to town looking for Diana."

"How does he know her?"

Jimmy looked pensive as he stroked his chin. "Turns out they're married, Mary."

"What? I had no idea Diana was married before."

"Yeah. According to Joe, they married just out of high school, and at some point, she ran off. Parker tried to find her, but he got himself in trouble not long after and went away to prison. They never divorced, and once he was out, he started looking for her again."

Mary cringed. "How long ago was this? She's been here for years."

"That, I don't know," Jimmy said. "Anyway, the state

bureau of investigations is now involved and working to piece together what happened at the apartment."

"Does Joe have any insight?"

"No, and Hippie Chick told him she doesn't remember much of anything. Did she tell you anything?"

"No," Mary said, shaking her head. "Not yet anyway."

"Maybe she will in time."

"Is that normal?" Mary asked, her concern for Diana growing. "Her memory loss, I mean."

"In traumatic situations, sure, it's been known to happen. But, Mary, it's no surprise that she and Bobby Moore had extremely high blood alcohol levels, plus significant traces of THC in their systems."

"I know she's a partier. But Jim, if she drank enough to black out, she may never remember."

"That leaves forensics." His phone rang, and he checked the caller ID. "Joe again." He swiped open the call.

Mary zoned out while the two men talked. She hadn't slept well the last two nights, and she doubted she would for the duration of Diana's stay.

Jimmy set his phone on the desk and shook his head.

"What?"

"Michaud's on his way from Philadelphia. He knows Diana was in the hospital, but not the details."

Mary shrugged. "George told us he was cleared in his wife's murder. Guess he's free to travel again."

"And I said as much to Joe. Apparently, Michaud didn't know about Moore's murder and is clueless about Diana's involvement."

"He won't be for long," Mary said.

"I just don't see it," Jimmy said.

"What?" Mary asked.

"What Hippie Chick has that some guys find irresistible."

"And it's a good thing you don't, buddy," Mary teased, grinning for the first time in days. "And if I were you, I wouldn't look too hard to find it."

"Never even crossed my mind," he teased, arching his eyebrows.

67

ROGER

"I UNDERSTAND you've been cleared in your wife's murder," Chief Vickers said as he sat opposite Roger in the station's small interrogation room. "Sorry for your loss, by the way."

Roger nodded. "Thank you, and yes."

"They've arrested your business partner for her murder, huh?"

"That's what I was told." He checked his phone, then said, "Chief, why don't we save us both some time and cut to the chase. I know I'm not here to talk about my wife or my business partner."

"Maybe not directly, no. But you are here because Bobby Moore was murdered earlier this week in the apartment of your girlfriend, Diana Forrester. I don't know about you, but I find it disturbing that he and your wife were murdered within weeks of each other."

Roger felt immediately sick to his stomach. "What? You've got to be joking."

"I am not. I am deadly serious."

"Are you accusing me of something?"

"No, sir, but I can't help wondering if there's some connection we're not seeing here. If, maybe, that connection is you."

Roger felt his face burning. "Fuck that. You're grasping at thin air if you think I had anything to do with Bobby's murder. I was five hundred miles away the night it happened. On house detention, no less."

"That's what I was told, so I might be grasping at thin air, as you put it. Did you know Miss Forrester and Mr. Moore were intimately involved?"

Roger felt a stream of sweat slip down his back. Of course, he knew, but in the past six months or so, he had come to believe that Bobby was no longer in the picture. Diana was available to see him every time he came to town, and they hadn't run into the kid at the bars since sometime last fall.

"Mr. Michaud, did you?" Vickers's voice interrupted his thoughts.

"I did," he admitted, swallowing hard. "But I was under the impression she'd ended it with him."

"Did she tell you that?"

"No, I just assumed."

The chief tapped his pen against the table. "I see."

Roger stood and began to pace the small room.

"Were you jealous of him? He was quite a bit younger than you."

Roger shook his head. "Hell no."

"You sure?"

"No. I mean, yes, I'm sure." He grabbed his bottle of

water and took a swig.

"Okay. Let me ask you something else. Do you think Miss Forrester was seeing other men? Besides Mr. Moore?"

Roger was getting pissed. "If I didn't know she was still seeing Bobby, how do you expect me to know if she was carrying on with other men? It's obvious she was keeping secrets from me, so why not just ask her?"

"I will when I talk to her again."

"What are you waiting for? If anyone knows who had reason to kill him, she does."

"You're probably right. Thing is, when I spoke to her in the hospital earlier this morning, I believed we had the murderer in custody."

"But you no longer believe that?"

"At the moment, Mr. Michaud, I'm not sure what I believe. Let's just say our investigation is ongoing."

"Is Diana in danger?" Roger asked, feeling a tug of concern beneath his consternation.

"She's in good hands, so not likely. Do you know Mary Branson?"

"Diana's friend?"

"Yes. Miss Forrester was released from the hospital this afternoon and is staying at the home of Mrs. Branson and her husband. He's retired law enforcement, and they're keeping a watchful eye out for her." He slid a business card across the table. "Miss Forrester's cell phone was destroyed the night of the murder, but that's Jim Branson's number if you want to reach out."

Roger's mind was spinning. He picked up the card and slipped it into his shirt pocket.

"You heading over to your house on Bald Head tonight?"

"After what you've told me, I think I will. Are we done here?"

"We're done, but I would like you to think about all this. Someone knows the identity of the person who killed Bobby. Whether or not they realize they have this knowledge, or they're simply holding out on me, I will learn the truth. So, Mr. Michaud, if anything comes to mind that might help with my investigation, please call me right away."

"I will, but I sincerely doubt I'll think of anything."

"You never know," the chief said. "Something may pop into your head when you least expect it."

Roger shook the man's hand, then returned to his car. As he drove toward the ferry terminal, the pain in his stomach steadily worsened. He was such a fool. But if he was honest with himself, Diana wasn't to blame. It was all on him and had been from the start. He was the married one when they first hooked up, not her. And he never promised or intended to be faithful, even after he suggested they go steady. What did it matter that she was sleeping with Bobby? Hadn't he jumped right back in the sack with Darla? There was no denying it, he and Diana were perfect for each other.

As he waited in line for the ferry, he began to feel better. He pictured Diana lying next to him on the beach. Making love. Dancing on the deck. Somehow, they would work through this. He pulled out his phone and dialed the number for Jim Branson.

68

DIANA

WHEN DIANA AWOKE, the flickering glow beyond her still-closed lids tricked her into thinking she was lying in the hospital with sunlight pouring across her face. But the sounds and smells were different here, and she opened her eyes and smiled when she recognized Mary's guest room.

She stretched and yawned. Her nap had been a good one, especially with the added benefit of the sedative she swallowed after Mary stepped from the room. Glancing around, she noticed a full glass of wine on the tray atop the dresser. She unraveled herself from the throw and padded over to it, sighing as the liquid slipped down her throat.

A knock sounded at the door, and Mary peeked in. "You're up."

"Just," Diana said. "Found the wine you left. Thanks."

"You were out cold when I came back in. Sleep well?"

"Very."

"We're about to put dinner on the table. Are you hungry?"

Diana thought a moment. "I could stand to eat something."

"Take your time, and we'll keep it warm. You should find everything you need in the bathroom."

"Thanks, Mary. I'll be just a minute."

SITTING at Mary and Jimmy's table, Diana thought back to the first time she joined them here for dinner. Her antics that night were the reason Jimmy still didn't like her much. Lucky for him, there was zero chance of a repeat tonight. Her pot stash had no doubt been confiscated during the investigation into— She stopped herself mid-thought.

"I got a call from a friend of yours while you were napping," Jimmy told her.

She looked at him, puzzled. "I'm sorry?"

"Roger Michaud called about an hour ago. On my cell. Asked me to tell you he'll see you tomorrow."

"Aw," she whined. "I wanted to see him today."

"He planned to come by," Jimmy said, "but he got waylaid at the police station talking to Chief Vickers. He was heading to the Bald Head ferry when he called."

Diana felt a flash of ire. "You should have woken me."

"But you needed your rest," Mary said, rubbing her arm soothingly.

Diana shook her head and took a deep breath. "No, you're right. How'd he sound?"

Jimmy shrugged. "Given that I've never spoken to him before, I'm probably not the best person to answer that."

"I'm sure he's worried about you," Mary offered. "You can call him on my cell after we eat if you want."

"Thanks, Mary. I think I will."

"HEY, THERE," she whispered when Roger answered. She was curled in a wicker chair on Mary and Jimmy's front porch, a glass of wine on the table beside her. A warm breeze drifted in from the salt marsh across the street, and the smell of plough mud was unmistakable.

"How are you feeling?" he asked. He sounded a little drunk.

"Tired. Fuzzy."

"But otherwise, you're okay?"

"Yes."

"That's good to know."

"I suppose. I heard you talked to Chief Vickers. What did you tell him?"

"About?"

"I don't know. I guess he told you about Bobby."

"Uh-huh."

She heard ice clinking against crystal and pictured him sipping Scotch in front of the fireplace. She would give anything to be sitting next to him.

Diana gulped some wine for courage. "Are you mad at me?"

"I don't really have a right to be," he said.

"I never meant to hurt you."

He was quiet for a moment, and she was afraid he'd hung up.

"Roger, talk to me."

"What do you want me to say, Diana?"

"I don't know. Tell me what else Vickers said."

"He thinks I know something that will help with his investigation."

"Why does he think that? I mean, you weren't even in town."

"He knows. They have someone in custody already, but he isn't one hundred percent certain he's the killer."

"What do you mean he's not sure? He arrested the man outside my building. He has to be the one who murdered Bobby."

"Do you know this guy? I mean, there must be a reason he broke into your apartment. And then to kill the kid. My God, Diana. He could have killed you, too."

"But he didn't." She sighed deeply. "Roger, can we talk about this later? I'm getting really tired."

"Sure."

"Will I see you tomorrow?"

"If you want to."

"Of course, I do. Maybe I can go back to Bald Head with you." Her voice choked. "I wish I'd never left."

Roger sighed. "Me too. But the chief says you're safe at the Bransons, at least til they're sure they arrested the right guy."

"I guess. Will you call me when you wake up?"

"Yes. Good night, Diana."

"Wait, don't hang up," she said.

"What?"

"Mary told me they arrested someone for Vanessa's murderer. I'm so, so glad."

"Yeah, me too. I just wish.... Oh, never mind."

"We'll talk, Roger. I promise. We'll get past this."

"I hope you're right." He disconnected the call.

Diana finished off her wine, then allowed the tears to fall.

69

MARY

MARY'S NERVES were on edge, and when she dropped her brow pencil for the second time, she cursed.

"What's the matter?" Jimmy asked, coming into the bathroom.

"I'm jittery."

"Why?"

"I don't exactly know," she said. "It's not like we haven't had guests for dinner before."

"It's not a party, Mary."

"I know that, Jim. I'm still nervous."

He walked behind her and kneaded her shoulders. As the knots unkinked, she felt herself relaxing.

"Better?"

"Mm-hm. Thanks."

"What time is Michaud getting here?"

"Diana said around six, so you have exactly thirty minutes to shower and dress."

He opened the shower door, then asked, "How's she doing? Is she as fidgety as you?"

"More so, I think."

"I would be, too, if I had to explain to my lover how the dead body of my other lover ended up in my bed." He rubbed his palm together. "This should be fun."

"Please don't embarrass her," Mary pleaded. "Or me."

"I won't," he said. "I'm fairly certain Hippie Chick will take care of that all on her own."

"Let's hope not," Mary said. "Are you sorry we invited her to stay with us?"

"No," Jimmy said, stepping into the shower stall. "I only wish I'd thought to hide a video recorder in the kitchen."

Mary shook her head, then left the bathroom to dress. She selected a black jumpsuit with a Western-style belt and booties which, she was hoping, would lasso Jimmy's attention long enough to give Diana and Roger time to talk without an audience.

Because Diana's apartment was still off-limits, she had loaned her a silky blue wrap dress and a pair of beaded ballet slippers. Not something her friend typically wore, but she looked lovely, nonetheless.

Jimmy had ordered takeout from Castucci's, which he picked up a short while ago. As Mary laid out the final place setting, the doorbell rang. Diana, who was waiting nervously at the island, startled, sloshing wine onto the countertop.

"Sorry, Mary," she apologized as she reached for a napkin.

"No worries," Mary said, taking the napkin from her hand. "Go answer the door."

Diana grimaced, then asked, "Do I look okay?"

"You look fetching," Jimmy said, coming down the stairs. "But if you're not going to greet our guest, should I?"

Diana gave him the evil eye and strode past him.

Mary joined Jimmy in the foyer in time to watch Diana fling herself against Roger. Pulling Jimmy back to the kitchen, she said, "Let's give them some privacy."

"Aww," he whispered, "you're no fun."

A few moments later, Diana and Roger came into the room. Diana was holding onto him for dear life, but Roger looked decidedly uncomfortable. "Mary, Jimmy, this is my dear friend, Roger Michaud. Roger, you remember Mary, don't you?"

"I do," Roger said, although Mary doubted his veracity. "And you must be Jim. We talked yesterday." The two men shook hands.

Diana quickly poured a glass of wine for Roger, handing it to him before refilling her own. It would be her third glass, Mary noted, although a few drops from the second had spilled when the doorbell rang.

"To friends," Diana toasted enthusiastically.

Roger smiled awkwardly and held up his glass before taking a sip.

"Pull up a stool, Roger." Mary suggested. "We've got appetizers before dinner." She retrieved the tray of antipasti from the fridge and set it on the island.

"This looks great," Roger said. "I'm starving."

"Good," Jimmy said, snagging a toothpick-skewered ball of mozzarella. "There's enough here for a small army."

70

MONKEY

MONKEY LAY on the rickety cot, staring up at a buzzing fluorescent fixture hanging from the ceiling. The flickering light was headache-inducing, but he couldn't look away. It, and the small, cinder-block cell, reminded him of Mountain City. Despite the fourteen plus years lost while incarcerated there, it had been his home. The similarities to this place were comforting in some small way. Difference now was he hadn't done nothing to get locked up this time.

"Parker," a voice called out as the door slid open. "Come with me."

Monkey blinked, then rolled off the mattress, a crooked smile lighting up his face. "About time," he said, holding out his wrists for the man to cuff.

"What's your hurry?" the corrections officer asked. He was a beefy man with arms the size of Monkey's thighs.

"I shoulda never been locked up. You ain't got nothin' to hold me on."

"Yeah. You and everyone else," the man replied.

He was led to an interrogation room, slightly larger than the one at the Southport station. He recognized Chief Vickers sitting beside a stern-looking woman wearing a dark suit. The public defender Monkey met earlier sat on the opposite side of the table.

"Take a seat, Mr. Parker," the woman ordered.

"What's going on?" he asked the court-appointed attorney.

"Shh," the man scolded under his breath.

"Mr. Parker," the woman addressed him again. "I'll get right to the point. Your fingerprints were found on the door-knob to the apartment above the Seaside Siren on South Howe Street in Southport. The very apartment where Robert Moore was murdered Tuesday night. What, sir, were you doing there?"

Monkey shook his head. "Before I say anything, I need to know who the heck you are."

"Just answer her," his attorney ordered with teeth clenched.

"No, he's right. I should have introduced myself," the woman said. "I am Mavis Peele, Assistant District Attorney for Brunswick County,"

"Nice to meet you," Monkey said with a smile and a nod.

"Very well, now that the niceties are out of the way, I'll ask you again. What were you doing inside the aforementioned building on Tuesday night of this week?"

"Just so we're clear, you might have proof I was there, but you have zero proof I was there Tuesday night." Monkey looked askance at his attorney. "Some defense attorney you are," he muttered under his breath.

"No, you are correct on that point," the DA agreed. "Care to tell us what night you were there?"

"I already told the chief here."

"You did, Mr. Parker," the chief confirmed, "but for the benefit of ADA Peele, please repeat your story."

"Waste of time, seeing how I done nothing wrong," Monkey complained. "I was looking for my wife."

"Diana Forrester?" Peele asked.

"You might know her as Diana Forrester, but truth be told, she's Ina Rose Parker. Mrs. Michael Parker."

"I see. And you were there looking for her."

"Isn't that what I just said?"

"How did you gain access to the building?" the woman asked.

"The door was open, and I walked on in."

"And once inside, what then?"

"I climbed the steps and sat on the floor."

"Mr. Parker, we have proof you did more than just sit. You touched the door handle."

"So, what if I did?"

"I'm simply trying to understand your actions. First, you drove all the way from Tennessee to Southport, North Carolina in an effort to find your wife. Once in Southport, you located your wife and gained access to the building that houses her apartment. You walked up the stairs inside that building and, at some point, you touched the handle of the door to her apartment. You did not knock on said door, but instead, you sat on the floor in the stairwell outside her apartment. Do I have that right so far?"

"Yes. I was gonna knock, but I heard voices inside." At the memory, Monkey swallowed back an urge to puke.

"Whose voices?"

"Ina Rose and some man."

"Did you hear what they were saying?"

"Only bits and pieces."

"Why did their conversation, of which you heard only bits and pieces, stop you from knocking? From letting your wife know you were there? I mean, in my humble opinion, it's the least you could do given how far you'd come to find her."

"Wouldn't have done no good. I was too late." He felt the tops of his ears burning. The sick feeling in his belly intensified.

"Ah," the woman said. "I get it now. You were too late to stop your wife from having sex with this other man." She said the word *sex* as though it were nothing. "And that upset you?"

"Course it did," Monkey snapped. The heat inside him threatened to explode, and when the PD elbowed him, he turned to glare at the man.

Vickers poured a glass of water and slid it across the table. "Calm down, Mr. Parker, and tell us what you did next."

"I already told you, Chief. I left."

The DA smacked the tabletop. "You expect us to believe that you did nothing? Your wife is this close," she held her thumb and forefinger a centimeter apart. "You realize she's having sex with another man, yet you simply walk away. In my experience, a tougher man would've broken down that door and put a stop to whatever was going on behind it. Maybe even beat the living crap out of the guy screwing his wife."

"Shut up!" Monkey shouted, pushing out of his chair.

The CO rushed into the room, but Peele waved him off

as she addressed the public defender. "Please control your client, or I'll have the officer here take him back to his cell."

The PD held up his hands in defeat.

Monkey took a deep breath, then exhaled slowly. When he regained control, he sat down. Closing his eyes, he said, "I did want to pummel him, to drag Ina Rose out by her hair. But it wouldn't have changed nothin'. Not that night anyway. I figured to come back later when Ina Rose was alone."

"And that's why you were outside the building Wednesday morning," Vickers said.

Monkey nodded. "I was there to take Ina Rose home with me, where she belongs."

The DA stood. "I think I've heard quite enough." She turned and left the room.

Vickers smiled at Monkey, then followed the DA out.

"What now?" Monkey asked his attorney.

"Damned if I know," the man said, wiping sweat from his brow.

71

DIANA

DIANA WAS FEELING relaxed and more like herself. It had been awkward at first. Roger barely kissed her when she threw herself into his arms, and he hardly looked at her for quite a while after. But a few glasses of Jimmy's delicious wine loosened everyone up, and the entire atmosphere changed for the better.

She beamed at Roger now, sitting beside her at the table. He was so handsome, and, it turns out, quite the entertaining conversationalist. Of course, she always loved listening to him, but she'd never seen him in a social setting like this. Usually, when they were in the company of others, it was at a bar or restaurant. Tonight was different, more intimate.

Mary was, as always, a gracious hostess, and Jimmy seemed quite loose, laughing as Roger regaled him with tales of his glory days playing professional hockey. The two men talked on and on and on, and by the time the antipasti was devoured, Diana was more than ready to change the topic of conversation.

Mary brought out pans of penne a la vodka, sausage and peppers, and the old standby, spaghetti and meatballs. "Something for everyone," she announced. "Fix a plate, then take a seat at the table."

Yes, her friend made everything appear effortless. Diana envied her poise and grace. She also envied the way Jimmy looked so lovingly at his wife, even when she didn't see him doing so. Diana witnessed it several times, and she wondered if Roger ever looked at her that way. Like he was proud of her.

She picked at a meatball, then laughed at something Jimmy said. She had no idea what it was, but since everyone else found it amusing, she joined right in.

"This is so much fun," she gushed. *Did I say that aloud?* Mary was nodding and smiling at her, so she must have.

"It is," Roger said, putting his arm over the back of her chair and stroking her hair. "Thanks again for inviting me."

"Of course," Mary said, getting up to grab another bottle of wine.

Thank God, Diana thought, holding out her empty glass. Mary filled it, then offered to fill Roger's, but he covered it with his free hand and shook his head. "Thanks, but I've had more than enough."

As the conversation continued on, Mary motioned for Diana to join her at the island. "Please let Roger know he's more than welcome to stay here," she whispered. "If he wants to drink more, that is."

"Why don't you," Diana suggested. "It'll mean more coming from you."

"Okay," Mary agreed. She then turned to the men.

"Who's ready for dessert?"

"Oh, God," Roger groaned, patting his belly. "I couldn't possibly. But what do you have?"

"Cannolis and tiramisu."

"I'll take a small one of each," Jimmy said as he pushed back from the table. "Sit back down, Diana. Mary and I have this."

As he and Mary prepared coffee and dessert, Mary said casually, "Roger, we have after-dinner liqueurs here. Please feel free to add some to your coffee or pour yourself a snifter. You're more than welcome to stay the night with us."

"Thank you, Mary. I just might take you up on that." He squeezed Diana's shoulder, then stood. "What can I get you, honey?"

"I'll take a cannoli and more wine, please," Diana said, giggling as she held out her empty glass.

At the island, Roger poured himself a snifter of Frangelico, then carried it and an open bottle of wine to the table. "Thanks," Diana said after he filled her glass. "So, will you stay here with me?"

He nodded and patted her knee. She breathed a deep sigh of happiness. *I'm forgiven*, she thought.

As they munched on the sweets, Jimmy said, "I hate to bring up a painful subject, Roger, when we're having so much fun here, but what will you do with all your stores now that your partner is out of the picture?"

Diana turned to Roger, and her heart ached at the sad look on his face. She took his hand and laid her head on his shoulder.

"I've been thinking a lot about that, Jim," Roger said.

"We don't have to talk about this now, honey," Diana told him, crinkling her nose at Jimmy.

"No, I've had a couple weeks now for Vanessa's death to sink in, and to be honest, Nixon's arrest doesn't alter the direction I've been leaning."

"What direction's that?" Mary asked.

"Well, I'm meeting my financial adviser next week, and I plan to task him with finding a buyer for the entire company."

"Wow," Jimmy said. "How many stores are there?"

"Six," Roger said with a grimace. "I don't know what I was thinking. I was crazy to open the last two."

"Once they're sold," Mary said, "what will you do with yourself?"

Diana pursed her lips and looked down, crossing her fingers beneath the table.

"There'll be a period of adjustment, for sure," Roger admitted, "but I'd eventually like to transition full-time to Bald Head Island."

Diana squealed. "Yes! That's what I was hoping you'd say."

"Calm down, Diana," Roger said. "It could be a year or more before I extricate myself completely from the business. And I still have to sell both the house in Radnor and the cottage in Delaware."

"What's the real estate market like up there?" Jimmy asked.

"Whew," Roger said. "That's a good question. I believe the commercial market's strong, and the stores should garner a great deal of interest. As for the housing market, frankly, I don't know. What I do know is that before I can list the Radnor house, I need to do some fairly substantial remodeling."

"I'm sure it's quite lovely," Mary said. "Like so many others on the Main Line."

"It is," Roger agreed, "but unfortunately, my wife, in her infinite wisdom, eliminated two perfectly good guest bedrooms, plus a large part of the third-floor attic, to create her own private princess suite."

Diana laughed and clapped her hands. "Mary, you should see it! There's a massive closet filled with hundreds of beautiful gowns, all with matching shoes, and a huge crystal chandelier above an entire wall of mirrors. Not to mention this incredible canopy bed and a bathtub the size of a small swimming pool. God, what I'd give to live there."

She stopped to catch her breath, then closed her eyes, smiling dreamily. After a moment, she realized the room had grown very still. She slowly opened one eye to find Mary and Jimmy staring at her with bewildered expressions. She grew hot and felt the color drain from her face. With a heavy sense of dread, she turned to look at Roger. His mouth hung open, and his eyes were dark with what she could only define as a blend of fear and fury.

"How do you know all that?" he demanded, pushing his chair away from her.

"You, you told me," Diana stuttered. She reached out and grabbed his hand.

"I did not," Roger spat. He yanked his hand from her grip.

"Yes, you did. You just don't remember." She smiled pleadingly and motioned across the table. "Besides, you just described it to us. Right, Mary? Jimmy?"

"My memory's perfect, Diana. I didn't tell a soul about that room before tonight." He threw his napkin on the table and stormed from the kitchen.

"Roger," she screamed at his retreating back. "I love you. Please don't go. I can explain." She jumped up from the table and ran after him, sobbing.

72

MARY

JIMMY POINTED to Mary as he pulled out his phone. "Go after her, and I'll call Joe."

Mary ran out to the porch in time to see Roger's car tear up the street. Diana stood at the foot of the drive, shrieking at the top of her lungs.

"Diana!" she called. "Come back inside." The wind had picked up, and the swooshing of leaves drowned out her voice. As she moved down the drive, Diana bent at the waist, sobbing. She approached and held out her hand. "Diana, honey, let's go inside."

"No. I need to wait here for Roger to come back." She slapped at Mary's hand.

"Not tonight you don't." Mary hardened her voice. "What you need is sleep. Your meds and all that wine aren't letting you think straight."

"I'm thinking just fine, Mary!" She stumbled as she

stepped off the curb. Dropping to her knees, she began to crawl in the direction Roger had gone.

A slipper came off her right foot, and Mary picked it up. She grabbed Diana by the shoulders and attempted to help her to her feet, but she dropped to her belly. "Leave me alone."

Mary was reminded of two-year-old Cathy throwing a tantrum in the middle of the grocery aisle. At the time, she'd picked up her twenty-five-pound daughter and carried her from the store. That wouldn't work here.

"Have it your way, Diana. But just so you know, you're embarrassing yourself. In front of my entire neighborhood, I might add."

"I don't care," she replied petulantly. "Roger will be back. He just has to."

"Mary," Jimmy called from the porch. "Let her go. Joe's on his way."

Diana pushed to her knees and shouted at Jimmy. "What? Roger's on his way?"

"No, Diana," Mary said, reaching again for her arm. "He's not."

Diana recoiled, and her face crumbled. "You're lying to me, Mary. You're both lying to me." She turned and began to run up the street, oblivious to the missing shoe. At the stop sign, she paused, looking in both directions as if uncertain which way to turn.

Jimmy came up behind Mary, wrapping his arms around her. "You can't help her now, Mary. Let Joe handle this."

Mary's shoulders began to tremble as tears fell from her eyes. She took one final look at Diana, who stood dazed and confused in the middle of the intersection, then allowed Jimmy to lead her into the house.

. . .

FORTY MINUTES LATER, Joe Vickers knocked at their front door, and Jimmy let him in. He and Mary had cleaned up the kitchen, and Jimmy led him there now. Mary offered him a cup of coffee, and he nodded, taking a seat at the island.

"How is she?" she asked, feeling utterly drained.

"I don't know. We haven't found her yet," he said. "I was actually hoping she'd come to her senses and returned here."

Mary felt sick at the thought of Diana out in the darkness, drunk and desperate. "If she's stumbled into the marsh, she'll never find her way out."

"The fire department is setting up their spotlights to conduct a more thorough search, but that's the most we can do until daylight."

"Our neighbors will be thrilled when they're driven from bed by blinding lights," Jimmy said.

"Screw the neighbors," Mary said. "Diana could be hurt! Or worse."

"Least this time of year, we don't have gators to worry about," Jimmy said. Mary punched his arm.

"So," Joe said, "tell me again exactly what she said."

As Jimmy gave him a play-by-play, Mary went to the front window and stared out over the lawn. Her heart was in her throat as she listened in the background to the two men talking. It was as if she were listening to a recap of a movie, not something that had taken place in her own home, in real time and in real life.

Joe got up from the barstool and headed into the foyer. "I'll go back to the station and put a call in to the PA police, but in the meantime, call me if she comes back." He tipped his hat, then offered, "Sorry for your trouble, Mary."

"Thanks, Joe," she said as Jimmy closed the front door.

Jimmy pulled her to his chest. "Why don't you go up to bed, Mary. I'll wait up."

"No, I'll never be able to sleep."

"Might be a long night," Jimmy warned.

"Not as long as Diana's," she replied.

Jimmy kissed the top of her head. "Be that as it may, something tells me Hippie Chick is getting exactly what she deserves tonight."

73

ROGER

A LOUD JANGLING WOKE ROGER, and he cursed as dueling jackhammers proceeded to pound craters behind his eyeballs. After locating the phone under his pillow, he tentatively opened one eye. The room was dark, but he recognized his own bed. And he was alone. With relief, he recalled racing away from the Branson house and catching the last ferry back to Bald Head. Once home, he set about forgetting the nightmare dinner by getting rip-roaring drunk.

"Yeah," he managed as his parched tongue stuck to the roof of his mouth.

"Mr. Michaud, Joe Vickers here."

"What do you want?"

"I'd like you to come by the station this morning. A Detective Molino from the Radnor PD is on his way to

Southport right now, and he's asked to talk with you here in my office. I believe you know him."

Roger groaned. "Not going to happen." He hung up.

THREE HOURS LATER, he walked off the ferry and spotted Chief Vickers waiting for him dockside. "No need to retrieve your car," the man said. "You can ride with me."

Roger dropped his head and followed Vickers to his SUV. Minutes later, he was sitting in the same small room from two days before, but this time, they were joined by the a-hole detective from Radnor. The one who'd taken him into custody the night he found Vanessa's body. God, that seemed forever ago.

"Talk," he told them, shimmying uncomfortably in the stiff chair.

"Mr. Michaud," Molino started, "as of this morning, Bart Nixon has been cleared in the death of your wife, and he is no longer in police custody."

Roger huffed and shook his head. "First me, then Nixon. You guys are O and two."

Ignoring him, Molino continued, "After last night's revelations at the home of James and Mary Branson, we believe Diana Forrester, or rather—" he looked at his phone, "Ina Rose Parker—is responsible for Mrs. Michaud's murder."

Roger looked confused. "Ina who?"

"Miss Forrester's legal name is Ina Rose Parker," Vickers explained.

"No kidding?" Roger said. "And to think it only took her drunken revelations for you to figure this all out."

"Well, what about you?" Molino asked, ignoring the jab. "I mean, sure we didn't catch on, but if anyone knew what she was capable of, it was you. You're what connects the two women, so if you ask me, you're her *raison d'etre*. And if you don't speak French, it means Diana Forrester is a murderer because of you. The only question remaining is whether she's a murderer *for* you."

Roger jumped to his feet and pointed a finger in Molino's face. "That's going too far, Molino, and if you so much as think it again, I'll sue your ass for defamation."

"Calm down, gentlemen," Joe said, motioning for Roger to sit. "We need to cover more ground here, so let's get beyond this, shall we?"

Roger took his seat and crossed his arms, seething.

"Just so you know, Mr. Michaud, we also suspect Miss Forrester of killing Bobby Moore."

"I thought you had someone else in custody for that," Roger said, shaking his head.

"We did, but he was released late yesterday."

"So, she's confessed to both murders?" Roger asked.

"No, not yet, she hasn't," Vickers said, "but the evidence is piling up against her."

"Is part of that evidence the knife she used to kill Vanessa and the baby?" A vision of Vanessa's slashed throat and the single wound to her stomach flashed before him. He closed his eyes to quell an urge to throw up.

"We found *a* knife," Vickers said, "wrapped in a towel that was duct-taped to the backside of a cabinet in her office. We're currently testing it for fingerprints and DNA."

"We won't find your prints on it, will we?" Molino asked, his eyes directing daggers at Roger.

Roger didn't take the bait. "Why don't you redirect that animus to the one who deserves it? Grill Diana instead of me."

"We'll do just that once we locate her," Vickers said.

"I left her at the Branson house last night. Start there."

"We did, but she ran off after you," the chief explained, "and has since disappeared, seemingly into thin air."

"Well, I don't know what the Bransons told you about last night's dinner, but I swear she's certifiably insane. You could see it in her eyes." He shivered at the memory.

"Insane or not, she's undeniably a mistress of deception," Vickers said. "Did you know she was married twice before?"

"No, but nothing surprises me at this point."

"That first man we pegged for Bobby's murder? Turns out he's husband number one. Still is legally."

"But you say you let him go?"

"We had to," Vickers explained. "He was never in her apartment, so he couldn't have killed Bobby."

"And the second chump?"

"That one was brought to our attention this morning after the Las Vegas PD saw our APB. Seems a local casino owner was stabbed to death in his bed some years back. At the time, the victim, a Mr. Alejandro Vila, was unlucky enough to be married to a dancer by the name of Ivy Blue. When Mr. Vila's body was discovered, Miss Blue was nowhere to be found."

"Let me guess. This Ivy Blue and Diana are one and the same?"

Vickers nodded. "The photo and prints are a match."

Roger stood. "I think I've heard quite enough, so if we're done here, I've got far better things to do."

Chief Vickers nodded. "We'll be in touch if we learn anything else, but in the meantime, keep your guard up. When last seen, she was chasing you down."

"Then do your jobs and find her before she finds me."

"I still believe you had role in all this, Michaud," Molino said.

"Then you're as crazy as Diana," Roger replied.

"Or you are," the detective rebutted. "Until there's proof positive you aren't, in some way, behind these murders, I won't stop digging."

"Knock yourself out," Roger said before slamming out the door.

74

MARY

MARY AND JIMMY boarded the plane and settled into their seats. She laid her head back and released a deep sigh of relief. It had been an intense six months since the night of Diana's drunken disclosure and disappearance, and they were finally getting away for ten days of recovery and relaxation. Cathy was joining them in Cancun, and their small family was spending a much-needed vacation at an all-inclusive resort on Isla Mujeres.

As the flight attendant reviewed the safety instructions at the front of the cabin, Jimmy squeezed Mary's hand and whispered, "Close your eyes. I know the drill and will save you if it comes down to it."

"You always do," Mary whispered back.

Try as she might to nap once the flight leveled off, she couldn't pause the unbroken loop going round and round in her head. It started with that pre-dawn text from Diana, zipped through the whirlwind that followed, then rewound itself after the search for Diana's body in the marsh across from Mary and Jimmy's house had been called off.

In between, there'd been Bobby Moore's funeral, a day of mourning for the entire community. Mary still couldn't figure out why the beautiful young man had to die, and no excuse Diana could ever give would suffice.

WITHIN WEEKS OF THE MURDER, Mort Baxter, the old pharmacist, announced he was auctioning off the contents of the Seaside Siren, as well as Diana's apartment upstairs. He then put the entire building on the market, and Maria and John Franklin promptly bought it. They were now in the process of moving Maria's expanded design studio into the first-floor space. Mary and Jimmy were becoming fast friends with the Franklins, but Mary wasn't sure she would ever again step foot in that building.

George Purnell visited for a few days after Easter to help Mary outline the Philadelphia angle of her upcoming novel. Jimmy hadn't wanted her to write the story at all, fearing it would be too difficult for her, but he eventually understood that it's what she needed to close the chapter on Diana. There was a lot of writing left to do—she was taking it very slowly—but she hoped to send the completed manuscript to her editor by the end of the year. For reasons she couldn't quite comprehend, she occasionally found herself missing her friend.

George kept them abreast of Roger Michaud's activities. His half-share in Slap Shots was quietly transferred to Bart Nixon, and the Main Line mansion and house on Bald

Head Island were unloaded shortly thereafter. Rumor had him now living in the small cottage on the Delaware shore.

JIMMY NUDGED MARY, and she opened her eyes. "I know you're not sleeping, so how about some wine and a movie?"

"Sure," she replied. "We're on vacation, so I might as well indulge."

After Jimmy paid the flight attendant for four miniature bottles of Merlot, Mary lifted the arm rest and snuggled into her husband. As the opening credits played on the small screen in front of them, she smiled. Life was good, and she was happy. They were happy.

EPILOGUE

INA ROSE DRIFTED in and out of sleep. It was painfully uncomfortable lying on her back for hours on end, bound as she was to the headboard and footboard. She opened her eyes and stared at the ceiling. Dust motes danced in the light streaming through cracks in the boarded-up windows. If she squinted just so, the dust looked like tiny angels floating down from heaven.

"Monkey," she called out. "I need to use the bathroom."

Light from the hallway flooded the room. "I guess you do by now," Monkey said. "You sure must have needed your beauty rest, sleepy head."

He released the restraints, massaging her wrists and ankles before helping her slide her legs off the mattress. "Now gimme your hands." She held them out, and he hoisted her to a standing position. "Woo-wee," he teased. "You're heavy."

"Of course, I am," she pouted as she smoothed down her nightgown. "You never let me exercise. I've gotta get back in shape, Monkey."

"Ain't no need for that anymore, Ina Rose. I love you just the way you are." He pinched her cheek.

She stomped her foot. "Let me at least practice my yoga some. I can't even bend over and touch my toes anymore."

"Why would you even want to?" he asked. He ran his calloused hands over her bare arms and down her hips. She shuddered at his touch and pushed him away.

He grabbed her and kissed her hard, then spanked her rear end. "Now hurry up before you pee yourself again. Breakfast is on the stovetop waiting on you."

As Ina Rose shuffled to the bathroom, she cast a furtive glance down the hallway to the front door. Last night, like most nights since Monkey brought her home, she dreamed of escaping. She was running through the salt marsh, toward someone just out of view. Was it Roger? She couldn't see his face in the swirling fog, but it had to be. She called his name, but he didn't hear her over the wind blowing through the grasses.

She'd cried out in her sleep, and Monkey rolled over and wrapped his arms around her. He smelled of body odor, lube oil, and exhaust fumes. Nothing at all like her Roger.

She plopped down on the toilet, sighing as her bladder released. When the stream finally ended, she leaned back against the tank and closed her eyes. The tiny bathroom was her only sanctuary, a place of sweet respite from the chains that bound her to the bed, the table, the sofa, or to Monkey himself on the rare occasion he took her outside.

"Ina, come on out of there," Monkey called through the door.

"Coming," she said, pulling herself up and flushing the toilet. She splashed cold water on her face, then looked at herself in the mirror. She hardly recognized the woman staring back. Her face was puffy, her complexion sallow, and her hair was now more gray than blond. She'd asked Monkey to pick her up a box of hair color at the pharmacy, but he'd refused, saying he didn't care what color it was so long as she brushed it every night while he watched.

Monkey knocked three times hard, and Ina Rose turned the knob. "Come on, food's getting cold," he said.

"I'm not hungry," she complained as he pushed her ahead of him into the kitchen.

"I don't care, Ina. Sit."

She obeyed and pulled out a dining chair, one of the many new pieces of furniture Monkey bought before he came looking for her. She was pleasantly surprised, to be honest, by how nice the place looked after so many years. Clean and sparkly, even.

"It's so pretty," she had told him, hoping to make him believe she was happy to be home. "Where'd you get the money?"

"From a guy who didn't deserve it," was all he said.

The following week, he handed her a yellow envelope.

"What's this?" she asked.

"I call it our insurance policy."

Ina Rose opened the envelope and withdrew a stack of photos tied together with a length of black ribbon. She slipped off the ribbon, then picked up the first photo. She turned it one way, then the other, snorting with surprise when she figured it out. A man stood with his back to the camera, bent at the waist and grasping his ankles. He was wearing high-heeled black leather boots and a lacy black thong that did little to cloak his hairy scrotum.

In the second photo, the same man was on his hands and knees as a woman stood behind him, grasping a leash that was clipped to a ball-gag jammed in the man's mouth. She was dressed in combat boots and a Nazi military uniform, and strapped to her belt was a long, spiked dildo, buried halfway up the man's rectum.

Ina Rose dropped the photos and slapped her hand to her mouth. "Some insurance policy, I'd say."

"Like I said, he didn't deserve the money."

Now, she picked at the pancakes and runny eggs on the plate in front of her. She was, in fact, quite hungry, but she dreaded the prospect of gaining even one more ounce. She didn't have a scale to weigh herself, but she figured she had packed on at least ten pounds, maybe more. She needed to convince Monkey to let her exercise, or at least allow her to dance a little. When the opportunity arose, she wanted to be strong enough to get away, to run as far as she could without stopping.

She would have gotten away that night, too, if she weren't so drunk. If she didn't take two sedatives before she started in on the wine. So much wine. When the pickup truck pulled to a stop in front of her, it nearly blinded her with its headlights. And when the passenger door flew open and someone yelled for her to get in, she swore it was Roger. Without even thinking, she climbed into the cab, and the truck sped off before the door latched. By the time she realized her error, that the voice called out for *Ina Rose* to get in, not *Diana*, it was too late.

"Eat," Monkey said, smacking the tabletop.

"But I'm not hungry," she whined.

Monkey reached over and pulled her head back by her long hair. When she cried out, he shoveled a spoonful of eggs into her mouth.

"Chew," he demanded.

She did, trying hard not to gag. When the food finally went down, she breathed deeply until the queasiness passed.

"Now, that's better, isn't it?" Monkey said, wiping her mouth roughly with a napkin.

Ina Rose sniffled and tried to stand, but he pushed her back onto the chair. "You are feisty this morning, woman. Just a few more bites, and I'll let you get back to bed so I can go to work."

"I've had enough to eat, Monkey, and I don't want to go back to bed. I want to stay up. I want to live like a normal person." She turned her head and squeezed her lips together.

"Listen to me, Ina Rose Parker," he said, grabbing her chin. "You had your freedom for years and years, and where did that get you? In trouble, that's where. So until I say otherwise, you are no longer free to do whatever you please. You will eat what I tell you to, and you will rest when I tell you to."

"I've been obeying you for months already," Ina Rose cried. "How much longer before I earn back my freedom?"

"Need I remind you, little lady," Monkey said, smiling as he patted her belly, "that you're almost forty years old and considered at a high risk for complications. By my calculation, you have three more months to grow our baby inside you. So all things considered, you'll earn back your freedom in about eighteen years and three months."

The End

ALSO BY CAROLYN COURTNEY LAUMAN

AGAINST THEIR WILL: A Thriller Conceived From True
Events

The Deceptive Series

Book One: DECEPTIVE WATERS

A THRILLER CONCEIVED FROM TRUE EVENTS

AGAINST THEIR WILL

CAROLYN COURTNEY LAUMAN

FROM THE AUTHOR OF *AGAINST THEIR WILL*

CAROLYN COURTNEY LAUMAN

DECEPTIVE WATERS

A NOVEL

THE FIRST BOOK
IN THE DECEPTIVE SERIES

PRAISE FOR DECEPTIVE WATERS

Wonderful Suspense Novel. Loved this story, so many twists and turns.

A real page turner!! Couldn't put the book down.

Great read. On the edge of my seat til the end!!

ABOUT THE AUTHOR

Carolyn Courtney Lauman is a former international business woman and interior decorator who now writes novels of suspense and mystery. *Deceptive Affairs* is her third novel, and the second in her *Deceptive* series. She resides in the United States of America with her husband.

Made in the USA
Columbia, SC
09 May 2022